Love is in the air at Smith High School! Tuxes are being rented. Dresses are being fitted. The magic of prom is only one month away . . . and the question on everyone's mind is will that special somebody ask me to the dance?

Three of Smith High School's geekiest students are about to find out. . . .

Praise for the Smith High Series by Marni Bates

"From scandalous stories to hush-hush flirtationships to a few doses of drama, *Invisible* has just the right mix of all our fave genres—perfect if you're looking for a fun summer beach read!"
—*Seventeen* magazine on *Invisible*

"Ever wonder what it's like to go from being the shy girl no one notices to basically a celeb? *Invisible* by Marni Bates will put those thoughts to rest. Walk in Jane's shoes as she realizes that being noticed might not be as great as it seems."
—*Girls Life* on *Invisible*

"[Bates keeps] the wit dialed up to 11 in a comedy of errors . . . but Jane also learns some solid life lessons about bullying and courage, and she teaches some lessons about friendship to her own circle as well."
—*Kirkus Reviews* on *Invisible*

"This light story of self-actualization and romance will have wide appeal for lovers of high school rom-coms."
—*VOYA* magazine on *Invisible*

"A quick, enjoyable read . . . made for a good story on timely topics—namely, bullying, insta-celebrity via the Internet, and social responsibility."
—Examiner.com on *Invisible*

"Readers get an inside view into the good side of the popular girl, showing that she has as many insecurities as the geeks do; she just hides them more successfully. Another funny, lighthearted romp from Bates."
—*Kirkus Reviews* on *Notable*

"Fun and humorous coming-of-age story . . . For fans of Meg Cabot and Louise Rennison."
—*School Library Journal* on *Notable*

"Very funny. Should please lots of readers, awkward or not."
—*Kirkus Reviews* on *Awkward*

AWKWARDLY EVER AFTER

More by Marni Bates

AWKWARD

DECKED WITH HOLLY

INVISIBLE

NOTABLE

Published by Kensington Publishing Corp.

AWKWARDLY EVER AFTER

Marni Bates

KENSINGTON PUBLISHING CORP.
www.kensingtonbooks.com

K TEEN BOOKS are published by

Kensington Publishing Corp.
119 West 40th Street
New York, NY 10018

All Kensington titles, imprints, and distributed lines are available at special quantity discounts for bulk purchases for sales promotion, premiums, fund-raising, educational, or institutional use.

Special book excerpts or customized printings can also be created to fit specific needs. For details, write or phone the office of the Kensington Special Sales Manager: Kensington Publishing Corp., 119 West 40th Street, New York, NY 10018. Attn. Special Sales Department. Phone: 1-800-221-2647.

Kensington and the K logo Reg. U.S. Pat. & TM Off.

eISBN-13: 978-0-7582-9517-0
eISBN-10: 0-7582-9517-0
First Kensington Electronic Edition: July 2014

ISBN-13: 978-0-7582-9516-3
ISBN-10: 0-7582-9516-2
First Kensington Trade Paperback Printing: July 2014

10 9 8 7 6 5 4 3 2 1

Printed in the United States of America

This book is dedicated to my loyal readership. It's because you kept asking "What comes next?!" that I had to make sure you got your Awkwardly Ever After.

I want you to know that you are special. That you are smart. Beautiful. Talented. And absolutely overflowing with potential.

But I know that those words can be incredibly difficult to believe.

It's so much easier to see yourself as disposable.

You're not.

So if you feel like you could disappear off the face of the earth with nobody the wiser, *please* call a suicide prevention hotline. If you dial 1-800-273-8255 in the United States, a trained professional will be there to listen. They can help.

My best friend made that call, and I can't even begin to express how grateful I am that she did. That phone call saved her life. I think it saved my life too.

This is my way of paying it forward.

All my love,

Marni

Acknowledgments

It's hard to say good-bye.

These characters have been my constant companions for the past five years. We've journeyed together to four different continents, visited seven countries, and explored countless cities. They've given me advice on a wide array of subjects. They've been there for me through the good, the bad, and the "meh" times.

And they would exist only in my mind if it weren't for a whole bunch of people.

I'm so incredibly grateful that Megan Records, Alicia Condon, and everyone else at K Teen wanted to publish my crazy ideas; that they said yes to awkward teenagers, arrogant rock stars, and even one very nasty Cambodian drug lord. They believed in the beauty of my dreams . . . even when I wanted to consume the entire contents of my fridge instead of editing.

I need to thank Laurie McLean for representing this series. It has been quite the ride! The lovely Marina Adair's critiquing skills have saved my sanity on more than one occasion. She's my best friend, my colleague, and a constant source of inspiration. I hope to one day have a relationship as adorable as hers.

The writing lifestyle is often wearisome, especially for the author's family! Thank you for being so patient and understanding with me. The highest honor I will ever receive is that of being a Hoosfoos.

But I think the biggest debt of gratitude goes to my readers. Thank you for loving my characters every bit as much as I do. Thank you for letting them live in your hearts.

I can't even begin to express how much that means to me.

Thank you all!

Awkwardly yours,

Marni

Contents

Awkwardly

Chapter 1

Love is in the air at Smith High School! Tuxes are being rented. Dresses are being fitted. The magic of prom is only one month away . . . and the question on everyone's mind is, will that special somebody ask me to the dance?

—from "Preparing for Prom,"
by Lisa Anne Montgomery
Published by *The Smithsonian*

There's no good way to tell your friend that you've got a crush on her little brother.

It's not the kind of thing that I could imagine slipping into a casual phone conversation.

"Hey, it's Melanie. Listen, is Dylan around? Because I was kind of hoping the three of us could hang out together. Why would I want to do that? Well, you know how you just see him as your annoying little brother? Yeah, nothing about him seems brotherly to me."

Oh yeah, *that* wouldn't get weird or anything.

In fact, mentioning Dylan at all seemed downright dangerous for my health. It's generally considered a bad idea to provoke an overly protective person, and beneath the thin layer of insults Mackenzie and Dylan enjoyed slinging at each other, there was an intense sibling loyalty. All it would take for Mackenzie to go into full mother grizzly bear mode was the vaguest rumor that some high school girl was interested in dating her middle school brother.

I doubted she would care that there was only a one-year age gap; that next year he would be a freshman and I'd be a sophomore. Or that the year after *that,* he would be a sophomore and I'd be a junior.

Perfectly normal.

Except for the whole little brother factor—which I couldn't imagine Mackenzie Wellesley *ever* overlooking—the two of us would barely raise eyebrows as a couple by next year's prom.

Just over twelve months from now.

"Um, Melanie? You do realize that you're staring at my boyfriend's butt, right?"

Actually, I hadn't. My mind had been wandering and apparently my eyes had made a little side trip of their own. Mackenzie's eyes were glinting with amusement, so instead of trying to deny it, I leaned back in my chair and took another sip of hot chocolate before I gestured to the rink in front of us where the Smith High School hockey team was practicing.

"Not my fault. It's . . . wow."

"Yes, it is." Mackenzie's smile only broadened as Logan skated past with a look of pure concentration on his face. "But if *he* sees you staring, it might get a little awkward and . . . oh no!"

I turned just in the nick of time to catch Patrick Bradford checking Logan hard, sending him sprawling across the ice. My nose wrinkled in contempt—the standard expression whenever I was forced to share the same room with Patrick. Thankfully, it didn't happen all that often because he didn't exactly associate with lowly freshmen. He was far too busy trying to climb the Smith High School social ladder to spare a second for someone who wouldn't propel him up a rung.

Patrick's delusions of grandeur wouldn't have bothered me if I hadn't seen Mackenzie's devastated expression when she finally figured out that he was more interested in her sudden rise to YouTube celebrity than he was in her as a person. She had looked absolutely shredded. I still felt a twinge of guilt every time I thought about that night. My first high school party. My first party, period. I was supposed to have been going as moral support for Mackenzie. Instead, I had accidentally let her drink to the point that she couldn't walk in a straight line, because I was too preoccupied flirting with her little brother to notice.

To be fair, he had started flirting with me first.

Although that still didn't make him any less off-limits.

So even now that Mackenzie was obnoxiously happy with Logan Beckett, I still blamed Patrick for the way it had gone down. Maybe I would have tried harder to let bygones be bygones if Patrick would stop taking cheap shots against his own team captain to prove some kind of stupid guy point.

But probably not.

Mackenzie let out a quiet breath of relief as Logan picked himself off the ice and his best friend, Spencer King, skated over and glowered at Patrick. There was no doubt in anyone's mind that Spencer was more than ready to throw a few punches if it turned into an outright brawl.

"Okay, all good." She smiled at me. "You were saying?"

I decided to test whether she would actually be able to focus on me with a testosterone-fueled display only a few feet away on the ice. "Um . . . that your boyfriend is cute?"

"Right. Yes. That's undeniably—oh, *seriously!*"

Logan said something to Patrick that had the other boy glaring and moving within striking distance.

"So I take it things are still kind of awkward there."

"Uh-huh . . ." Mackenzie nodded absentmindedly. She

jerked upright in her seat as Patrick tossed his stick aside and launched himself at Logan. "If he gets a concussion, I'm going to kill him. It's hard enough getting him to concentrate already."

"You sure that doesn't have something to do with your being more than just his tutor now?" I asked wryly. It wasn't exactly a secret that Logan Beckett hated his AP U.S. History class—something that had actually brought the two of them together before Mackenzie's embarrassing YouTube video launched her into fame. Now that they were dating, though, I had a feeling he was trying to find new ways to distract her from the books.

And judging by the blush that crept up her neck, his efforts weren't entirely unsuccessful either.

"Nope, I'm sure that has nothing to do with it."

I rolled my eyes.

"That's my story and I'm sticking to it."

"Sure, Mackenzie. And that hickey I see peeking out under your shirt is a coincidence, right?"

"Absolutely."

I laughed until I saw Logan haul off and slug Patrick in the stomach. "Okay, yeah, coincidence. Don't sic your boyfriend on me, please."

She laughed. "We both know that Logan's totally harmless."

It didn't look like Patrick would agree with that statement as the rest of the team rushed over to surround the two boys. I barely caught a glimpse of Spencer grabbing a solid handful of Patrick's jersey and cheerfully pulling him away from his friend. From where Mackenzie and I were sitting, I couldn't be certain if Spencer had tripped Patrick up in the process, but I definitely enjoyed watching the jerk slide five feet across the ice . . . on his face.

"Um, okay. *That* was impressive."

Mackenzie swiveled toward me and it didn't take a genius

to figure out that her brain had jumped to the wrong conclusion. "Really? Because I happen to know that Spencer is very single."

"Uh . . . good for him."

"And the two of you would make a really cute couple, Melanie. Kind of a *Beauty and the Beast* thing."

I glanced over at Spencer, who had taken off his helmet and was explaining the situation to the coach while Patrick sulked and Logan scowled. Spencer's blond hair flopped charmingly across his forehead while he gestured animatedly from one boy to the other. It looked like the guy honestly *enjoyed* breaking up fights. Although I had a feeling he would've enjoyed it even more if he had gotten in a few blows of his own.

"In this scenario, I'm guessing I'm the beast?"

"You're right, Melanie. I took one look at you and thought, *Wow, that girl needs a total fashion makeover.* Oh wait, nope. That's what you gave *me.*"

To be fair, it was Mackenzie's friend Corey who had been most adamant about giving her a fashion makeover. I just happened to tag along, the lone freshman on their island of misfit toys.

"I guess technically it would be a beauty and the beauty scenario." Mackenzie rolled her eyes. "I still stand by my earlier statement."

I flipped a page in the textbook that I should've been concentrating on from the very beginning of our "study session" instead of staring out at a rink full of hockey players. Next time I crashed a practice session, I needed to make sure I didn't actually have to accomplish anything. Maybe if I could distract myself long enough with the guys on the hockey team, my feelings for Dylan would just evaporate.

My best friend, Isobel Peters, would've had no trouble poking holes in that plan. Then again, Izzie also wasn't preoccupied deflecting a conversation away from Spencer King.

"So, about this whole Boston Tea Party thing . . . did anyone actually drink the tea, Mackenzie? Or make crumpets to go with it? Because that sounds delicious."

"You're using American history to make me shut up about Spencer, aren't you?"

"Yep."

"That's pretty nefarious."

I grinned, willing to bet that a true history nerd like Mackenzie would combust in a matter of minutes if she didn't answer my questions. "Scones, maybe? With, uh . . . clotted cream. That was a thing, right?"

Mackenzie's smile widened as the team began filing off the ice, and she closed my textbook with a faint thud before she began packing up. "You're not going to distract me that easily. I think the two of you would be cute together. He might act like he only cares about partying, but he's a really great guy once you get to know him. And he's loyal to a fault."

"Riiight," I snorted. "That's why he gave you all those tequila shots at his party. Because he's such a stand-up guy."

"He was trying to make my night a little better."

I remembered the panic that had sharpened Dylan's soft brown eyes when he realized how trashed his older sister had become while he was preoccupied dancing with me. And it had gotten worse when Mackenzie started drunkenly rambling about their dad.

That's when his face had turned into a cold, unreadable mask.

Dylan barely spoke another word to me for the rest of the night, even after we'd successfully hauled Mackenzie's drunken butt into Logan's passenger seat. Instead, he had mumbled something about helping Spencer police the party, and disappeared into the crowd.

Leaving me standing alone outside like a loser, until Corey stopped by the party and offered us a ride to the Wellesley house on the way back from a date of his own.

Not that I'd been on a date with Dylan.

It doesn't count as a date if the other person randomly decides to avoid you for hours on end.

"Yeah, Spencer definitely went out of his way to make that night special. If he had 'improved' it any more, your stomach would've been pumped."

"That was my fault," Mackenzie protested. "I'm the one who kept drinking even after he tried to cut me off. And I learned my lesson. Tequila and I will never be on speaking terms again. But that doesn't make him a bad guy. In fact, I'll prove it to you."

I eyed her suspiciously. "Just what do you have in mind for—"

"Nice skating, Spencer. Hey, have you met my friend Melanie?"

Well, I walked right into that one.

My cheeks felt unnaturally warm, as if I had been the one exerting myself on the ice instead of sitting on the sidelines with a cup of hot chocolate. Then again, it was hard to act cool when I had one of the most popular guys in the junior class sizing me up.

"Well, hello again, Pocahontas."

I winced at the nickname. I've always found it annoying when people comment on the fact that my skin happens to be *slightly* darker than the average Oregonian—not much of a feat in a state where pale is the norm. Back in elementary school, I landed the role of Sacajawea while everyone else got to be part of Lewis and Clark's expedition every single year.

"Hello, arrogant jock."

Mackenzie kicked me under the table again as I smiled innocently.

"What? I thought we were giving each other cute nicknames based purely on first impressions."

Spencer at least had the good sense to meet my eyes directly. "Okay, not my best opening line. Does it help if I admit that I had a thing for Pocahontas as a kid? I mean, that

'Colors of the Wind' stuff was hot." His smile quirked up at the side and I began relaxing in spite of myself.

I shrugged. "Yeah, I'm still not thrilled with the comparison."

"It's the long brown hair," Mackenzie pointed out.

"And your eyes."

"And my skin tone. Not exactly a secret here, guys."

"I think mainly it's your eyes." Spencer leaned closer, as if an intense examination was required to settle the matter. "They're almost the same shade of dark chocolate as your drink."

I blinked up at him. "Okay, I get it. You weren't *trying* to be a jerk. Message received. You can tone down the flirting now."

He laughed and glanced over at Mackenzie. "Does she give everyone such a hard time?"

Only when I'm not entirely clear what game someone wants to be playing with me. If I think it will prevent a mess in the making, I have no trouble speaking up. Probably because I can't afford to clean up after anyone else—not without crumbling inside. That's why I only truly relax around a handful of people who don't push me too far.

Except that doesn't apply to my feelings for Dylan.

"Um, actually she never has be—"

"Hey, Mack." Logan Beckett interrupted her words with a quick kiss. Not that she appeared to mind, judging by the way her fingers gripped his hockey jersey. "Did you catch the show?"

"Nah, I hardly noticed you at all." The foolish grin plastered all over her face gave her away. "Melanie and I were discussing the Boston Tea Party."

He groaned. "No more history lectures, I beg of you."

"Actually, I was thinking the four of us could get together to watch *Pocahontas.*"

Oh crap.

Logan glanced over at his best friend, whose face I now

found impossible to read. "Um . . . I'm not so sure Spencer enjoys discussing historical accuracy, Mack."

"He was just telling Melanie how much he loved that movie as a kid. Weren't you, Spencer?"

"I—"

"Great! It's settled. We'll see the two of you at Logan's house for movie night tomorrow. Say . . . six o'clock?" She was already pulling on her backpack and entwining her fingers with Logan's. The two of them were so fricking adorable together it was almost nauseating. "See you then!"

And just like that they strolled out of the ice skating rink together.

Leaving me alone with a hockey player who had just been shanghaied into a movie date with me that I didn't even want in the first place.

Because I was still stupidly hung up on someone else altogether.

I was *so* screwed.

Chapter 2

The ballots for prom court will soon be passed amongst the student body. And while Smith High School sophomore Samantha "Sam" Wilson has loudly protested this tradition, calling it "nothing more than a popularity contest that only strengthens the patriarchal culture of this country," many people believe this is merely because she isn't in the running. . . .

—from "Preparing for Prom,"
by Lisa Anne Montgomery
Published by *The Smithsonian*

"So, on a scale of one to ten, how uncomfortable are you right now?"

Spencer's obvious amusement about the whole thing made me grin right back. I mentally began revising my estimation of him. At least he had a solid sense of humor . . . something we would both probably be needing with Mackenzie's brain tuned to matchmaking mode.

I shrugged. "Mackenzie means well. I'm not sure about her judgment when it comes to, y'know . . ."

"Me?"

"Yeah."

He flopped into the seat that Mackenzie had recently vacated. "Fair enough. She has a terrible track record. I mean, that guy she's dating? No good. I don't trust him as far as I can slide him on the ice."

I mentally replayed the way he had hauled Logan away from Patrick, and smiled at the joke. "Yeah, Logan's just the worst."

"That's what I've been saying for years. I'm biding my time now. Waiting for my parents to buy me the captaincy."

His parents could probably do it. Everyone knew that the new wing in the gym was courtesy of the King family fortune. I studied him carefully, searching for even a trace of truth behind his joking words. Spencer's green eyes were bright, but I suspected that it had less to do with hockey and more to do with messing with my head.

"Would you really want to be team captain?"

"Nah, probably not. That would mean I'd have to give all the pep talks." Spencer scoffed. "Show up early. All of that cr—garbage."

I didn't know what to make of his quick bit of verbal sanitation, whether it was his way of trying to impress me with his chivalry or if he considered it bad form to swear in front of an impressionable freshman girl. The sardonic edge underlying his every statement left me wondering if he ever meant *anything* he said, or if life was one big joke to him.

"Would all of that be such a bad thing?"

"It certainly would be for Patrick." He glanced down at his phone. "Listen Poc—Melanie. It was fun meeting you, but I have places to go, people to see, and parties to crash."

I rolled my eyes. "Of course you do."

"So I'll be seeing you tomorrow night." Spencer stood and I knew that if I kept my mouth shut he would saunter out of the hockey rink as if he owned the place, which he sort of did. His parents had paid for its remodel after all.

"I don't get it," I blurted out, before he had taken more than two steps. "We have nothing in common. Why on earth would you want to hang out with me? If you really wanted to get out of this, you could convince Mackenzie to let it drop easily enough."

His smile quirked up at the side. "That's for me to know . . . and you to find out."

"*Seriously?* You couldn't come up with anything more original than that?"

"Nope, but I'll do better next time." Spencer winked. "Catch you later, Melanie."

That was the last thing I needed. Especially if Spencer developed real feelings for me and I had to explain to Mackenzie why I was reluctant to give one of the hottest guys in the junior class any of my time.

Sorry, Mackenzie. I'd just rather date your little brother than your boyfriend's best friend. That's fine with you, right?

The only thing I found myself dreading more than trying to explain *that* to Mackenzie was introducing *anyone* to my dad. Not when he passes tipsy and moves on to getting thoroughly trashed before five o'clock every evening. Just because my dad wasn't an angry drunk didn't really change anything; I still hated watching him stare at the television for hours on end while he poisoned himself into an early grave.

I absolutely refused to let anyone else see him that way.

Which was why I waited until the next morning before school to corner Izzie for advice.

"So, hypothetically speaking, if someone tried to set you up on a date with Spencer King . . . how would you worm your way out of it?"

Izzie barely glanced up at me from the AP Statistics textbook she had propped open against a tree, giving herself an excellent view of her surroundings while remaining relatively invisible.

Not that Isobel Peters ever needed help going unnoticed. "I would let my trusty dragon take care of the situation. Or ask a warlock friend to intervene. Those things are way more likely to happen than a date with Spencer King. At least for *me*. What's going on, Mel?"

"Okay, so let's say someone was trying to set me up on a date with Spencer King. Hypothetically."

She shoved her glasses higher up her nose and stared at me in disbelief. "Nothing about this conversation seems hypothetical. Do we need to review the definition again?"

"Fine. It's . . . well, honestly I'm blaming Mackenzie for this one."

Izzie grinned and closed her textbook with a resounding whump. "Let me guess: Mackenzie wants to set you up with Spencer because he is Logan's best friend and she feels guilty about interrupting their bromance time."

She might not like being the center of attention, but that's never stopped Izzie from paying attention to the intricacies of everyone else's lives. That, combined with her analytical nature and her inability to lie with anything even remotely resembling a straight face, made her the world's best confidant. I could trust Izzie to keep my secrets safe. I imagined it'd be similar to admitting my sins to a priest; what happens in the confessional, stays in the confessional.

Forgive me, Father. I've been having some thoughts about my best friend's little brother that probably don't meet up to your godly standards or whatever. . . .

Yeah, I didn't think saying fifteen Hail Mary's would really help in this particular situation. I'd also kept my embarrassing crush on Dylan to myself. And luckily, Izzie had never needed to know every particular to point me in the right direction, which was why I considered her undeniable talent for giving advice as one of Smith High School's best kept secrets. Nobody would think to ask a girl who acted like she had a supercomputer chip wired into her brain for relationship pointers. Izzie might be good at understanding people, but she didn't exactly come across as a people person.

"I think Mackenzie's in the mood to play matchmaker, but I don't think her relationship with Logan has anything to do with it."

Izzie laughed outright. "If that was the case, don't you think she would have noticed by now that you're head over heels crazy about her little brother?"

"What are you talking about? I'm not—"

The three-minute warning bell cut me off and I watched in stunned silence while Izzie began methodically packing up her backpack.

"Sorry, was that supposed to be a secret? You mention him all the time, Mel." Izzie pitched her voice higher, which sounded doubly absurd coming from her. "So I spent the night at Mackenzie's house and Dylan told us the *funniest* story about his soccer practice. And then he challenged Mackenzie to a game of basketball, but when she pointed out that he had an unfair advantage, he said they would play on *rollerblades!*"

I felt my cheeks turning redder. "I don't remember going into that much detail."

But Izzie was into her act now, and I could tell by the sparkle in her eyes that she wasn't going to let it drop.

"So they took Mackenzie's rollerblades to a nearby court and both put one of them on and used me as the referee." Izzie's voice finally dropped to her normal husky register. "This is the point in the story when you get a glazed look in your eyes."

Yeah, it was. Because that's when I started thinking about the way Dylan's dark hair had looked windswept and tousled as he focused on beating his older sister, only to look up at me and flash a bone-melting smile.

"You're doing it again."

I forced myself to concentrate on Isobel.

"Look, Dylan isn't . . . we're just—I'm *not* . . ." I stumbled incoherently.

If anything, Izzie's grin only widened. "Uh-huh, that clears everything right up."

"Nothing can happen between us, okay! Not without jeopardizing my friendship with Mackenzie. So . . . drop it."

She instantly sobered, met my gaze squarely, and nodded. "Consider it dropped. But if you ever need to talk, well, I'm here."

The last part usually went without saying. *Of course* Izzie would be there for me. That's how it works when you've been best friends since the first day of middle school. I mean, if you can make it through *that* without hating each other, you've got a pretty firm foundation for friendship. Although the real test had come in seventh grade when she dropped by my house unexpectedly and saw my dad passed out in a drunken heap on the couch. I had been mortified; frozen in place by an overwhelming rush of shame. And I had desperately hoped that somehow she wouldn't notice him—or the noxious smell of stale beer that filled the room. I had braced myself for the inevitable; I waited for her to turn on the pity eyes and start making excuses to bolt.

I forgot, there's . . . somewhere else I need to be. Right now. Sorry, Mel. See you tomorrow. Or . . . whenever.

I couldn't even imagine an alternative. Nobody in their right mind would want to deal with the rank reality of my home life—not if they caught one good whiff of it. There were days when I thought I could wash my clothes a thousand times and never completely remove that smell. Days when I checked the recycling bin outside so I would know what to expect when I opened the front door. Nights I spent hovering over my dad, listening for the next quiet intake of air just to make sure he was still breathing.

Then I'd leave a large glass of water and an aspirin on the nearby coffee table for him.

If there had been a way out, I would have taken it a long time ago.

So even as I had braced myself for Izzie's knee-jerk reaction to flee, I didn't resent her for it. I accepted it as the way things worked.

Except instead of splitting, Izzie had tentatively placed one hand on my shoulder and said, "What do you need me to do?"

That's why I didn't care if everyone at Smith High School thought it was weird that I chose to spend my time with a girl they'd already dismissed as a chubby nerd when I could be hanging out with the most popular kids at school. All I had to do was ditch Izzie and every lunch from then on I could be eating at the most prominent table in the cafeteria with the rest of the Notables.

Never going to happen.

Because if I had to pick between joining the Notable clique or staying Isobel Peters's best friend, it wasn't even a contest.

"Thanks, Izzie."

"So you were saying something about Spencer King." Izzie's lips curved up into a half-smile. *"Hypothetically . . ."*

I laughed. "Mackenzie made a big deal out of inviting us both to watch a movie at Logan's house tonight . . . and I don't know how to get out of it. Which is why I need *you* to give me some of that genius-level advice of yours."

Izzie rolled her eyes. "I've got fantastic advice all right, if you want to get a jump on prepping for the PSATs. Guys like Spencer King—ones who are good looking and rich and could get away with murder—yeah, not my area of expertise."

"Come on, Izzie! Pretend I'm asking for an anthropological study of the . . . *Homo,* um, make that *Hockey erectus* clan. How can I turn him down without pissing him off?"

Izzie's expression turned thoughtful. "He's proud, right? Probably used to getting his own way and equipped with a competitive streak a mile long. So make it seem like *his* idea. As long as you distract him with a bet or a dare—some kind of feat to prove his manliness—he'll probably forget you even exist." She zipped up her backpack and then paused as if reconsidering the last part of her statement. "Sorry, he'd forget that *I* exist. You're too pretty for that, so . . . not sure how you'll pull this one off. Keep me posted, though."

Izzie brushed off the dirt on the seat of her pants and started walking toward her science class while I tagged along beside her. I probably should have let the subject drop and left for the English wing, which happened to be located in the opposite direction, but I couldn't let it go. Not without a solid, workable plan in place. Not when it was entirely possible that Mackenzie was scheming how best to throw me at her boyfriend's best buddy.

I needed a wingwoman.

And it looked like Izzie was it.

"You know what would make a really great distraction, Izzie? Having someone else come along to keep it from being a double date. That would really help keep the pressure off." I looked pointedly at her. "I just need to convince someone I trust to play the role of the fifth wheel for a single night."

Izzie feigned ignorance. "Oh? Well, I'm sure you won't have any trouble locating a volunteer. From what I've seen, all Spencer has to do is grin and almost any girl here will leap into his arms."

Funny, but I never noticed anything special in his smile. I mean, yeah, the guy was good looking, but he always seemed a bit too . . . polished. His whole attitude was a little too slick for me; he knew exactly how he came across and used it to his advantage. I could totally picture him naming his dog something obnoxious like "Babe Magnet" and *still* walking away with phone numbers in his pocket.

Part of me couldn't believe that anyone would fall for his lines, especially at a small high school where everyone knew *exactly* what you did last summer because they were probably there with you—or they knew someone who was. Maybe that explained his sudden interest in me, though: He was expanding his dating pool to include freshmen because he had already hooked up with everyone else.

Or at the very least dated everyone else's best friend, thereby invoking the Girl Code. Although I suspected plenty of girls would be willing to overlook the code for a shot at Spencer King. And that an equal number of girls felt gut-wrenchingly foolish when he launched into his whole *I don't do serious relationships speech.* Everyone at Smith High School knew about his talk, and yet somehow heartbroken girls still ended up crying in bathroom stalls while they crossed out the hearts they had drawn around their linked names.

Dylan's smile, on the other hand . . . yeah, his name was something worth etching into the ugly chipped blue paint on the stall doors.

Not that I ever would.

Probably.

"I don't care if other girls would be interested in him. I need you, Izzie. Please say you'll go with me. *Please.*"

She picked up her pace and pretended to consult an imaginary watch. "Oh, will you look at the time? I've got to—"

"One night, Izzie. We'll watch a stupid movie with them and then head to your house for our classic Sunday night sundaes."

"I don't want to go."

I shoved back a strand of long brown hair that had some-how found its way into my mouth. "But you'll do it, right? For me?"

Izzie groaned. "You owe me one for this. And you better believe that I'll be collecting."

"Deal! You're the best, Izzie!" I fought the urge to do a celebratory fist pump as other students began swarming the hallways around us. Instead, I did an abrupt turn and hurried against the flow of traffic in the hallway, pausing only to call over my shoulder. "The absolute best!"

But not even the promise of Izzie's stalwart presence lessened my panic when my phone vibrated with a text message from Mackenzie.

CHANGE OF PLANS. MOVIE AT MY HOUSE
INSTEAD! SEE YOU SOON!

Which meant that not only was I going to be avoiding the advances of a smug, *I can get any girl I want* jock; I'd also be stuck navigating around the one guy I wanted but couldn't have.

Just freaking great.

Chapter 3

Prom court reflects the best and the brightest of each class. And all eyes have turned to the juniors this year. Will hockey captain Logan Beckett once more be crowned? Or will his relationship with Smith High School's Ambassador of Awkward, Mackenzie Wellesley, strip him of the title?

Many people are speculating that Spencer King might live up to the family name yet. . . .

—from "Preparing for Prom,"
by Lisa Anne Montgomery
Published by *The Smithsonian*

"Let's go over this one more time. If I start coughing . . ." Izzie glanced around the parking lot outside the high school as if she expected Logan to appear at any second and whisk us away to Mackenzie's house. "Then I change the subject."

"And if I glance down at my watch?"

"I explain that we should probably head to your house because we promised your mom that we'd help her paint the living room."

"Right again. Okay, last one." Izzie shoved her glasses higher up her nose as she waited for me to spit it out. "If I say, 'Oh, hi, Dylan? Fancy seeing you here.' "

She screwed up her face in mock concentration. "Let's see . . . I call the cops and hustle you out of there, right? Or do I take it all the way to the feds?"

"You're hilarious. Now answer the question."

"I pull you out of there by any means necessary. We've been over this, Mel. I've got it. You're not exactly asking me to solve Fermat's Last Theorem here."

"Okay, I'm going to pretend like I know what that means." I took a deep breath as I felt anxiety begin creeping up my back, one vertebra at a time. "You know, if you could come up with a few brilliant ideas for a preemptive escape, right now would be a great time to share them. So . . . feel free."

Isobel lowered her voice as Mackenzie approached the pair of us. "Don't you think you're blowing this out of proportion? It's a movie with some friends. How bad can it get?"

Oh, I don't know . . . *nuclear fallout bad!*

Hey, it could happen. Theoretically . . . I decided not to mention it, though. The last thing I needed was to be on the receiving end of another one of Izzie's *are you actually saying that out loud?* looks.

"Hey, Isobel!" Mackenzie said, conveniently interrupting our conversation as she drew within speaking distance. "Are you meeting up with Sam?" She swiveled around as if expecting to see the most unconventional of our mutual friends come striding over in a fifties style dress and a pair of motorcycle boots.

Izzie shook her head. "Nope, she's in detention. Again. I don't think she'll be free to hang out for a while. As in, she might stage a jailbreak in time to catch the tail end of this year's graduation. Maybe."

Mackenzie grinned. "What did she do this time? Oh wait, let me guess . . ."

"Did she toilet-paper the principal's office?" I suggested.

"Maybe she submitted a strongly worded letter to the editor for *The Smithsonian.*" Mackenzie pursed her lips thoughtfully. "I wouldn't blame her. The article Lisa Anne wrote about her was total crap. Then again, the only people on the staff of our school paper who would give Sam even an inch for a rebuttal is Jane. *Maybe* Scott. And since Jane's focused on getting her fiction publication up and running, and Scott's primary interest centers around his camera . . . I can't see that happening anytime soon."

I was just grateful that Jane had seemed to mellow out around me. Maybe it was because Mackenzie and I had bonded so quickly post-YouTube video and Jane's nose got a little out of joint, but I'd been getting a serious *back away slowly* vibe from her for weeks. It was only when Scott began dogging her every move that she'd eased up around me.

Probably because her photographer boyfriend was keeping her preoccupied.

A guy who *wasn't* related to our mutual best friend.

Some girls have all the luck.

I quickly tried to move the subject away from Jane. "Maybe Sam vandalized the boy's locker room with anti-rape pamphlets?"

Mackenzie positively lit up as she yelled, "I've got it! Sam was busted trying to organize a protest for prom! Now she's stuck making glittery signs for the school dance during detention."

Izzie shook her head, but I could tell she was enjoying our little guessing game too. "Um, none of the above, actually. She was caught passing out condoms in the hallway."

"*Again?* Either she needs to mix things up a little or she needs to get a whole lot sneakier." I crossed my arms. "She's going to get suspended soon."

Izzie merely shrugged. "That's up to her, Mel. She told me yesterday that she has no intention of letting abstinence-only education send her fellow classmates out into the world with an inadequate understanding of sex. So . . . I'm guessing she's not going to be easily swayed from her mission. Although I'll be sure to mention all of these suggestions to her; I bet she'll love them."

"They weren't really intended as suggestions," Mackenzie pointed out, but Izzie's smile only widened.

"Uh-huh. Yeah, you can try explaining that to Sam. Let's see how far you get."

I doubted Mackenzie would even make it a foot. Our school principal could personally attest that when Sam cared about something, she would go to great lengths to take a stand, even if that meant forming a one-woman picket line or roping us into joining her.

We'd be the ones stuck making glittery signs . . . about various means of contraception.

"So, if you're not waiting for Sam . . ." Mackenzie let her voice trail off, probably because she realized halfway in that it might sound as if she didn't want to be involved in Izzie's plans. "Um, do you want to come to my place? We're just getting together to watch a movie, but I'd love to hang out. If that works for you."

Mackenzie might have a habit of sticking her foot in her mouth, but at least her heart was always in the right place.

"Izzie would love to join us," I announced, just in case she tried to weasel her way out of it. "Isn't that right, Iz?"

"Um . . . right. I'd love to join in," Izzie parroted back weakly, and I knew that I was the worst friend ever. When it was just the two of us, Izzie was all snarky and self-confident, but with most other people, she sort of crawled into her shell. The shoulders would go up, her glasses would be adjusted, and my brilliant, sarcastic friend would shrivel up into a little ball. And even though Mackenzie on her own might not produce the full hermit effect, the addition of the two hottest juniors on the Smith High School hockey team definitely would.

If the roles had been reversed, Izzie wouldn't have pulled me into her mess. She would have faced the freaking *gallows* alone, nervously pushing up her glasses the entire time, but on her own nonetheless. She never would have roped in anyone else along the way.

I should have let her back out.

But Izzie's chin was jutting out, and despite a rigidity in her shoulders that hadn't been there before, it looked like she really wanted to do this. Okay, she didn't *want* to do it, exactly. More like she felt she had something to prove to herself.

I was selfish enough to feel relieved—and proud. Really freaking proud of my best friend for pushing beyond her normal comfort zone.

"Are Jane and Scott coming too?" she asked Mackenzie.

"They can't make it. Something about the school paper. Again."

Izzie looked disappointed and I felt a quick surge of guilt. Jane and Izzie were no longer just bus buddies with a casual friendship created by a mutual desire not to sit alone. That had all changed when Alex Thompson, the biggest jerk at Smith High School—one who made Patrick look like nothing more than a vaguely irritating moth—ridiculed Izzie's weight in front of everyone in the school cafeteria. He'd been under the impression that neither of the girls would protest too loudly.

He had been wrong about a whole lot of things that day.

I would have given anything to see his expression as good-girl Jane Smith hauled back and slammed her fist right in his face.

Actually, I would've given anything to be there five seconds earlier so that I could have beaten Jane to the punch.

But I had been stuck trying to come up with a good explanation for Mrs. Paralov as to why I'd been late for her class eight times that semester without mentioning the fact that each morning my daily ritual included making sure my dad wasn't still so drunk from the night before that he was unable to drive me to school. Or that my dad insisted he was merely coming down with a case of the flu when the binge the night before left him with a particularly nasty hangover.

Yeah, I had no intention of mentioning any of that.

Which was why I was stuck making evasive, *mm-hmm* noises and promising to be more punctual while Jane Smith was defending my best friend.

The only part of that catastrophe that I witnessed was the aftermath. The way Isobel spent the next few weeks listlessly moving her food around with a fork instead of actually eating it. Izzie still wouldn't be caught dead at the ice skating rink. Not when that would only increase the risk of encountering Fake and Bake (Mackenzie's rather fitting nickname for two of the most popular girls in school) along with a whole horde of their Notable cohorts.

Izzie barely managed to curl her mouth into a lackluster excuse for a smile when she spotted Spencer and Logan walking right toward us. We both knew that she wanted to jackrabbit out of there. I subtly nudged her with my shoulder in what I hoped passed as a silent show of support, while I mentally reviewed the game plan one last time. Isobel's advice had seemed so simple earlier.

Distract him with a bet or a dare—some kind of feat to prove his manliness—he'll probably forget you even exist.

Brilliant in theory. A whole lot harder in execution with Spencer grinning broadly at the three of us. Especially since I was already smiling back, and not because I had any interest in flirting with him either. There was just something infectious about him. Maybe it was knowing that we could have been ninety-year-old nuns and the megawattage wouldn't have wavered an iota. Spencer was a natural charmer who enjoyed putting everyone at ease with a few casual jokes. Well, everyone except Izzie. She only appeared more tightly wound than ever as she shoved her glasses higher up her nose.

"Hey, *Melanie,*" he said, not even trying to disguise how impressed he was with himself for remembering my name. Then again, for all I knew, the golden boy had enough girls in rotation to make my head spin. "How's it going?"

"Um, fine. Have you met Isobel?" I practically shoved my friend forward in my haste to distract him. "She enjoys, um . . . reading, solving difficult math problems, and—"

"Long walks on the beach?"

I grimaced. So much for playing it cool and keeping it casual. I was introducing Izzie as if she were entering a pageant. An absurd image of my best friend strutting over to a raised podium in a bikini had me fighting not to laugh. Izzie would rather take her finals three times in a row than enter one of those competitions.

And she would probably come up with some incredibly brilliant way to avoid the thing completely even if someone tried to railroad her into it.

Izzie glared at both of us and her chin jutted up ever so slightly. "She likes the beach just fine. But you know what she *really* enjoys? Speaking for herself—without using the third person."

Spencer blinked in surprise, probably because he had written her off the instant she had fiddled with her glasses instead of making eye contact. His smile kicked up at one end, revealing a dimple that should have been at odds with his bad-boy reputation. The slight tinge of pink I noticed flushing Izzie's cheeks also made me wonder if maybe she was enjoying herself after all.

That fleeting thought probably jinxed everything.

Because any trace of good humor—in Spencer, Izzie, Logan, or Mackenzie—vanished as soon as Fake and Bake, better known as Steffani Larson and Ashley McGrady, rounded the corner and locked their sights on our little group.

"Okay, can we move this to Mackenzie's place?" Technically, it was a question, but Spencer didn't give any of us an opportunity to refuse before he began hustling us toward the parking lot. "Now. Move it along right now."

"But I was going to—"

"Keep walking, Mackenzie," Spencer ground out, "one foot in front of the other."

Logan rolled his eyes at his best friend. "Running scared already, Spence? Prom isn't for another two weeks. If you can't deal with this now, how do you expect to handle it when things really heat up?"

"Later." There was nothing even remotely resembling a smile on Spencer's face now. Nothing in his eyes except deep frustration, and if I wasn't mistaken, a dash of panic as well.

It answered one question of mine, though: Spencer had definitely lied about his leadership abilities the day before. If the guy was half as good at exerting his will on others on skates as he was on foot, he would have no trouble keeping his teammates in line. One gruff order from him and the four of us were instinctively fleeing from the two reigning queens of evil.

"Almost there," he murmured encouragingly. "We're almost there . . ."

Mackenzie twisted, probably hoping to see if the Axis of Evil were drawing close, lost her balance, and tripped. One second she was keeping pace with the rest of us and the next . . . not so much. Logan was instantly kneeling on the pavement next to her.

"You okay, Mack?" His voice was soft with concern, although I thought I detected a hint of amusement in it too. "Need a hand up or are you, um, practicing yoga again?"

I had a feeling that "practicing yoga" was Mackenzie's new not-so-subtle way of covering up her clumsy moments.

And given how often Mackenzie managed to stumble over nonexistent obstacles in her path, she probably found herself making up excuses fairly often. Not that any of us— Mackenzie included—expected Logan to actually believe any of it.

She smiled up at him but batted away the offered hand. "That's right. I'm just practicing the downward-facing klutz position." Mackenzie rose and brushed off her jeans where dirt clung at the knees.

"Act injured. Right now," Spencer ordered desperately, but it was too late. Steffani Larson was already close enough to all of us to stick her cosmetically altered nose into our business. I actually kind of felt sorry for Fake. I had glanced once at Mackenzie's freshman high school yearbook and Steffani's face had far more character when there was a slight bump in her nose and dirty blond hair that didn't come from a bottle.

Well, maybe *sorry for her* was a bit of a stretch. The girl got her kicks making the easy targets in the freshman class feel as uncomfortable as humanly possible. Sympathy has never been something that I extend to bullies. But that didn't prevent me from having a morbid curiosity as to how she could've transformed herself so quickly into someone completely, well . . . fake.

"Hey, Spencer," she said breathily, as if she were auditioning for the part of Marilyn Monroe. "Long time no see."

"Uh, yeah. Long time. Funny how that happens." Except he didn't look like he found any humor in the situation whatsoever.

Ashley beamed at him, too, her white teeth looking particularly bright against her orange tanning salon skin. No way would anyone start calling *her* Pocahontas, though.

"You promised to come talk to me after your hockey practice yesterday," Ashley pouted. "What happened?"

"Oh, you know," Spencer said evasively as he took one

rather large step backward, accidentally positioning Izzie in front of him like some kind of shield, placing her right in the line of fire. And my brilliant best friend was completely oblivious to the danger in becoming a target, probably because she was staring at all parties involved as if watching a particularly riveting daytime drama.

"I think it's pretty obvious that they want you to go into more detail. Maybe you should try using really small words. Two syllables or less," Izzie muttered under her breath.

Something I happened to find pretty damn funny. Unfortunately, this time I was in the minority. Everyone else was staring at her in disbelief.

"Are you calling me *stupid?*" Steffani demanded, ignoring Spencer as she tried to incinerate Izzie with her eyes.

"Nope," I interrupted before the situation could slip even further out of control. "Izzie's just worried we won't make it to that . . . thing on time." I glanced down pointedly at the beatup watch on my wrist. "Oh, man, we've got to go. See ya!"

That earned me a grateful smile from Spencer as we booked it for the boys' cars.

I only realized as I clicked my seat belt on that earning his gratitude was the absolute last thing I was supposed to be doing given that my goal was to stay well within the Friend Zone.

So much for following Izzie's advice.

Chapter 4

Speaking of the illustrious King family, this reporter has heard rumors that there may be another substantial donation headed to Smith High School that is earmarked for making this year's prom unforgettable. While this has proved impossible to substantiate, Principal Taylor has hinted that an announcement may occur after the King's twenty-sixth wedding anniversary.

If the high school prom is even half as decadent and exclusive as their yearly extravaganza, this is going to set an unreachable standard for years to come.

—from "Preparing for Prom,"
by Lisa Anne Montgomery
Published by *The Smithsonian*

"Okay, Spence, want to tell me what *that* was all about?"

It was weird hearing Mackenzie address a hockey player so casually, because pre-fame she would've been every bit as frazzled by his presence as Izzie. Now she was acting like it was totally normal for Spencer to pull up to the curb and saunter over as if he hadn't peeled out of the parking lot like the hounds of hell were nipping at his heels.

To be fair, that wasn't far from the situation . . . and maybe for Mackenzie this was the new normal.

Spencer smiled, clearly ready to go back into full-on charm mode again. "Nothing. I'm curious about that yoga move you mentioned, though. Does the downward-facing klutz transition into any other interesting positions?"

Mackenzie reddened, but she didn't look like she had any intention of backing down.

"I'm serious, Spencer."

"Oh, me too. Have you and Logan tried any advanced poses together? Because I'm more than happy to give my buddy here some pointers."

"Spencer is having some girl troubles right now," Logan answered for him, which probably broke some friendship rule. Although I was willing to bet that a quick punch on the shoulder would be enough to wipe the slate clean.

Izzie didn't make much of an effort to hide her disdain. "Why? Has he run out of girls to sleep with or something?"

She was probably already calculating the most likely percentage of girls he'd had sex with in each class.

"Not yet, obviously. But I'm more than happy to remedy that error." Spencer gave her a slow once-over and I could've sworn the tips of Izzie's ears reddened. "What do you say, Isadore?"

"Isobel."

He shrugged. "You say potato, I say—"

"My *name*. Correctly." She shoved her glasses up higher. "His girl troubles no longer surprise me. I'm just amazed he's ever able to keep one interested long enough to have a problem."

Spencer laughed outright at that, but sobered when Mackenzie tried to discreetly elbow him.

"Yeah . . . the problem is that they won't leave him alone."

I couldn't help staring in disbelief, first at Logan as his words began to sink in, and then at the imperturbable Spencer King.

As far as problems went . . . that was a pretty great one to have.

"I fail to see the problem here," Izzie said abruptly. "He clearly has a short attention span. So why exactly is it a bad thing that he's the one being pursued?"

Spencer moved forward, and though there was nothing overtly threatening about the sudden movement, I watched Izzie's shoulders instantly hunch as he drew near. He paused only when they were well within touching distance—within kissing distance—forcing Izzie to struggle to hold her ground. I'd expected her to trip over her own feet in her haste to put some space between them.

But she stuck it out. Barely.

"There is showing interest and then there is pursuit. I don't happen to enjoy it when people don't respect my boundaries." He cocked his head in a thoughtful examination as Izzie struggled to breathe naturally. "How do you like it?"

I couldn't tell if he was coming on to my best friend, making a point, or terrifying her; either way, I instinctively wanted to put a halt to it.

Izzie wasn't prepared for Spencer's kind of games, and the last thing she needed was to get all wound up over a guy who didn't stick around. She was just back to eating normally. If Spencer ended up kicking her to the curb for Fake and Bake, I wasn't sure how long it would take to raise her self-esteem out of the gutters.

Logan interceded before I did, though. "Shut up, Spencer."

Which looked like exactly the response Spencer had wanted, given the way his shoulders relaxed as he leaned against the front porch of Mackenzie's house. "No problem."

Then he began whistling cheerfully.

Izzie and I traded looks. Hers said quite clearly, *What the hell am I doing here? You've got to find a way to get me out of this!* I shook my head just to make sure she knew that there was no way she was ditching me now.

Not when awkward tension was already filling the air.

Still, Spencer was true to his word; he didn't speak while he waited for Mackenzie to unlock her front door. But then it swung open as if we were all cast in some painfully overly choreographed play.

And on the other side of it stood Dylan Wellesley.

He was absolutely filthy. Dirt was smeared on his face, in his hair, and down his whole left side, so that it looked as if he had decided to rub himself against the side of a mountain or fought a losing battle with a landslide. Seeing him so thoroughly coated with dirt should have been funny, but I couldn't manage even a hoarse laugh because my body seemed to go on the fritz. My heart started beating too quickly, my pulse started racing as if we had a whole pack of Notable girls armed with hairspray and tweezers sneaking up behind us. I shoved my hands in my pockets because any second they were going to start shaking with nerves.

It was ridiculous. I half-wanted Izzie to tug me out of sight and force me to snap out of it. Dylan wasn't the first boy to make me go a little weak at the knees. He also wouldn't be the last. Although I still freaking *hated* that he had this effect on me.

I mean, let's be real: Most high school relationships end. They fray under the pressure of waiting for college acceptance letters and come completely unraveled as soon as a long-distance relationship becomes a reality. And sure, some people defy the odds and end up marrying their high school sweethearts. Some people find a way to stay together despite everything life throws in their path. Some people also win the freaking lottery—that didn't mean the odds were in my favor. The very last thing I needed was a relationship complicating things even further. Not when I had classes to pass, tests to take . . . guidance counselors to impress when they inevitably poured over a handful of standardized tests and tried to use it to divine my future.

Ahh . . . you scored well on your SAT II for the Spanish language exam. That might help compensate for your abysmal score in math. Congratulations, you might not be doomed to a crappy minimum wage job after all!

Too bad my racing pulse wasn't willing to consider all the reasons why getting involved with anyone—let alone someone as intertwined in my life as my close friend's little brother— was a bad idea right now.

"Um . . . hi, Dylan," I mumbled. "Fancy seeing—I mean, it's . . . uh, good to see you."

I glanced over at Izzie to see if she had even noticed my near fumble with our code. She seemed a little preoccupied giving her glasses a quick cleaning.

So much for having a brilliant observer of human nature watching my back every step of the way.

Dylan grinned, as if seeing me on his doorstep automatically canceled out every annoyance that might have accrued over the course of the day. The interest, the keen sense of attraction that I was determined to keep under wraps, was written all across his face for everyone to see, right beneath the mud and dirt that streaked his jaw, the left side of his nose, and his temple.

I wanted to dismiss him as cute—adorable, even—in an open, puppy-doggish kind of way. To shrug it off as some fleeting infatuation from some kid who was going through a stage and be content knowing that when Dylan Wellesley looked back at his life, he would have fond memories of his first crush on Melanie Morris. That he would idly wonder whatever happened to me before he shrugged and then greeted his perfect girlfriend, who was probably just returning home from her morning run. He deserved that kind of happiness;

the cup of coffee with his soul mate over breakfast every day thing.

And that girl was never going to be me, because I wasn't cut out for that kind of life.

Not when I needed to devote a large chunk of my time to making sure my dad didn't choke to death on his own vomit.

Which didn't stop Dylan from self-consciously wiping at his cheek to remove the mud. "Hey, Melanie. I haven't seen you since—"

"Yeah, long time no see." I winced when I realized just how closely my words echoed the ones that Spencer had used to shoo away Fake and Bake. "Um . . . we were just going to watch a movie, but I actually have a lot of homework waiting for me, so . . ."

For some reason Dylan refused to take the hint. I could tell that he was hearing my message loud and clear; his eyes narrowed, his jaw tightened, and he nodded slightly. But he didn't appear discouraged.

And he never took those enigmatic espresso brown eyes off me.

"I'm betting my sister would be happy to help you with your homework," Dylan said easily, as he stepped out of the doorway. "Isn't that right, Mack?"

"Of course, but I thought you felt pretty good about your history test after our study session yester—"

Mackenzie never got a chance to finish that sentence because Izzie interrupted. "Do you have popcorn?"

At least Izzie was following our previously established protocol.

"I've been sort of craving . . . popcorn recently." The freshly cleaned glasses were shoved higher up her nose again. "So if you don't have any, I was thinking maybe Melanie and I could pick some up before we start the movie. Maybe . . ."

Izzie was just as bad at covering for me as I was at doing it myself, but oddly enough it seemed to work. Mackenzie didn't suspect a thing. She just slung an arm across Izzie's shoulders and led her inside, right past where Spencer stood examining them both with one sardonically raised eyebrow.

"I think we have some popcorn. Unless Dylan has already eaten the entire contents of the house. Again," Mackenzie said.

Dylan lifted his hands in mock innocence. "I haven't touched it. The Pringles, on the other hand . . . yeah, those are history."

Mackenzie laughed and gave her brother a playful shove, but Logan lagged behind her. He paused and then looked pointedly from me to Dylan as if he wanted to deliver some kind of warning but found himself at a loss for words. I almost felt sorry for the guy; it had to be hard picking up on social tension that went straight over his girlfriend's head, especially since it involved her only sibling. Thankfully, he held his tongue and followed the girls inside. Spencer trailed after Logan, but his smirk made it clear that he knew I had something unfinished with Dylan. Then again, we had hit the dance floor at his party together before everything went to hell.

Maybe he had remembered that when he accepted Mackenzie's invitation. That's certainly how it looked to me when he winked before he sauntered inside.

Leaving me completely alone with Dylan.

I seriously considered making a run for it. Just booking it across the weed-strewn lawn, leaping over the mud-caked soccer ball resting against the base of the single tree on their property as I sprinted for the street. Three blocks from where I stood was an elementary school, a block past that was a chain store where I could probably lose him if he decided to pursue.

Except I would have to explain to Mackenzie later why I had fled from her younger brother. And considering that he had never once done anything to me, unless smoldering glances counted, that wasn't something I wanted to discuss. Mackenzie might be oblivious sometimes, but she wasn't stupid.

At some point she would figure it out if I didn't keep my feelings tucked away.

"So are you avoiding me now?" Dylan asked, his words at odds with the total unconcern in his face. "Or is there some other reason you look like you're ready to head for the hills?"

Crap. Apparently there was nothing subtle about my reactions.

"No. Nope. Not at all . . . I don't know what you could be talking about."

Dylan merely grinned. "You want to rethink that answer? Because the last time we were alone, I had my hands on your waist and then I moved them to your—"

My face flushed as I mentally replayed that moment at Spencer's party. I didn't need to hear Dylan remind me how great it felt to have my arms wrapped around his neck, my fingers toying with his hair, my body pressed against his, as we moved in time to the music. Just like I didn't need him to make any comments about the way his hands had slowly moved down my back in a caress that I could easily have broken if I had wanted to protest.

But I hadn't.

I blew out a frustrated breath as I forced myself to walk toward him. "I remember it, thanks. I just don't think we need to talk about that night. It was obviously a mistake. So . . . let it go, Dylan."

"Let it go?" Dylan pretended to consider the idea as the distance between us shrank.

My body felt all tingly as I drew up within touching distance. I had half-hoped he would step back into the house so that I could pass him in the hallway with my sense of personal space perfectly intact.

Yeah, like that was really going to happen. Even with ten

feet between us there was something about his gaze that left me feeling like I was pressed against him as closely now as I had been on the dance floor.

"There's just one thing stopping me from doing that, Melanie. Something you seem to be forgetting."

"Oh yeah?" I said with false bravado as I pressed myself against the doorjamb so that I wouldn't accidentally brush against him. "What's that?"

Dylan leaned forward and I fought the urge to remove a clump of mud from his hair. "You made me promise to stay close."

My breath caught as he inched forward.

"And I always keep my promises, Melanie."

Chapter 5

Prom tickets will be going on sale this week and run $12 for one ticket and $20 for a pair. So time to pluck up the courage to ask the person who has your heart. Don't forget: The memories you create this night will follow you for the rest of your life.

So go big or stay home.

—from "Preparing for Prom,"
by Lisa Anne Montgomery
Published by *The Smithsonian*

Mackenzie called my name and I used the distraction to scramble past Dylan.

It wasn't like he didn't already know how his proximity got to me. Dylan was an observant guy, and there was no way he had failed to notice my pulse thrumming erratically in my neck, my uneven jerky breathing, the way I had forced my fingers to cling to the pockets of my jeans so they wouldn't be tempted to venture anywhere else. I felt like I had pretty much plastered an enormous sign on my forehead that read, *Melanie Morris has a crush on Dylan Wellesley.*

And I knew that if I told him to back off, he would instantly give me space.

All I had to say was, "That's one promise I don't want you to keep anymore, Dylan," and he would respect my wishes. He wouldn't even consider going around them, because if anyone tried to pull that crap with his sister, he would go ballistic. Logan and Dylan seemed to get along just fine, but there was no doubt in my mind that if Dylan heard Mackenzie crying, he would get right in the hockey captain's face.

I doubted Dylan would appreciate it, but the word that most readily came to mind when I thought of him was *sweet*. Hot chocolate sweet. The kind that made me feel warm and safe while I melted like a marshmallow.

So he didn't try to stop me from hurrying over to the others even though I knew he'd probably been hoping I'd answer the one question that always seemed to hang heavy in the air between us.

Am I willing to give us a shot or not?

And all I'd been able to determine with any real sense of certainty was . . . not now.

"There you are, Melanie." Mackenzie held up the DVD of *Pocahontas* and gestured at the couch where Izzie was perched nervously between two Notable hockey players, a bowl of popcorn sitting on her lap. "Are you ready?"

"Um . . . sure."

Izzie tried to stand up but couldn't seem to manage it without risking the upheaval of the snacks. "Here. Take my spot, Mel." Her eyes were full of desperation.

"That's okay." I didn't want to get close to Spencer King any more than she did. I wasn't about to discount the way he had winked at me earlier. So instead of allowing Izzie a safe escape, I sat down on the floor and leaned against the couch, effectively trapping her behind me.

Izzie leaned forward so that she could whisper in my ear. "I will kill you for this, Mel. Someday. When you least expect it."

I forced out an incredibly fake-sounding laugh. "Good one, Izzie."

Spencer eyed us suspiciously. "Want to share the joke?"

"No . . . just, y'know, classic Isobel Peters humor. This girl. Laugh a minute."

Izzie's hands clutching the popcorn bowl turned white and I suspected it was because she was fighting the urge to dump it on my head.

"That's me, all right," she said dryly, as Mackenzie popped in the DVD and reclaimed her seat on the couch next to Logan, scrunching Izzie even closer to Spencer in the process.

I couldn't help but notice the way Izzie drew her finger across her throat in the universal signal for impending murder. When Spencer glanced at her, she used that hand to hurriedly adjust her glasses as if that had been the plan all along.

I doubted Spencer bought it for even a second, especially since his mouth quirked upward into an amused grin. Logan couldn't have cared less about any of us. Mackenzie was cuddled up against his chest and judging by his smile, that automatically meant all was right with the universe. Meanwhile, I settled back against the couch, ready to watch the movie, play it cool, and get the whole awkward double date setup over with already.

Then I heard the unmistakable sound of water running.

It made sense. Dylan probably didn't enjoy hanging around with a coating of mud and sweat on his skin. *Of course* he would shower after coming back from his soccer practice.

Of course he would.

Unfortunately, even knowing that there were three rooms and two doors between us, I still felt jumpier than hell. Worst of all, I felt guilty about it. Because what kind of a person agrees to watch a movie at a friend's house and then spends the next twenty minutes trying not to imagine what her little brother looks like under the spray.

It was just . . . wrong.

Izzie seemed equally tense and one of her legs next to me began vibrating with impatience. She also kept snacking away on the popcorn, as if that would be enough to keep the discomfort at bay. If the prickles on the back of my neck were correct, none of our behavior was going unnoticed by Spencer.

Mackenzie was the only one of us who looked thoroughly engrossed by the movie, and that was probably because she was kept busy pointing out historical inaccuracies. Which wasn't exactly hard to do given that the movie totally glossed over the treatment that the Native Americans received at the hands of the English. Still, every few minutes she would pipe up with some random factoid.

"Yeah, they have the wrong flag on the ship," Mackenzie murmured while I debated how quickly I could flee from the room . . . and just how much trouble I'd be in with Izzie later. "Great Britain wasn't united under that flag until 1707."

Logan shook his head in disbelief. "Okay, seriously, Mack. How do you know that stuff?"

She reddened a little as she turned to face her boyfriend. "I may have Googled it."

"God, you're cute."

Okay, yeah, it was definitely time for me to leave. I wasn't even going to make it to the whole "Colors of the Wind" part. Sue me, I wasn't in the mood for adorable animated raccoons or historically inaccurate representations of America. If I was going to be stuck in a lecture, I preferred it to happen in a classroom.

At least at school I was legally obligated not to bolt.

"Well, this was fun, but I think—"

Dylan sauntered into the room, part of his hair still waterlogged, with spikes going in all directions because he had obviously toweled off as quickly as possible. He grabbed a chair and settled in to enjoy the movie.

Right.

Because *Dylan* enjoyed nothing so much as watching a Disney movie with his older sister, his older sister's boyfriend, the girl he wanted to be dating, the best friend of the girl he wanted to be dating and . . . Spencer.

"What were you saying, Melanie?" Mackenzie asked distractedly.

I lunged for Izzie's popcorn, shoved a handful of it in my mouth, and sat back down on the floor. "Mmmphing."

Spencer didn't even try to contain his laugh of disbelief at that one. My cheeks heated and I decided right then and there that Izzie had the right plan all along: Just keep eating popcorn and wait for the awkwardness to pass.

The movie could last for only so long. And then I could flee without having to answer any of Mackenzie's questions.

I just had to sit it out until then.

No big deal . . . until I literally hit rock bottom. Bowl bottom. Whatever.

"Um . . . will you look at that! We're out," I said, yanking the bowl out of Izzie's grasp, probably earning myself another black mark in the column with the title, *Number of times Melanie Morris has thrown me to the wolves.*

I owed her some serious groveling.

But unlike Izzie, I usually don't have a problem taking the easy way out. Not when the hard way involved obsessing over whether my best friend's little brother was intentionally trying to make me admit we were "soul mates" or something equally insane. So much for simply enjoying the movie in peace. To be fair, it wasn't like anyone else was really paying much attention to it either. Izzie's sole focus had been on the popcorn, Logan and Mackenzie had been playfully stealing kisses when they thought nobody else was looking, and Spencer was doing his whole *I'm the coolest person in the room and I could be partying it up right now* routine by glancing repeatedly at his watch.

"I'll, uh, get us a popcorn refill," I said lamely, hoping that nobody would remark about the way two freshman girls had been able to kill a snack faster than two of the star players on the Smith High School hockey team.

"I'll help you with that." Dylan stood easily and I instantly wished that I'd been smart enough to mention the idea of a refill when there was still enough popcorn at the bottom to make it semi-plausible that I had just changed my mind.

"It's popcorn. I think I can handle it."

Dylan just shot me an amused look. "Do you have any idea where we even keep it?"

"I'm guessing in the kitchen."

Okay, I admit it, maybe that was a bit snarkier than necessary, but the prospect of once again being alone with him already had me so jumpy, I felt like I had downed three energy drinks in a row. I couldn't handle it.

Not when his hair was still damp from the shower. Not when his sister would be only one room away.

"What kind of a host would I be if I let the guests fend for themselves?"

"The kind of host who isn't so much a host as an accidental party crasher?" I pointed out. I sort of thought that would put an end to it—all of it—the flirting, the glances, the incredibly unsubtle attempts to spend time with me alone.

I thought that all it would take was a little confirmation that, yes, I could be that bitchy and rude. Usually, I tried to keep that side of me from showing, but when provoked . . . well, let's just say I have a tendency to be a little on the defensive side. Maybe some of that comes from years spent bracing myself for a comment about my dad. There were only a few times a year that the amount of liquor he bought at the supermarket didn't raise eyebrows: Saint Patrick's Day, Super Bowl Sunday, Thanksgiving, and Christmas.

Every other day it was painfully obvious that he wasn't celebrating anything with a large circle of family and friends. He was just trying to numb himself a little bit more.

Dylan didn't react, though, not outwardly, with anything more than a speculative gleam in his eyes. Which only served to annoy me more. Was there some special guy class that I had missed where all the jocks were taught how to look skeptically at each other as some kind of demented means of intimidation?

I was willing to believe it.

Instead of waiting for me to make a move, he snagged the empty bowl from my hands, turned on his heel, and headed right to the kitchen. I could have sat down and pretended nothing had happened, but with the mixture of confusion (Mackenzie), disapproval (Izzie), and disbelief (Logan and Spencer) coming at me from every side of the room, I hastened to make my exit.

I trailed silently after Dylan and prepared myself to apologize for my rudeness. To end whatever it was between us that kept making me act like such a head case. To break whatever knotted thread appeared to be binding the two of us together. Case closed.

"Listen, Dylan . . ." I began, determined to say the words before I could chicken out again. "I'm sorry, I was way out of line. But I don't want to give you the wrong impression. We're friends, right? I think we're friends. And I think we should, y'know . . . stay that way. So . . . no hard feelings?"

"I'm just curious; how many classic breakup lines did you consider before settling for the *I just want us to be friends* approach?"

I crossed my arms defensively. "This isn't a breakup. You have to be *together* in order to be broken up."

There was a flash of pain in Dylan's dark brown eyes and I instantly felt like crap. Correction: I felt like a dung beetle stuck on a pile of crap, even though I was the one trying to make the best out of a really shitty situation.

Better that I hurt him a little now than to let him think that there could be something between us.

"If it's not a breakup, then why the grand speech? The last time I checked, I hadn't mailed a declaration of intentions or a love letter to your house. Not that I even know where you live since the one time I walked you home, I seriously doubt you let me come within two blocks of it."

Three blocks, actually.

But that had nothing to do with Dylan. Not really. I just didn't want to become evasive when we reached my doorstep. And I definitely didn't want him coming inside.

I'd learned early on that compartmentalizing my life was the key to surviving it.

Dylan was part of the outside world. And I needed him to stay there.

So I had walked the last three blocks by myself and hoped that he wouldn't read too much into it. Apparently, he had.

"Look, I just . . . I'm here with Spencer," I blurted out. "So I thought we should clear the air."

The microwave beeped, but Dylan's attention didn't waver from me as I consigned myself to a lower level of hell for lying to him. Again.

The scary part was that if Mackenzie got her way, I would be telling the truth.

"Interesting," Dylan said slowly. "I don't see him with you now."

I curled my lip in disgust. "What does *that* mean? I'm not a fire hydrant that you can pee on to stake your claim over all the other dogs on the block."

He laughed and for a second I could almost believe that we were actually friends again, the way we had been right before that party. Right before we'd complicated things by flirting with each other for hours. . . .

"Nice analogy there. And here I was going to unzip and—"

There was a hesitant knock on the door that thankfully cut him off. There are some things that are better left unsaid, and I had a feeling that was one of them.

Dylan glanced from the door back to me. "Are you expecting anyone else? There's still time to give Spencer the *let's be friends* talk so that you'll be free to date whoever is on the other side of the door."

"Very funny," I snapped as the knocking grew louder.

"Dylan, are you going to get that?" Mackenzie called out, and I knew that if I didn't answer the door, the whole group of them would investigate the source of the racket.

The last thing I needed was to be on the receiving end of any more of Izzie's panic-stricken looks or Spencer's dissecting stares.

"I've got it!" I hollered, moving quickly for the door before Dylan could comment that I'd made myself right at home. I yanked it open just as the dark haired man at the door lowered his fist. He looked like he was in his mid-fifties and was dressed in what I suspected he considered "business casual" with a pair of tailored khaki slacks and a button-down shirt with a few buttons undone at the collar. He looked like he should be at a golf course or heading to the Katsu sushi restaurant downtown, not dropping by the Wellesley house in the late afternoon.

"Um, can I help you?" I asked uncomfortably. If this guy was some kind of honorary uncle or godfather or something, then I was probably making a royal mess out of the situation.

"Mackenzie? You've grown and . . . gotten some sun."

I burst out laughing, because the idea that someone would

confuse the two of us was downright, well . . . laughable. "She's inside. Do you want me to get her or—"

"Don't bother." Dylan cut me off and I turned to look at him, expecting to see a full-fledged grin on his face. There wasn't even the slightest trace of a smile. "Long time no see . . . Dad."

Chapter 6

Am I the only person already sick of hearing about prom? It seems like everywhere I turn there are signs declaring that Smith High School should get ready to get wild with the Mardi Gras theme. Seriously. Seriously? Because nothing says "Prom in Oregon" quite like sparkly dresses, bauble necklaces, and jazz, right? Oh wait. Nope. Not even a little bit.

—Anonymous letter to the editor
Published by *The Smithsonian*

"Maybe I should, uh, get Mackenzie?"

I probably should have kept my mouth shut, but I couldn't let Dylan go through whatever this was alone. Not when tension and hostility were radiating off him in waves.

"That sounds great! It's nice to meet you."

The stranger—Dylan's *father*, I mentally corrected myself—nodded enthusiastically at the exact same moment his son said, "Leave her out of this."

I wasn't entirely sure if Dylan was referring to me or to

Mackenzie, but his dad clearly had no intention of turning around and going anywhere.

"I've missed you, Dill-pickle." The nickname rang hollowly as I watched Dylan absorb the comment. The guy who made sarcastic comebacks in the face of rejection had morphed into a brick wall. Sure, there were nicks and cracks in his composure, but I knew he wasn't going to budge an inch. At least not until there were miles of space between him and his father.

"Yeah, you seemed really broken up in all those holiday cards you sent us over the years. How are Chase and Adam doing? You all looked like you were having a great time in the Christmas photo."

"They're doing well."

"Neither of them need a kidney transplant?"

His dad looked taken aback by the question. "No kidney transplants."

Dylan nodded. "Okay, then. Great. Glad to hear it. Because honestly that's the only way I would give you even five more minutes of my time. Now that we've got that settled, leave."

"I was hoping we could talk." He glanced over at me and shifted uncomfortably. "In private."

"And I was hoping that you'd be able to keep your pants zipped when you were married to Mom. Looks like we're both destined for disappointment." Dylan surprised me with the total matter-of-factness with which he dropped that bomb. Then he turned to me and said calmly, "Melanie, would you please step back? I think this moment calls for a door slamming in his face. I know it's overdone and kind of childish, but what the hell. You only get to brush off your deadbeat dad once, right?"

"Um," I said articulately. "Are you sure you want—"

"What's the holdup, Dylan?" Mackenzie rounded the corner, took one look at her brother's stony expression, and bolted forward. "Everything o . . ." Her voice trailed off as she saw the visitor at the door. "Holy crap."

It was the first time I had ever heard Mackenzie swear, and even though the expletive was pretty mild, it still sounded wrong coming from her. Dylan didn't hesitate any longer. He pulled me back and slammed the door shut.

Right in his dad's face.

Then, ignoring my presence entirely, he focused on his older sister. "He says he wants to talk to you."

"Is it about Chase or Adam?" Mackenzie asked.

Out of everything, that detail surprised me the most. They had two half brothers I had never heard either of them ever mention by name. Heck, I'd never heard them even bring up their dad. I always figured he had died in a car accident or something when they were young.

It was kind of funny, because if there was one person who should have known better than to make assumptions about an absent father figure, it was me.

"They're fine."

Mackenzie nodded, but there was a dazed look in her eyes, one that had been plastered across tabloid covers when her embarrassing YouTube video went viral. "How are you?"

Dylan's mouth kicked up at the side, but there was a grimness there that I hadn't seen before. I couldn't help thinking that if his father had shown up even a few hours earlier, he would have seen Dylan coated with mud. Somehow that seemed more appropriate given that this emotional battle was definitely going to get dirty.

"Fine," Dylan lied so confidently, I might have believed him if I hadn't witnessed his reaction to his father firsthand. "How do you want to play this, Mackenzie? I don't think he's going to budge from our doorstep anytime soon. He seemed pretty determined to talk to you."

"I can't imagine why," Mackenzie admitted. "Not when he hasn't bothered to swing by since . . . what? Elementary school?"

"Yeah, well, that was before you became America's Most Awkward Teenage Girl. My guess, he wants to sell the heart-warming story of your reunion to the tabloids."

"Still . . ." Mackenzie didn't appear to have any idea what to say on *that* topic, so she shifted back to the more pressing matter. "What do you think we should do?"

He shrugged. "He's not here to see me, Mackenzie. If you want to rehash the past or whatever, that's up to you. If you don't want to say a word to him, I can make sure he keeps his distance while Logan drives you to his place. But either way, you need to make up your mind now."

"Why are we going to my house?" Logan asked from behind me, and I jumped before swiveling around to see that at some point Spencer, Isobel, and Logan had gotten curious.

"Mackenzie?" Dylan said calmly. "Tell me what you want and I can handle this."

Her eyes were wild, and I could tell that she really didn't want to be the one making such a huge decision. It wasn't hard for me to relate. I mean, if my dad stopped drinking and I found myself in a position where he was asking me for forgiveness for spending years wasting away in front of the television, I'm not sure how I would respond either.

Don't get me wrong; I'd be thrilled.

I just would have a really hard time believing he meant it.

At some point, well . . . even the most heartfelt apology can be too little too late.

Although from where I was standing, I didn't see much of an apology going on. There had been no protestations of love from Dylan and Mackenzie's father. He seemed to think that if he acted like nothing had ever happened, his children would fall in line.

Apparently he didn't know the first thing about either one of them.

"I want to talk to him," Mackenzie decided at last; then she repeated her words as if she needed extra convincing.

Logan slipped his hand into hers in a silent show of support and I found myself absurdly jealous of that small action. Not because I wanted to be holding hands with Logan, but because I wanted the freedom to do the same for the person I knew was hurting.

Even if he was pretending that the entire scene was nothing out of the ordinary.

"Okay." Dylan nodded slowly before he turned to Logan. "You're staying here with her."

It wasn't a question; it was an order.

"Yeah, I'm staying."

"Hey, isn't that *my* call?" Mackenzie pointed out, probably in an attempt to lighten the mood a little. Dylan was having none of it.

"No, it isn't. Not when you want to bring . . . *him* into the house. As for the rest of you—" Dylan briefly looked at each of us, although I doubt he noticed that Izzie's shoulders had hunched as if that would make her less intrusive during this incredibly personal moment, or how Spencer was already reaching into his pocket and pulling out his car keys. And if he had any thoughts about me . . . well, none of them showed. "You'll make sure they get home safely."

That was aimed at Spencer. Once again Dylan wasn't really making a request.

"I can see myself home," Izzie said quickly. "And give Mel a ride too. So why don't I just call my mom and—"

"You afraid to ride in a car with me, Isosceles?"

"That's a triangle." Izzie shoved her glasses higher up her nose and glared back at him. "And no, I'm not."

Spencer grinned. "Excellent. Then why don't you go grab your stuff from the living room while I—"

But before Spencer had a chance to finish that sentence, Dylan had tugged open the door. I half expected his dad would have left. Based on everything I had just overheard, the guy had a reputation for bailing when things got rough. No reason for him to start sticking around now.

He was standing right where we had left him, though. Actually, he had moved a few inches to the right so that he could lean against the porch railing, but I hardly thought that little detail was significant.

He didn't appear to be going anywhere.

I couldn't resist turning to Mackenzie to see how she was handling all of this. It sounded like this was the first time she'd seen her dad in *years*. And this probably wasn't the way she had imagined their reunion playing out. Given Mackenzie's love of history, she probably would have wanted more time to formulate her plan of attack. Time to create an intricate web of excuses should she need to fall back and re-strategize.

At least she had her boyfriend by her side.

Logan wasted no time stepping forward, as if placing his body between Mackenzie and her father could somehow protect her emotions.

"Hi . . . Dad."

Dylan flinched as if hearing those words emerge from his sister's throat had somehow registered as a slap across the face. The kind that would leave a handprint afterward.

"There's my girl! How's my little Mack-Attack?"

Mackenzie ignored the question entirely. Probably because she didn't want to snarl that he'd lost the right to use all nicknames when she was back in elementary school.

"You should have called."

Spencer cleared his throat lightly and edged his way to the door. "Thanks for suggesting the movie. It was . . . interesting. Come on, Poca—Melanie. Time for us to go."

But I couldn't seem to move. My feet were transfixed as I

stared at Mackenzie and watched a virtual rainbow of emotion transform her features. Discomfort. Anger. Hurt. Hope.

The air was thick with years of unexpressed pain.

"I did call. A few times. Your mother promised to give you the messages."

Mackenzie jerked back and her eyes instantly flicked over to her younger brother. "And I told her that I wanted nothing to do with you. You should have taken the hint."

"Speaking of hints . . . *Melanie. We're. Leaving. Now,*" Spencer hissed as he moved past Mackenzie's father and headed straight for his car. Izzie didn't need to be told to get out of there. She was uncomfortable enough with the scene taking place to willingly spend one-on-one time with Notable royalty.

Which meant that I now owed her about a billion more favors.

"Why don't we discuss this privately, Mackenzie? I know a great little Mexican restaurant—"

"I'm pretty sure that eating anywhere with you would spoil Mack's appetite. And last time I checked, she had a strict 'no asshole' policy with her life." Logan raised an eyebrow skeptically as her dad straightened in an effort to look as intimidating as possible. "Interesting. I always pictured you with more of a weasely face. I'm kind of disappointed, actually."

Mackenzie jabbed him in the side. "Not. Helping. Logan."

"Really?

"Really."

He squeezed her hand. "Sorry."

And that simple apology was enough. But I didn't exactly have a chance to *awww* over the cuteness of Mackenzie's relationship because Dylan nodded one last time, not in response to anything in particular, but as if he had just confirmed something for himself.

Then he turned very deliberately and walked right past his father.

He didn't shoulder-check him.

There were no snarled insults or teeth-baring or any other kind of alpha-male display to assert that the son had taken up the role of man of the house. Dylan made sure that he didn't so much as brush against his father as he walked away at a steady, deliberate pace while everyone else gawked at his retreating figure.

For half a second I hoped he was going to climb into Spencer's car and order the Notable to start driving. That the four of us would go see some new action movie or something. Nothing like a postapocalyptic society to put your life into perspective, especially when combined with the brain-numbing power of subzero movie theater air-conditioning.

Dylan didn't slow down.

He passed the car without even sparing Spencer or Izzie a glance. That's when I knew that I would be owing Izzie even more favors. A lifetime of them, in fact.

Because I wouldn't be accepting that ride home with her.

I started running down the street after Dylan.

Chapter 7

Dear Anonymous,
The Mardi Gras theme was selected by the prom committee. Maybe instead of whining, you should try to join in some leadership position. And if you're really that sick of hearing about prom—then stay home!
Sincerely,
Lisa Anne Montgomery

—from "Hello Anonymous,"
by Lisa Anne Montgomery
Published by *The Smithsonian*

I'm not sure what I expected to happen.
If my life were a romantic comedy, I probably would call out Dylan's name and watch him pause. Then there would be a slow-motion running scene where my long hair would ripple beautifully behind me. I would draw up to him, attractively out of breath and yet remarkably sweat-free, and he would singe me with a kiss.

"I knew you would come after me," he'd murmur right before I plastered my mouth against his again.

"Always."

Roll credits.

Too bad real life didn't work out that way.

"Hey! Wait up, Dylan!" Even as the words left my mouth I knew that I would have a better chance trying to convince Izzie to wear three-inch stiletto heels to school than I'd have slowing him down.

At least he didn't pick up the pace. He kept his stride long, but he wasn't running and as long as I could keep my feet smacking the pavement in a rhythm that rivaled a full-out sprint, I was only seconds away from drawing up to his side. There wasn't anything glamorous about the way I was sweating.

Dylan didn't so much as glance my way, though.

"Now isn't really a great time, Melanie," Dylan said calmly, as if he were running a few minutes late for a dentist's appointment.

I didn't say anything—partly because I was still struggling to keep up with him and partly because what was there for me to say? *Hey, buddy, sorry your dad is such a jerk. If it helps, my dad spends most of his days staring at the bottom of a beer bottle.*

Yeah, *pass.*

"Uh . . . where are we going?" I asked finally when I had regained my breath.

He shrugged. "Does it matter?"

"I guess not." We descended into silence for another block . . . then two . . . then three.

We passed the elementary school and the blacktop where only a few weeks ago I had been cracking up with Dylan as Mackenzie did a celebratory dance after finally making a shot in rollerblading basketball.

I wondered if he was remembering that or something else entirely. Some distant moment from his childhood back when his dad was actually a part of his life. I tried to picture him as a toddler wobbling around the adjacent soccer field, a wide grin splitting his face, and found myself wondering how long it had been since he'd felt that carefree.

"So I take it you don't want to talk?" I said eventually. One of us needed to break the silence at some point, and it didn't look like it would be him.

"Not particularly."

"Mind if I talk anyway?"

He shrugged, but he didn't make eye contact. "Nothing stopping you."

I took a deep breath. "Okay, well, I'm pretty sure I owe you an apology."

"Oh yeah?" There was a slight hitch in Dylan's step, but he didn't allow it to happen a second time.

"Well, there are a few things, actually."

"Start wherever you'd like. Alphabetically. Numerically. Categorically. It's all the same to me."

Great. He wasn't giving an inch and now I had talked myself into one hell of a situation. I had planned to say that I was just trying to be a good friend—to help him deal with his dad and then split—but I hadn't realized that any apology would inevitably lead to the truth: that I liked him back.

And I still wasn't sure what to make of my feelings.

"I shouldn't have treated you that way back at the house."

He considered that for a moment and then turned to look at me—really look at me—for the first time since Mackenzie had agreed to talk to their dad. "Care to be more specific?"

I kicked at a pinecone and sent it careening forward as my guilt kicked into high gear. "You know . . . when I was making popcorn?"

He slowed, slightly, but I had a feeling that one wrong word and I'd be left in the dust. "That was . . . what? Fifteen minutes ago? Yeah, Melanie. I remember our conversation just fine."

"It was an intense fifteen minutes. You saw your dad again for the first time in years and—"

"Get to the point," Dylan interrupted.

"I'm just sorry about some of the things I said."

Dylan pulled up short. It was funny that I'd been hoping I could make him stop for the past six or seven blocks, and yet now that he was truly stationary and staring me down, I would have gladly accepted any interruption. I would have welcomed a phone call—a text, heck, even a tweet—if that would provide an excuse for me not to face Dylan head-on. The frustration and pain that gleamed in his deep brown eyes made my stomach lurch and twist.

"I'm really not in the mood for one of your head games right now, Melanie. I mean, I'm *never* in the mood for them. But now is a particularly bad time. You say you're more interested in being with Spencer? Fine. Go find him. I'm not stopping you."

"That's not—"

"Not what?" Dylan cut me off again. "Not what you want? Are you sure about that? Because I have a feeling he's *exactly* what you want, Mel. He's one of the most popular guys in school. He's not just a Notable—he's a freaking *legacy!* And then there's the added bonus that as a junior he could actually take you to prom. That probably sounds pretty exciting to you too. So why don't you go pick out your dress and leave me alone?"

"Because he's not you!" I blurted out and then clapped a hand over my mouth as if that could help me magically take the words back. No such luck. So I was stuck standing there while Dylan gaped at me in disbelief.

"Are you for real right now? You don't want me, Melanie. So if you're feeling guilty for blowing off your best friend's little brother—get over it. I certainly will."

I sucked in a deep breath and reminded myself that he was hurting right now. That I deserved a rejection after unintentionally toying with him. He was right about the mind games. Or at the very least, I had been sending some seriously mixed signals.

Still, I'd hoped that the first time I ever told a boy I liked him, you know, *that* way, I wouldn't be feeling quite so vulnerable. That his whole face would light up at the words.

"What . . . what if I didn't want you to get over it?"

He took a step back and then glanced over his shoulder as if he needed to make sure that this wasn't some elaborate prank. Dylan slowly cleared his throat before answering. "Then I would say I never realized you were this selfish."

That stung.

In fact, it burned.

"What. Do. You. Want. Melanie?" Dylan enunciated each word and I felt them all like a backhanded slap.

"I-I don't know! We can't be together. You know we can't be together, so—God, I just don't know anymore!"

Dylan crossed his arms. "Want to run that logic by me again? Why exactly can't we be together? Overlooking the whole *I never asked you to be with me* thing for a moment."

I glared at him. Maybe he hadn't asked directly, but he had made his intentions more than clear. And when he put it that way . . .

I sounded absolutely nuts. Borderline delusional.

But I knew it wasn't all in my head, and if it hadn't been for the fact that he was—

"You're Mackenzie's little brother!" Somehow I managed to get the words out. "There are rules against that sort of thing!"

"No, there aren't. We can go to any state—hell, any *country*—and be together if that's what we wanted. Nobody has legislated against dating a friend's sibling."

"It's the Girl Code," I mumbled, embarrassed to have to say the words.

"Sorry, I didn't catch that."

Liar, I thought bitterly, but Dylan deserved a straightforward answer. Maybe he would never be able to get one from his dad, but he certainly could from me.

"Girl Code," I repeated defiantly.

The excuse sounded increasingly stupid as it hung heavy in the silence between us.

"Oh, *Girl Code.* What rule am I breaking, exactly? I'd really love to take a look. Here I thought that involved dating your best friend's ex. Apparently I need to look over the rules again."

"Well . . . yeah. But—look, I really value Mackenzie's friendship, okay?"

Dylan began walking again and I scurried to keep up. "Okay, then you probably shouldn't try to date Logan. Beyond that—"

"What happens if we have a fight?" I blurted out. "A big one. You want me to go somewhere with you and I can't go and—"

"That's your idea of a fight?" Dylan's eyebrows had shot up in disbelief, but his eyes kept boring into me, past the fake confidence that functioned as a veil and hid my nervousness from sight, right to the heart of the girl who was sick of pretending to be fine.

I flicked a long strand of hair back away from my face, using the movement to cover some of my discomfort.

"Well . . . yeah."

"If I wanted to go somewhere and you couldn't make it, I'd be disappointed. That's it."

"Right," I laughed hoarsely. "You'd just be disappointed if I didn't make it to your middle school graduation because it would make me feel like a cougar?"

"One year, Melanie. I am *one year* younger than you are. And yeah, it would suck if you didn't show up. Is that what you want to hear? Hell." He started walking, only to stop abruptly in his tracks. "You want to know why I hate my dad, Melanie?"

I did. I wanted to know all his secrets. To be the one person he could confide in even when his whole life felt upended.

But now I was terrified by what I might hear.

"Yes." I couldn't manage anything beyond that single word. Dylan didn't need a bigger opening, though.

"He bailed. That's why I hate him. He could have been my father and still raised two other kids with his home wrecker. I would have been furious about the way he treated my mom—I'm not sure I could *ever* overlook that—but I still would have loved him."

I nodded speechlessly.

"But he wanted a fresh start. That's why he pretended that Mackenzie and I never existed. He took the easy way out. He bailed."

Those two little words began repeating over and over again in my head.

He bailed. He bailed. He bailed.

My stomach sank as it hit me that I was doing the exact same thing to Dylan. Making him believe that for reasons beyond his control he wasn't good enough for me.

"And I never confronted him about it."

"You were what? Five at the time, Dylan?"

He acknowledged that point with a brittle smile. "Yeah, but as you can see, I'm a whole lot older than that now. And I never called him up. Never yelled at him over the phone. None of it."

I bit my lip as I searched for the right words. "Do you want to—I mean, should we turn around? Do you want to talk to him now?"

Dylan shook his head. "I don't need to anymore. Mackenzie may need to have him answer her questions, but I don't. I already got mine years ago: not interested. That came through loud and clear."

I flinched. That was the same message I was supposed to be giving him.

Isn't it?

I didn't even know anymore.

"I don't hide now, Melanie. Not even for you. So if you actually want to do this thing—well, you've got my number."

This time when he started walking, I stayed in place.

I didn't feel I had the right to be anywhere near him.

Because I had been lying; not on purpose, but I'd been misleading him nonetheless. Dylan wasn't too young for me. He wasn't too immature. He wasn't lacking *anything.*

I'm not good enough for him.

And it was only a matter of time before he realized it too.

Chapter 8

The whole notion of prom is fundamentally flawed. It's meant to be one long romantic night; arrive in a limo with your One True Love in a dress with a matching corsage that elicits gasps from everyone in attendance.

Except if my One True Love is at Smith High School—well, I haven't met him.

And I'm not willing to lower my standards to the point of kissing frogs.

—from "Promising Too Much,"
by Vida Condon
Published by *The Smithsonian*

I walked home.

I didn't really see any other viable alternative, given that Isobel probably wasn't speaking to me since I had ditched her with Spencer back at Dylan's house. And the last thing Mackenzie needed while having a conversation with her dad for the first time in *years* was for me to call, asking if Logan could give me a ride.

My mom was still at work and wouldn't appreciate getting

a phone call during business hours at Sew Creative. And it wasn't as if my dad would be in any condition to give me a lift home, even if he was working weird shifts in the hardware store this week. Assuming that he was at home, he was probably on his third beer and his fourth episode of *NCIS*. Or maybe it was *SVU*.

All of his TV shows blurred together for me. Someone was murdered. A concerned group of "good guys" tried to piece it all together. The case was solved. The theme music blared.

I had a case for him to solve: the one of his deteriorating liver.

That would be a much better use of his time.

Then again, my dad wasn't looking for a good use of his time. He was looking for ... actually, I wasn't quite sure. Numbness, maybe. Or maybe he had just been drinking for so long that he'd stopped asking himself that question. What he wanted was a beer. And then another.

It didn't matter that my mom and I desperately wanted to him quit.

Still, I'd never asked him to stop.

I had just accepted this as my way of life. Wake up. Make breakfast. Go to school. Come home. Maybe cook dinner. During most of the time we spent together, my dad would be quietly nursing a drink. We'd talk a little—stuff about my day, the idiocy of some people who couldn't tell a Phillips head screwdriver from a wrench—normal, boring stuff like that, while he worked his way through the first one or two drinks. Then he would graduate to drinks three and four when I started making noise about going to my room to do my homework. He was usually on number six by the time my mom came home with a new quilt store sample project in her tote bag.

Unless he switched to something a whole lot harder.

Then there was no telling when I might find him passed out on the couch.

But I had never confronted him about it directly. My mom and I had discussed staging an intervention a few times, but it never went anywhere. We wanted to give him an ultimatum, but we couldn't cope with the consequences if he called our bluff. If he didn't stop drinking, then we would do what exactly? Leave him?

He would be dead by the end of a week. Not from starvation or general incompetence, but because if the alcohol didn't numb the pain of that rejection, he would use a bullet instead. That's how I thought it would play out. And given the choice of watching my dad, the man I loved despite everything, drink himself slowly to death or getting that phone call from a neighbor that they'd heard a gunshot and that nobody was answering the door . . . yeah, I would pick the drinking.

I still couldn't shake Dylan's voice in my head.

He bailed.

So had my dad. Maybe Dylan had a point. It was time for me to stop running.

From everything.

I barely paused to scan the recycling bin—five beer bottles, one bottle of cheap gin that he had consumed last night—before I took a deep breath and forced myself to unlock the front door.

"Hi, honey." My dad's voice didn't have the faintest hint of a slur to it, which meant he hadn't made it even halfway through his latest six-pack. Good. "How was your day?"

I didn't even know how to answer the question.

Really freaking terrible. I mean, I got to spend time with this guy I've been crushing on. So that would have been great if I hadn't just totally screwed it up with him. And I'm not even sure why I said half of the things that I did. Why it scares me so badly to admit that I like him.

"Fine," I lied. "Could we, uh . . . talk?"

My dad tipped his head quizzically. "I thought that's what we were already doing."

"No, I mean, yes. But—" I gestured awkwardly at the couch. "Could we really talk?"

He settled down on his preferred side of the couch, the place that had one enormous wet ring in the fabric from all the drinks he had rested beside him over the course of the past ten years. The couch we had before this one probably had a similar stain.

"What's this about? Is someone giving you trouble at school?" My dad took a long pull from his beer as if he were bracing himself for the worst. Or maybe it was just because he wanted more.

There were times I didn't know who made more excuses for my dad's alcoholism: him or me.

"I . . . I'm, uh—" I stuttered before I froze.

There would be no taking back this conversation. So I hovered there, knowing that as soon as my silence was broken, my life would never be the same. My relationship with my dad would forever be altered by the outcome.

"I'm worried about you," I blurted out in a breath. "Your drinking is out of control, Dad."

He laughed.

That was one option I had never imagined. I'd anticipated a series of somber nods before he took yet another sip, or . . . for him to get defensive. Grumpy. Uncommunicative. Distant. *Something.*

Instead, he was acting as if I had pulled some childish prank on him.

"You had me scared for a moment, Melanie. I thought this was something serious," he laughed again. "I just like finishing the day with a cold one. Nothing wrong with that."

Denial.

I forced myself to remain outwardly calm.

"It's not a cold *one*, Dad. It's a cold *eight*." My hands

started shaking, so I pressed them flat against my jeans. "And if you had a long day at work—maybe a customer gave you a hard time about pipes or bolts or something—well, then time to break out the hard stuff."

He rubbed his forehead as if I were responsible for a pounding migraine. As if he had just come home from a long, grueling day of work and the last thing he needed was his daughter giving him a hard time about the way he chose to relax.

My mouth snapped shut, but I still couldn't find it within me to regret letting the truth out in the first place.

He bailed.

Maybe Dylan was satisfied with having that for an answer, but I had to try at least once to get through to my dad.

"I'm *fine*, Melanie. You're blowing this out of proportion."

What was there for me to say to *that? No, Dad, I'm not doing your drinking problem justice. It's so much worse than I'm making it sound.*

He kissed me on the forehead. A quick peck, a scratchy brush of stubble, and a whiff of the oh-so-familiar scent of liquor; then he ruffled my hair. I felt like I was back to being a six-year-old.

Because nothing, *nothing* had changed.

"I have homework to do," I mumbled, moving toward my bedroom as I heard the click of the remote and another murder show claimed my dad's attention.

I wanted to punch something. To rip something to shreds. Maybe throw a plate against the wall, shattering it into pieces. Something big enough that my dad would have to listen. Instead, I sank onto my bed and curled up so that I was hugging my knees to my chest while I tried to suppress the body-shaking heaves that wouldn't quit. I wasn't going to cry, though.

Not competent Melanie Morris. Not the girl most likely to

move confidently between the Notables and the Invisibles at Smith High School. She wouldn't start blubbering just because her daddy refused to change his ways.

Although I wish somebody could get that message through to my body, because the tears were definitely sliding down my cheeks in wavering lines. And no matter how quickly I wiped them away, there was always a fresh set to take their place.

I couldn't seem to move and once again, I heard Dylan's words playing over and over again in my head. Only this time he wasn't telling me that his dad had bailed on him. I heard him asking me a question.

What. Do. You. Want. Melanie? What. Do. You. Want. Melanie?

What. Do. You. Want. Melanie?

I wanted to scream, "I don't know!" but I couldn't get the lie past the lump in my throat. Dylan was right: I knew exactly what I wanted.

A father who would choose me over a beer bottle.

That was never going to happen.

My heart felt like it was being ripped to shreds by that simple truth. He was never going to be the man whom I needed. For whatever reason—assuming that a rough childhood with a disapproving mother I'd never met and a genetic predisposition to drink counted as legitimate reasons—that was beyond him.

I felt like I was being gutted. This, right here, was why I had fought so damn hard not to confront him. As long as I had been able to pretend that my dad would change if I ever mustered the nerve to ask him to do it, I had hope. I had a fantasy father who would face down his darkest demons for my sake.

That man wasn't real, though.

I had wanted and tried and failed.

And it hurt like hell.

But it was also a relief. That fantasy father would still haunt my daydreams with his alcohol-free breath and his clean-shaven jaw. But I couldn't keep beating myself up for not being good enough to make him a reality.

Okay, maybe that was an exaggeration; there was no escaping the what-ifs that constantly swirled around my brain. What if a proper intervention could convince him to enter rehab? What if we took him to an Alcoholics Anonymous meeting? What if my mom and I left so that he could finally hit rock bottom?

What if he required his life to get *that* bad in order to make a change?

Yeah, I would be wondering those questions for years to come. And that was only if I got lucky and he didn't drink himself into the grave first.

Still, I had spoken up.

I had *finally* admitted what I wanted, and there was a comfort in that knowledge even in the wake of rejection.

Now I had to face the unavoidable fact that you can't always get what you want.

If it matters enough to you, then it's worth crying through the pain.

And there was someone else who mattered enough to me.

So the real question was whether or not I had the courage to face another rejection.

Chapter 9

"It's not fair!" Bethany Smarson pouted as she turned to face her part-time friend—and full-time rival—Ashleigh Brody. "We're totally, like, the most popular girls at this school. How is it even possible that we don't have dates to prom yet?"

Ashleigh contemplated that deep theological question while she checked to make sure her spray tan wasn't blotchy. "Well . . . who do you want to go with?"

"Nobody in particular," Bethany murmured coyly.

It was a lie and even Ashleigh knew it.

—from "Prom and Backstabbing,"
by Jane Smith
Published by *The Wordsmith*

Dylan had told me to give him a call when I figured out what I wanted, but I didn't think he meant that literally. I didn't think I could handle having that conversation any other way than face-to-face. Although I couldn't help imagining his reaction if I tweeted him.

HEY @DYLANWELLESLEY, I LIKE YOU. WANT TO BE SEEN IN PUBLIC WITH ME? ON A DATE? #SORRYABOUTYESTERDAY #MYBAD

Yeah, that wouldn't be uncomfortable at all.

Especially if his response didn't require anywhere near the 140 allotted characters.

NO THANKS, @MELMORRIS.

And, okay, it wasn't like a private phone call would have any chance of turning into a public humiliation. But it also wasn't exactly romantic. I mean, best-case scenario? He would forgive me and then we would have to awkwardly discuss our schedules in an attempt to seal it with a kiss.

My pulse raced so quickly at the thought of *finally* feeling his lips against mine, I very nearly backed out of my own plans.

In some ways a rejection from Dylan would be worse than having my dad pretend his drinking wasn't a problem. My dad was a permanent fixture in my life and for all his flaws, I knew he loved me unconditionally. But Dylan?

It was entirely possible that I had already used up his patience.

I was already sick of dealing with myself.

But hey, he had managed to like me even after I shut him down right after the party. He had even tried to chat with me—twice—at his house. So maybe it wasn't a total lost cause.

Then again, all of that had happened before I had pointed out that I didn't want to be seen in public with him. Hard to imagine him just shrugging that one off. In fact, it was hard to see him wanting to speak to me at all. Ever.

It wasn't like he would have any trouble finding someone to replace me in his affections either. There was probably a whole host of girls in his class who'd be perfectly willing to stand in the bleachers during his soccer games so they could see him flash a wild grin beneath a coat of mud.

I had to keep repeating to myself that if he wanted someone else, I would be happy for him. I would back off gracefully. I wouldn't be as selfish as he had accused me of being yesterday. If he didn't want me back, well, that might not be the worst thing to happen to him, considering that I was a mess.

And I wasn't trying to hide that fact from myself anymore.

I kept my head down at school the next day and avoided Mackenzie at all costs so that I wouldn't be tempted to dig into how Dylan was doing in the wake of all the dad drama that had just gone down at their house.

I couldn't avoid Isobel, though.

"You have no idea what you got me into," she hissed as she dragged me away from my locker and the prying ears of a small group of wannabe Notables who might try to climb their way into the in crowd by shoving us further down the social ladder.

"Yeah, about yesterday . . . I owe you an apology."

Isobel's eyes were frantic. "An apology?!" she choked. "Oh, you owe me a whole lot more than that! You talked me into going to Mackenzie's house only to ditch me with *Spencer King*!"

Ouch. Yeah, I definitely wasn't going to be getting a best friend of the year mug.

"Any chance the two of you got along brilliantly?"

Isobel shoved her glasses up her nose, but the lens did nothing to obscure the withering glare she shot me. "You also didn't take any of my phone calls!"

I was tempted to tell her why. To explain that I had spent the night grieving for a father I would never have. That I'd been busy trying to tamp down the brutal, gnawing ache in my heart while simultaneously working up the courage to face my fears. To start making the kinds of decisions I'd look back on without regret.

But I still should have answered my phone.

Ignoring my best friend in her time of need wasn't exactly a source of pride. No doubt about it, I had dropped the ball.

"So what did the two of you talk about in the car?"

Isobel glanced furtively around us and then apparently decided that it still wasn't safe enough to disclose such top-secret information.

"Something that will probably lead to my death," she mumbled.

I rolled my eyes. "A bit dramatic, don't you think?"

"Not really. Steffani Larson never struck me as particularly bright, but Ashley McGrady might be able to poison me. She's probably got access to chemicals at whatever salon turns her orange on a regular basis."

"You're being paranoid, Izzie. You didn't make the best impression with them yesterday, but I hardly think they're out for your blood."

"You have no idea what's going on, Melanie," she snarled. "No. Freaking. Clue. I'm going to have to join witness protection and *then* where will you be, huh? Riddle me *that*, Batman!"

I stared at her in confusion. "Are you sure you're feeling okay, Iz? Seriously. I don't think I've ever seen you act this way."

She breathed out a long gust of air that succeeded only in flapping her bangs and mumbled something that sounded like, "*Doctor Who, this would be a really great time for you to show up in the TARDIS!*" before her eyes locked on to something behind me.

Or maybe I should have said someone.

Spencer King.

And he was headed right toward us.

"Crap!" Izzie squeaked. "Cover for me!"

Then she bolted. It wasn't a particularly impressive physical display. Izzie isn't exactly athletic, and her heavy footsteps resounded in the hallways as she sprinted away. Then again, I think the only thing she cared about was putting as much space as humanly possible between herself and the King of the Notables.

I turned on Spencer, ready to slice him to ribbons if I didn't like the answer to one simple question. "What did you say to her?"

"Oh hey, Melanie."

I moved closer, not caring who caught sight of me stalking toward Spencer. "If you hurt my best friend—"

"Relax. Instagram and I get along just fine."

"Isobel."

"Right. We're fine."

I shot him a disbelieving look. "Then do you want to explain to me why exactly she ran out of here as if Fake and Bake planned on using her for a makeup demonstration?"

"I have no idea what you're talking about," Spencer said easily. "But I'll be sure to ask her. She usually goes to the library after school, right?"

I found myself nodding instinctively. Then my brain caught up with my body. "Uh, no. She goes—"

Spencer grinned. "You're a terrible liar, Melanie."

"I really hate you right now."

His smirk only widened. "Like I said, a terrible liar. Don't feel bad; you look pretty cute when you try to pull a fast one. I've always liked that about you. It's probably for the best that I changed my plans, though."

And without bothering to explain that cryptic comment, he whistled as he walked away.

I had no idea what to make of any of it.

Maybe it was wrong of me to shrug it off and let Izzie sort it out on her own, but she seemed perfectly capable of keeping Spencer King at a distance.

Okay, and maybe a part of me was a tad curious to see how things would play out between the two of them without anyone's interference.

Then again, if I hadn't been so wrapped up trying to find the right words for my next conversation with Dylan, maybe I would have focused more of my energy on what was going on with my best friend. Once again, I was letting a boy keep me from my best friend duties. Except this time I didn't regret it, because I was finally going after what I wanted.

And even though I was pretty sure Izzie had every reason to complain about the way I'd been bailing on her recently, I also knew she'd be proud of me too.

Eventually.

Truthfully, I probably could have obsessed for hours about whatever weird thing was going on between Izzie and Spencer, and not have been any more prepared to talk to Dylan later that day. I couldn't come up with anything particularly witty or smart to say during my English class, or during my freshman history class, or at any time during my walk to his house. I was still coming up blank when I sat down on the front steps of the Wellesley house and waited. Dylan's scuffed-up soccer ball rested only two feet away from me and I idly wondered if I kept kicking it against the side of the house, would I be able to come up with something better than, "Heyyy, Dylan. Um . . . fancy seeing you here. At your house. What were the chances, right?"

Instead, I nervously twisted one of the silver rings on my left hand and tried to use willpower to make time speed up.

It felt like hours before I saw him approaching the house, his gait loose and easy. For a second I allowed myself to imagine that none of the events of yesterday had taken place. I hadn't shown up with his older sister and her friends. I hadn't tried to push him away. And his dad *definitely* hadn't showed up.

Once more Dylan was streaked with mud, undoubtedly the result of an intense soccer practice, and his eyes glinted with something extra when he caught sight of me.

Something that had my palms sweating nervously before he banked it and glanced around. "I thought Mackenzie was tutoring Logan today."

I stood up, hoping that the additional height would bolster my quickly fleeting sense of confidence. "Uh, yeah. I'm not— well, I was waiting for you."

Dylan never slowed and I battled a wave of panic as the distance between us shrank. Five feet. Two feet.

Six inches.

But instead of stopping when he reached me, Dylan reached into the pocket of his jeans, fished out the house key, and unlocked the front door as if he had high school girls waiting on his porch every day. As if this was such a regular occurrence, he would've been more surprised to find the steps totally vacant.

"You want to come in?" Dylan asked, his lips tilting up into a grin at my startled expression.

"Uh . . . sure?" I winced as it came out more like a question than a statement; he was totally unnerving me. I couldn't get a read on his emotions. If he was still mad at me over the things that I'd said the day before, he didn't let on.

I almost would've preferred it if he were pissed off. If he had seen me on the porch and told me to leave him the hell alone.

At least then I would have known where I stood.

But this whole *nothing bothers me* act he had going on only succeeded in rattling my nerves.

"Great. Why don't you make yourself at home while I

clean up?" He wrinkled his nose as if he caught a good whiff of *eau de soccer.*

Without waiting for a response, he headed right down the hall toward his bedroom, leaving me standing by the door looking in—fighting the urge to turn tail and run.

Crossing the threshold was enough to have the hairs on my neck prickling into the full upright position, but I forced myself to shut the door behind me.

No turning back now.

Chapter 10

Everyone at Mitch High School knew that Bethany and Ashleigh would ruthlessly pursue the title of prom queen. Underhanded insults intended to slash down the competition, malicious rumors spread throughout the hallways, none of it was too petty or too mean for the Terrible Twosome.

But there was only one way to get the crown, and that was by being the biggest, baddest ... Mitch the school had ever seen.

—from "Prom and Backstabbing,"
by Jane Smith
Published by *The Wordsmith*

It felt like an eternity before I heard the shower turn off. And then another millennium or so passed as I waited in the kitchen for Dylan to change. I felt every single tick of the clock above the sink as if I had swallowed it just like the alligator from *Peter Pan*. The fact that I was now thinking in terms of Disney movies didn't sit well with me either. I wanted to blame Mackenzie for the *Pocahontas* invite, except that was what had led to this upcoming talk with her little brother.

I couldn't quite decide if that was a good thing or a really, *really* bad one.

Probably because it all depended on this discussion with Dylan.

I began pacing in nervous circles around the room, trying to decide how exactly I should pick up the thread of the conversation. I couldn't exactly say, "So . . . nice shower?" or "Wow, you smell amazing. Want to have that talk?" even if I couldn't think of any other way to break the ice.

"You look serious. Do you want to take a seat or do you want to prowl around some more?"

I jumped. It was a ridiculous reaction given that I was in *his* kitchen, waiting for *his* arrival, and listening to *his* kitchen clock until I thought I was about to lose my freaking mind, but he had somehow managed to catch me off guard.

"I . . . uh . . . hi."

Dylan grinned and this time the expression reached his eyes. Suddenly, I felt . . . lighter. He was willing to hear me out—all the way—and I knew that he would actually listen.

It was all I could ask of him.

"My dad's an alcoholic."

Dylan stared at me mutely for a second, clearly trying to process what I expected him to do with that information. "So . . . you can't sit?"

My knees turned to jelly and I sank into one of the chairs that surrounded the kitchen table. "No! Yes! Of course I can. I just . . . I thought you should know."

"Okay," Dylan said slowly. Then he waited, probably because he didn't think I would just blurt out something so personal and then turn mute. But I couldn't seem to speak past all the emotions twisting and roiling inside of me.

Hurt. Fear. Shame. Guilt.

Anger.

So much anger that I thought I might choke on all the years' worth of unexpressed rage that I had kept to myself.

"Do you want to talk about it?"

They were my words from the day before, the ones I had used when I'd hoped a simple question might help Dylan find some kind of closure with his dad. Now I knew firsthand just how much it sucked to be on the receiving end of that question.

"Not much to say," I said stiffly. "He's an alcoholic."

"I'm familiar with the condition, Melanie. What kind of an alcoholic is he?"

I shot up from the chair and glared at him as adrenaline raced through my system. "He's not a violent drunk if that's what you're getting at!"

Dylan's chocolate brown eyes never wavered from mine. "I'm glad to hear it, but that wasn't what I meant."

I slowly eased back into the chair, my cheeks flushing hot with embarrassment. I was supposed to be explaining to Dylan that I wanted to try *dating,* not going for the jugular at the first mention of my father. Which was why I never should have brought him up in the first place.

"Does he expect you to cover for him?" The words were spoken so gently, I wanted to squeeze my eyes shut. It was so much easier to answer when I could pretend that Dylan was asking because he truly, genuinely cared about me in a way that went way beyond friendship.

"I . . . I guess," I muttered. "He's never asked me to do it or anything. It's just—someone has to, right?"

Dylan didn't say anything and I found words suddenly tumbling out of my mouth in a free fall. "Somebody has to make sure he doesn't die in his own vomit. Somebody has to make sure that he's okay, and my mom can't do it all. She tries, but it hurts her and I can't stand to see it hurt her, so . . . somebody has to step in."

"And that somebody has to be you?"

"Do you see anybody else around?" My voice cracked horribly on the question and suddenly I was crying again. It was as if my tear glands had somehow forgotten that they were supposed to be all tapped out after last night and had come back with a vengeance. I couldn't even *see* Dylan; my eyes were so full of tears that they obscured my vision.

Then I gave up even pretending I had everything under control.

Really gave it up.

I rested my forehead against the table, used my arm to pillow my nose, and sobbed for everything I knew wasn't going to happen. Saying it out loud, using the word "alcoholic" in conjunction with "my dad" made it real somehow in a way that it hadn't been before. It was like I had been living under a spell of silence, and all those years of tiptoeing around the issue had made me hope that as long as nobody applied that term to my dad, it wouldn't be real.

But it was painfully, excruciatingly real, and now I looked like a pathetic mess who started bawling at the drop of a hat.

I jerked my head up, and I knew I had to get the hell out of there before I somehow made this embarrassing breakdown even worse. I wasn't sure exactly how I'd even go about accomplishing that—maybe by blurting out that I *liked* him while he was trying to shuttle me out the door—but I didn't trust myself not to find *some* way to screw it up even worse.

"Sorry," I choked. "I didn't mean . . . I . . . sorry."

His face was right there. At some point while I was sobbing he must have moved closer because now he was only inches away. I could feel his arm stroking my back in a comforting motion that had nothing whatsoever to do with flirting and everything to do with silent support.

I barely managed a weak chuckle when he brushed away one of my tears. "Great timing, right? You see your dad for the first time in years yesterday and the very next day I show up here and have a meltdown over mine."

The pad of Dylan's finger lingered against my cheek and I almost wanted to keep crying just so he would have a reason to leave it there.

"It's okay, Melanie. I'm glad you're here." His mouth twitched upward into a smile that was every bit as soft as his words. "I'm always glad to see you."

"You weren't yesterday," I mumbled.

"Of course I was." Dylan's finger moved away from my cheek and a wave of disappointment crashed through me until he reached up and carefully tucked a long strand of my hair behind my ear. "That doesn't mean you can't annoy the hell out of me too."

That startled a laugh out of me. "So . . . you're not mad at me?"

Dylan dropped his hand and leaned back in his chair thoughtfully as I cursed myself for asking the question. Things had been going so freaking well, all things considered, before I had opened up my big mouth.

"I was more frustrated than angry with you, Mel," he said slowly, measuring each word. "I don't know what you want and I don't enjoy guessing, so . . ."

It was as good an opening as I was ever going to get.

"You," I said hoarsely. "I want you."

Dylan didn't move, and for one horrible moment I wanted to look over my shoulder just to make sure his dad hadn't entered the room again, because he was just as tense now as he had been when he'd found that unexpected visitor the day before.

"Do you mean it?" There was no sign of the cocky soccer player now, the one who had no trouble crashing a high school party, or flirting with a girl who was close to his older sister. And I wouldn't have wanted it any other way, because the anxiety in his voice, the fear and the hope all jumbled together, I felt it too.

But it felt right that we were scared together.

"Yeah, I mean it. I want *you*, Dylan."

A shutter fell over his eyes and he glanced away. "But not in public, right? You still want to pretend there's nothing going on between us."

This time it was my turn to advance.

So I leaned forward and kissed him.

It began awkwardly, partly because I didn't have the best angle to work from and partly because I knew he could taste my tears on my lips. I wanted our first kiss to be sweet, not salty. I pulled back just enough to look into Dylan's eyes and breathe the one word that had resonated in my mind, *"You."*

That's when Dylan pulled me back in and gave it his all.

And he showed me just how very sweet a first kiss could be.

Ever

Chapter 1

Smith High School now has a student-run publication dedicated to fiction called *The Wordsmith*
. . . and already it is proving itself to be fundamentally ill-conceived and horribly mismanaged. The
latest edition included a short story called "Prom
and Backstabbing" by junior Jane Smith that was
pettiness masquerading as fiction. There is no
doubt in anyone's mind that Smith is using her
new platform as editor of *The Wordsmith* to further her own personal vendettas.

It's time to pull the plug on this failed experiment.

—from "Stop the War of Words,"
by Lisa Anne Montgomery
Published in *The Smithsonian*

Melanie Morris was a dead girl.
Or at the very least she was going to be dead to me.
No more favors. No more expecting dorky Isobel Peters to
magically find a way to bail her out. Not.Going. To. Happen.

Rope me into hanging out with Notables once? Shame on me.

Ditch me outside Mackenzie Wellesley's house with the most obnoxious boy at Smith High School?

Shame on *you.*

Not that Melanie stuck around to hear my opinion of the *huge* violations to the Friendship Code that she was breaking. She was too intent on her pursuit of Dylan, in more ways than one, and if she hadn't just left me standing uncomfortably next to Spencer "I Practically Own This Town" King, I would have sympathized with her. She was obviously trying to pretend she felt nothing more for Mackenzie's little brother than . . . something vaguely little brotherly, but the only person she'd probably fooled was Mackenzie.

Normally, watching someone else's social life in a state of flux would have appealed to the future psychologist lurking inside of me, but I couldn't focus my attention on Mel when I was stuck next to a guy who was probably either a narcissist or a megalomaniac.

Or maybe he was just a garden-variety jerk.

Sometimes the simplest diagnosis gets overlooked for a flashier title. I should have known better than to discount the obvious, especially given that I was stuck in a high school that was chock-full of a range of jerks. They came in all sizes and, well, there wasn't a whole variety in color—Forest Grove being one of those communities in Oregon where everyone looked like vampires who would burn to ash if they ever left town without the protection of a daylight ring.

But regardless of their pallor, the jerks tended to brighten their days with a little geek hazing.

And since I happened to be the obligatory chubby freshman girl, I was often the target.

There were days when I really wished I could move and start over at some other high school—one where no football-playing jerk ever yelled, "Move your ass, *Fatty*," at me in the cafeteria at a decibel level that basically ensured everyone within a fifty-yard radius would overhear.

I was still trying to live that down.

Not that anyone mentioned it to my face. It was more of a hushed snicker that buzzed in the background every time I raised my hand in my honors psychology class. One that could have been "geek" or "loser," but that probably went right for the posterior: *fat-ass*.

So even though Spencer King himself hadn't treated me like trash for the past—oh, *year*—that didn't mean plenty of his ilk hadn't beaten him to the punch. Or that he wouldn't take advantage of Melanie's hasty departure by playing a quick game of *tease the fat chick*.

Yeah, that was a fun one.

Ten points if you make her cry.

Fifteen if you can make her run away.

"Are you coming or not?" Spencer didn't even pause to hear my answer before he opened the driver's side door and slid behind the wheel.

I glanced briefly at Melanie's retreating form and then over to the door of the Wellesley house, where only thirty minutes ago I had been pretending to watch a Disney movie. It seemed ridiculously PG now. Especially since having Mackenzie's dad show up was the emotional equivalent of dropping an atomic bomb on both Mackenzie and Dylan.

I didn't exactly want to stick around and observe the aftermath.

Well, that wasn't entirely true: I did want to soak it all in. Maybe even jot down a few notes while I was at it. But I had learned the hard way that most people don't enjoy being studied and treated like a case subject when they are at their most vulnerable—or at any time, actually.

And since I didn't exactly want to alienate the handful of

people at Smith High School who didn't feel the need to put a brainiac nerd like me in my place, I crawled into the passenger's seat and buckled in with sweaty palms.

I braced myself for an attack. Not a physical one. That would be too easy. No, it would be something snide and cruel that he could rationalize to himself later had "just been a joke"; if I was offended by it, that was because I obviously lacked a sense of humor.

Oh yeah, because nothing was quite as hilarious as being asked if I wanted to grab a muffin, only to have someone point to my stomach and say, "Never mind. You've got a muffin already!"

Although I didn't think there was anything worse than having someone lean in too close, gaze pointedly at the round swell that began right under my rib cage, and murmur, "Have you picked out a name for it yet?"

Fake had earned her fifteen points with that one.

"So where am I taking you?" Spencer looked totally unperturbed about being stuck with the biggest geek at Smith High School. I had half expected to hear him muttering about Logan sticking him with the chubster, but then again I hadn't counted for how unflappable he could be . . . well, all the time.

Okay, maybe he had looked a little flustered when Fake and Bake tried to corner him at school.

But he'd managed to stay a whole lot cooler through the exchange than just about anyone else—certainly better than me.

Come to think of it . . .

"Why were you running from Fake and Bake?" The words just kind of popped out of my mouth and I found myself nervously shoving up the bridge of my glasses while I waited for his response.

None of your business, Fatty.

Spencer glanced at me and there was something in his eyes I didn't quite trust. Something mischievous that made me achingly aware he was not going to be categorized into a personality type that fit neatly within my psychology textbook.

He was one-half bad boy and the other half . . .

I couldn't help shivering slightly with unease. The other half I doubted anyone at Smith High School knew at all. Well, nobody beyond Logan Beckett, and I had a feeling the hockey captain wasn't going to start spilling his best friend's secrets anytime soon.

"Steffani and Ashley," he said pointedly, while my cheeks overheated from my social slip, "have different interests than I do. That's all."

"They have *interests?*" I couldn't hide my fascination. "Really? In what?"

I wasn't being facetious. It was difficult for me to imagine either of them having any kind of passion for, well . . . anything. As far as I had seen, they were all about status, style, and securing their place in the high school yearbook so that someday they could toss their hair back and brag to their kids about how they'd been the queen of the prom.

"They want you for prom, don't they?" I could feel the rightness of the words in my mouth and I knew—I just *knew*—that I had nailed down the situation. "Let me see if I can get this right. Okay, so Fake and Bake both want to be crowned prom queen, but neither of their former boyfriends had the social power to make it happen. Which wasn't a problem back when Chelsea Halloway was at our school because it was obvious to *everyone* that she would be the one wearing the crown. But now that Chelsea goes to an entirely different school, there's a power vacuum and . . . they're trying to suck you in!"

"That's," Spencer coughed, "one, um . . . descriptive way to put it."

"So they're thinking it'll be easy; land Spencer King and take the crown." I couldn't help but whistle admiringly. "You know, they're probably right. The only real contender you've got for prom king is Logan, and now that he's dating Mackenzie and *your* family is picking up the tab for the dance . . . you're the safe bet."

"Well, thanks for telling me. Do I turn left or right at the stop sign?"

"Left," I said absentmindedly. "I'm missing something, though, right?"

"You're missing the scenery," Spencer pointed out. "I think we've probably passed some woodland creatures. Maybe a deer or—"

"You don't want any of it!" I crowed, unable to contain my excitement at figuring out the missing piece, moving that final bit of motivation until it clicked into place and formed a perfect picture.

Spencer raked one hand through his golden boy hair, which only succeeded in rumpling it perfectly.

Life was so freaking unfair.

"Would you mind dropping the inquisition and focusing on the directions?" His voice was slightly strained, which for all I knew meant that he was seriously pissed off. It was hard to tell with someone who was practically unflappable.

Although I suspected he was starting to get . . . flapped.

"Another left at the light." I drummed my fingers against my knee as I looked out the window without really seeing anything that was flashing past. "So you don't want to be prom king." I leaned back farther into the super-plush seat of his car. The luxury wasn't a surprise—nothing but the best for a member of the King family. "I thought that was part of your genetic code or something."

"It must have skipped a generation."

"Hold up!" I yelled, and Spencer smoothly drove to the shoulder of the road and idled there.

Spencer glanced around. "Are we near your house or something?"

"Nope." I swiveled in my seat to face him and then kind of

wished I hadn't. He was just too . . . everything. "You're not just ambivalent to this prom king thing. You actively don't want it. You're trying to sabotage your chances!"

Spencer took a deep breath. "Are you for real right now? You made me stop for *that*?"

"I didn't *make* you do anything," I muttered uncomfortably as I tried to escape from the look of utter disbelief that was aimed right at me. It's not exactly an unusual thing for me to be on the receiving end of snarky looks from the Notable crowd, but they never came in such close quarters. And I had never felt so trapped before.

He rolled his eyes. "You're unbelievable, Isotope."

"That's not even a name. An isotope is created when there are an equal number of protons but a different number of—"

"I get it!"

I looked at him doubtfully. Spencer wasn't exactly known for having a pristine academic record, but for the ridiculous ways he was able to scrape by with a passing grade. Most of the stories I had heard depended heavily on his charm and his parents' generous donations. "Do you, though?"

"Yes, you're an enormous pain in the ass. Thank you for confirming what before I merely suspected."

Well, crap. That hurt.

Do not react. No wincing, no flinching, no nothing. Poker face, Izzie. Keep it locked in place.

"You can turn right at the next light." I kept my eyes on the view through the windshield and waited for him to move back into the flow of traffic.

The car didn't budge. I fidgeted as the air seemed to thicken. Or maybe I was just imagining that, because at some point the seat warmer had apparently kicked in and the car now smelled like . . . money.

Loads of it.

"Do . . . do you want me to get out here or something?" I asked as my stomach lurched lower.

He did. *Of course,* he did. He probably wished he'd never agreed to play chauffeur in the first place. "I think I'll walk the rest of the way. Thanks for the . . . well, see ya!"

I tried to say the last part the way Melanie always did, effortlessly cheerful in a non-perky way. Less cheerleader, more casual and devil-may-care.

Too bad my voice cracked at the end of it.

"Spit it out already, Isadore. I know you're dying to ask."

I didn't even bother trying to correct him this time. "I have no idea what you're talking about, Spencer."

Saying his name out loud felt weird to me. Too familiar. We weren't friends, or even classmates for that matter, given that he was concentrating on wood shop instead of world history. We weren't anything to each other beyond acquaintances, and we were already failing spectacularly at that.

"You want to know why I'm not interested in being prom king," he said bluntly. "So ask away. I've got nothing to hide."

"I don't need to ask you anything." Spencer raised an eyebrow skeptically and I couldn't help grinning just a little as I continued, "I already worked that out for myself."

He snorted in disbelief, turned off the engine, and leaned back in his seat as if he had nothing but time. "Let's hear it, then."

I squared my shoulders.

Think like a psychologist, Izzie. Approach him as if he were just part of a case study. What is it that Melanie called them again? Hockey erectus.

"Well, you're loaded"—I gestured at the control panel of the car—"obviously. You throw the best parties."

"I thought you knew better than to put any stock in hearsay, Isolde. I know I've never seen you at any of my parties." He winked at me. "I would have remembered."

Yeah, a whole lot of people would have remembered a

party where mocking the freshman dork provided entertain-
ment for the night.

"Fine. You're *rumored* to throw the best parties. You have no trouble getting girls. That's also plenty obvious after your close encounter with Fake and Bake earlier today."

Spencer had no clever comeback for that, so I just kept right on going.

"My guess is that you've been around people like that your entire life. You've got an older brother who threw the same kind of keggers when he was in high school, and your parents probably still look the other way because it's expected. It proves that you guys are popular amongst your peers. And I'm also betting that your parents know of a cleaning company that can work wonders when it comes to removing beer stains from carpeting."

"Interesting theories, but it still doesn't have anything to do with prom."

"I'm getting there. So you're sick of it. Well, not really. I mean, you probably *love* the attention and the perks of popularity, but you *think* you're sick of it."

Spencer nodded. "Sounds . . . logical."

"Which leaves you in a bit of a bind. You could continue doing what you're doing—" I waved my hand at his perfectly tousled hair and the attractively rumpled button-up shirt he was wearing. "You could keep having random, meaningless hookups—"

"Hearsay," Spencer interrupted.

I ignored him.

"The problem with those . . . well, *one* of the many problems with those, is that we're approaching prom season and all those girls are hoping to score a place as your plus one. And I don't think you like disappointing people."

He drummed his fingers against the steering wheel. "What makes you think that? It doesn't seem in keeping with the rich, entitled asshole identity you've mapped out for me."

"You're Logan's best friend." I didn't realize that was even a factor for me until the answer tripped off my tongue. "You must have some redeeming characteristics. I'm betting that's one of them."

"Saved once more by Logan Beckett."

I wasn't sure about the "once more" part, but it didn't surprise me that Logan had to bail out Spencer on multiple occasions. What did surprise me was that I hadn't caught any snippets of it in the hallways. Mostly I heard girls crying over the fact that they thought Spencer would want to be in a relationship with *them,* but he hadn't called. Something along those lines . . . I had never paid it much attention.

"So that leaves you with door number two: Take yourself off the market. But for that you have to find the right girl. Someone whose feelings won't be hurt when you admit that there was nothing really going on between the two of you. There's just one thing I can't figure out."

Spencer stared at me hard and part of me froze under his intensity. This was a *Notable.* I had no business asking him anything, let alone expecting him to give me a straightforward answer.

But I also had nothing to lose.

"Yeah? And what's that?"

"*Why on earth would you ever try to use Melanie Morris as your beard?*"

Spencer momentarily looked too stunned to speak.

Score one for the freshman.

Chapter 2

Everyone here at *The Wordsmith* agrees completely with Lisa Anne Montgomery: It is unconscionable for someone to use a school publication to further a personal vendetta. However, that's *not* what we are interested in doing. We simply want to give students an opportunity to reimagine the world through fiction.

Any similarity to real people or events is entirely coincidental.

So back off, Lisa Anne.

—from "Censoring *The Wordsmith*,"
by Jane Smith
Published by *The Wordsmith*

"That's *not* what I was doing!"

It was funny watching him get all bent out of shape over it, especially because I couldn't shake the bone-deep feeling that I was *right*.

"You're not doing a very convincing job of faking it with Melanie," I said agreeably. "But that was the plan, right? Get Melanie to act like your girlfriend and wait for the social storm to blow over? No real feelings—how could there be when she's hung up on Dylan?"

Spencer laughed outright at that. "I don't think you were supposed to tell me that little detail. In fact, I'm positive you weren't supposed to let that slip."

I felt my cheeks flush guiltily. He was right. Melanie had trusted me with her secret and I had definitely let the cat out of the bag. But since it was out in the open now, there was no reason to let Spencer believe I couldn't hack an honest conversation—he was the one who constantly tried to be evasive.

"As if you hadn't already figured that out on your own," I said defiantly. "We both know better."

Spencer grinned. "You really hate being in the wrong, don't you?"

I crossed my arms tightly across my chest and sucked in a deep breath. Nothing to fear here. No reason to notice that when Spencer teased me, his eyes crinkled attractively at the corners. He would probably age like Robert Redford, with a cool sense of self-possession that could only come from years spent entirely satisfied with the person he'd become.

"I wouldn't know. It happens so infrequently. It's not exactly difficult to be right when everyone around you is inevitably wrong."

Okay, so I was overstating it a little. More than a little. It wasn't like there was *nobody* else at Smith High School who could keep up with me on an intellectual level. There were plenty of smart kids there, most notably Mackenzie Wellesley, Jane Smith, and Scott Fraser. Well, I hadn't actually taken a class with Scott because he had only recently transferred to our school, but I assumed he was smart. I couldn't picture Jane spending time with anyone who couldn't hold up his end of a conversation—let alone start dating him.

And since the two of them were every bit as adorable together as Mackenzie and Logan, I was willing to bet he had no trouble keeping up.

The only problem was that none of them was a freshman, and I wasn't exactly winning any popularity points with my classmates by being in all advanced courses. If it wasn't for my friendship with Melanie, I would probably have a bull's-eye painted on my back.

Okay, so I had Sam too. Nobody messed with Sam-never-Samantha. Not if they wanted to make it through their time at Smith High School without being besieged by flying condoms.

Spencer laughed at my bravado, and even though it wasn't the first time I had heard the sound coming from him, it still felt like a jolt to the system. A strange electric pulse that made me feel . . . alive.

Suddenly it made sense to me why there were always girls surrounding him, and it had nothing to do with his cash in-flow and class status. There was something about Spencer that was infectious.

I had no intention of coming down with whatever it was that he carried.

"You seriously need to unwind, Isobel."

I shoved my glasses frames higher, half expecting that the smile on Spencer's face was the product of my imagination or a residual thumbprint on the lens. I had trouble trusting my eyes, but there was no denying my ears. "You said my name correctly."

"Did I?" He shrugged with apparent unconcern, but his laugh lines deepened as he took in my openmouthed disbelief.

Spencer leaned closer toward me and for a millisecond my breath caught in the back of my throat. I felt like I was back in middle school, heck, maybe even *elementary school*. Back to having sweaty palms and a heartbeat that was pounding too quickly every time I interacted with the cool kids.

"Melanie's beautiful."

It was a total non sequitur, but it was the only thing I

could think of that would ease the pressure from my chest. The only way to get this conversation back on track. Spencer was still just the golden boy Notable and I was the pain-in-the-ass nerd who was trying to psychoanalyze his interest in my best friend.

"Yes, she is," Spencer said agreeably.

That was all it took to quell the quivers running up and down my side from his proximity. *Of course* he thought Melanie was beautiful. It was an undisputed fact. She was one of those girls who made everyone think enviously, *Man, it must be fun to glance in the mirror and see that looking back.*

At least that's what I inevitably ended up thinking.

"So why did you think you'd avoid being crowned prom king if you started feigning interest in her?"

I couldn't bring myself to look Spencer in the face as I asked that incredibly intrusive question, so I felt more than saw him stare out the driver's side window before he eased the car back onto the street.

"I wasn't feigning anything," he said carefully, which only made me snort derisively.

"If you were really interested in Melanie right now, you wouldn't be sharing the car with me."

It was the truth. He would have chased after Melanie instead and offered her a ride home. And if Dylan told her to leave him alone, Spencer would've been the safe shoulder to cry on, and from there . . . who knows?

Regardless of the outcome, I would have been calling my mom for a lift.

Spencer turned right at the light, which at least proved that he had been listening to my words earlier. I felt a soft glow of warmth at the thought that something I had said—even something as meaningless as driving directions—had made an impression on someone who was probably accustomed to calling all the shots.

"Melanie's nice," Spencer said simply. "I enjoy spending time with her. I wouldn't think that'd be news to you, since you claim you're best friends and everything."

It didn't seem like the right time to mention that I had every intention of killing my own best friend for putting me through this torture.

I need you, Izzie. Please say you'll go with me. Please.

I couldn't believe I had actually agreed. Melanie was now forever in my debt, no doubt about it.

"You had a plan. There's no way Mackenzie just happened to invite you to her house for a Disney movie if you didn't have some kind of endgame."

Spencer took his eyes off the road only briefly. "Are you this suspicious of everyone? All the time?"

Well . . . yes.

Then again, I wasn't a Notable either. I didn't have the luxury of strolling into a room and expecting that everyone in it would jump at the opportunity to hang out with me. Just the opposite, in fact.

"Okay, then let me try to explain something to you. See, most people don't need to have an *endgame* to hang out with their best friend and his girlfriend."

"Yeah, but you're not *most people.*"

Spencer's grin widened. "Now, if I didn't know better, I would think you had a crush on me."

My stomach jolted as he winked at me. It was probably meant to be friendly, but my palms only started sweating again. "You can relax, Isocrates. I know better."

"And . . . you've forgotten my name again." Except I didn't think he had. I was starting to think he'd known it all along and just enjoyed riling me up. Or maybe it was because he knew that as long as I could correct the obvious mistake, I wouldn't have time to obsess over the potential subtext of his every word the way I usually do.

Although it was entirely possible that I was giving him way too much credit.

"If I was to hazard a guess—"

"Oh, by all means, hazard one," Spencer interrupted.

"You thought that dating a freshman would be enough to keep you out of the running entirely. But you seriously miscalculated. Dating Melanie wouldn't sink your prom king potential. All those guys on your hockey team would just say, 'Hey, man, your new girlfriend is *hot.*'" I pitched my voice three octaves lower. "You *dah man!*"

Spencer burst out laughing. "Is that really how we sound to you?"

"Yo, bro, let's kick it at Spencer's house. His parties are *dope.*" It sounded ridiculous to my own ears, but then again, I wasn't exactly a member of the *Hockey erectus* clan. That was only to be expected. What I didn't anticipate was the rush of warmth that flooded through me at the satisfaction of making Spencer King laugh.

I might be a geek, but the King of the Notables found me funny. That had to count for *something*.

"So was I right?" I asked when his laughter died down enough for me to be heard.

"Nope, we don't sound like that at all."

"You did have a plan for Melanie," I persisted. "Turn left at the sign."

"A plan sounds so . . . planned. I'm not nearly as diabolical as you seem to think. Although I kind of like this villainous alter ego you've created for me. Feel free to spread it around. Maybe someday I'll be the inspiration behind a comic book bad guy." He paused to really consider it. "I think I'd like a double life."

"And I'd like to receive a reduced high school sentence for good behavior and then skip every single stupid reunion. Looks like one of us is going to be out of luck."

Spencer nodded sagely. "So do you think you'll go to the tenth anniversary or the twentieth?"

I laughed, but I couldn't help admiring his bravado. There was no doubt in his mind that he was going to get exactly what he wanted—because he wouldn't relent until he did. He lived his life like he was part of a freaking Nike commercial.

"Neither. What about you, Clark Kent? Planning on coming back to relive your glory days?"

Spencer shook his head admonishingly. "Now, that's shortsighted of you, Instagram. And highly prejudicial. You should probably work on hiding your obvious disdain for other people if you ever want to make it as a psychologist."

My mouth fell open. "How did you know I want to go into that field?"

"Well, the fact that I haven't been this pumped for details about my life since the last time I went in for the obligatory mental tune-up was something of a giveaway. I also know a bunch of people in your psychology class."

I stiffened automatically as I waited for the insult I knew was coming. *Yeah, my friends have all complained about the freshman who keeps screwing up the curve. Everyone wishes they could vote you out of the class.*

"Becka Cloober mentioned something about working on a group project with you a month ago."

"And you remembered that?" Maybe Spencer had a point about my prejudices; I never would have expected him to be capable of paying attention to anything except himself.

"Sure, it was the reason we had to push back our . . . date." He flashed his brightest smile and the car slowed down to a crawl.

"Are we close to your house?"

I pointed to the yellow two-story home that I had been born in. All through elementary school and even partway through middle school, my parents had taken my photo right next to the tree on the corner of the property. It was gnarled and rough, and it hadn't appeared touched by the years, and yet it always made me feel safe and small.

Spencer parked and turned toward me while I fumbled with my seat belt.

"You made a good point," Spencer told me before I could make my escape. His words pulled me up short.

"I made several," I said slowly. "Care to be more specific?"

"Dating Melanie wouldn't have been enough to sink my social standing."

My fingers pressed against the latch and the seat belt whirred quietly back into place. "Uh, right. Well . . . live and learn. I'm sure you'll have no problem concocting an equally insane plan B."

"I already have." The good humor that lurked in his eyes was still there, but this time he didn't look like he was kidding me. He seemed as serious as a wealthy party boy could get.

"Oh yeah? What's that?"

"You."

Chapter 3

High school is a popularity contest and at no point is that more obvious than during prom season, whether or not the school administration is willing to admit it.

—Anonymous letter to the editor
Published in *The Smithsonian*

"Me?" I squeaked. "No. No. *No. No. No!*"

"There's no harm in considering it," Spencer pointed out reasonably. Too reasonably. It had to be some kind of a setup. A new take on the classic *Carrie* story. Geeky girl goes to prom only to find out that it was one big joke cooked up by the popular kids at her high school. Actually, that wasn't even a new take on it. That straight up was the premise of the movie, minus the bloodshed and supernatural abilities.

Then again, I wouldn't put it past Fake and Bake to grab a bucket of pig's blood.

"Fine, I'll consider it." I paused briefly and then nodded. "Yep, considered. Rejected. Anything else?"

"You have to admit it makes sense," Spencer said, slowing

the car as we cruised through my residential neighborhood. "There's no way I'd become prom king if I say I'm dating you."

My expression must have given away how much that stung, because he winced.

"I'm sorry. I didn't mean that in a bad way."

"Is there a *good* way to be told that you could torpedo someone's popularity?" I said skeptically. "I think that's kind of like being forced to hear, 'I don't want to say I told you so,' when *obviously* if someone really didn't want to say it, they could have just kept their mouth shut."

Spencer raked one hand through his hair. "Look, I need to get out of this and I would appreciate your help."

I was getting really sick of hearing people dance around the words "I need a favor."

I shoved my glasses higher up my nose. "Let me guess, you need to pretend to be in a relationship with someone who would tank your social standing enough to kill any chance of being crowned, but not so much that you would have to hang with the geeks."

"I've hung out with a geek before. It was fun. She *knew* things. Lots of things. Not all of which you'll find in a textbook."

Spencer grinned, and even though I thought he was kind of kidding, he also sort of wasn't.

"Thanks for that very generous offer, but—"

"You haven't heard my offer yet."

"No, but I'm pretty sure I've seen it enacted for chick flicks over a dozen times. You're going to increase my popularity, right? Maybe find someone to give me a makeover? Well, screw you, Spencer. I *like* wearing sweatshirts and jeans!"

"I wasn't going to suggest that."

I raised an eyebrow in what I thought was a pretty good imitation of his go-to expression.

"Maybe you'll learn to lighten up a little, but that's it. I'm not trying to turn you into Chelsea Halloway."

"Because that would be impossible. There's only one Chelsea Halloway. Anybody who thinks they can take her place is delusional."

"Exactly. And since I'm not delusional"—Spencer paused to let me snort in disbelief before he continued—"I wouldn't attempt it."

"So you want me to pretend to be your girlfriend for a few weeks in exchange for . . . what exactly?"

"Name it."

"Excuse me?"

"Do you want party invites? Want me to introduce you to someone special that you've had your eye on but could never quite bring yourself to speak to at school? Money?"

"There is no special someone." Probably wouldn't be for a long time if my psych books were right about relationships requiring open communication. I had a hard enough time talking to Melanie, Jane, and Sam; considering that they were the three least judgmental girls at Smith High School . . . I was screwed. "And I'm not interested in your money."

"Okay . . . well, what *do* you want?"

The question froze me. It had been such a long time since I'd allowed myself to ask that, even if the words were only in my head. If I wanted something, I would be disappointed when I didn't get it. And most of the things I wanted only made me feel . . . guilty.

I wanted to be thin. To look in the mirror and think, *Hello, gorgeous, I have a closet full of clothing and none of it is going to make you look fat. What do you want to wear today?* I wanted to be able to walk within a fifteen-foot radius of a Notable without stiffening as I waited for the insults to fly.

Scratch that.

What I wanted was to look at the mirror and not care what anyone else said about me because *I* knew I looked fan-freaking-tastic. To give any jerk who dared to say different the middle finger and a *screw you* smile.

But I wasn't that girl either, and I couldn't exactly confess that what I really wanted was a much stronger backbone. I didn't want Spencer's pity.

Maybe because I actually kind of . . . pitied him.

"Does someone always want something from you, Spencer? Part of being a King, right? Part of the lifestyle. I bet you hear, *Hey, I could use a favor* more often than I do. And I've been hearing it a lot recently."

Spencer just stared at me in silence. After years of being the biggest geek in class, I was used to getting a look that was somewhere between *Did you actually just say that to me, loser?* and *Wow, weird girl has a point.*

"It happens," he said at last with a shrug, but I seriously doubted he was as calm about it as he let on.

"Is there anyone in your life who doesn't have an endgame?" I mused before answering my own question. "Logan. Okay, so you have one person. No girls, though, right?"

"Oh, I have plenty of girls." Spencer smirked.

I reached blindly for the door handle. "You want to keep acting like a pompous jerk, you can do that all by yourself. If you want to make a deal—"

"I'll keep my mouth shut," Spencer finished for me. "What were you going to say?"

"That you don't have any girl friends. And in case you didn't catch it; I'm putting a big old period between 'girl' and 'friend.' Not a girl who is *pretending* to be your friend because she's hoping it will turn into something more. A friend who also happens to be a girl. Do you have any of those, Spencer?"

"I . . . uh . . ."

"I didn't think so."

"So let me get this straight: You're offering to be my *friend?*"

It was the strangest moment of my life. Stranger than being invited by Melanie to watch a movie with some Notables. Stranger even than letting the King of the Notables give me a lift home.

I hadn't intended to psychoanalyze him, but now that I had . . . I couldn't back out.

Or maybe I could have, but I didn't want to do it. And not just because I was curious to see if I was right; if all the assumptions I'd been making about life as a Notable were accurate. It sounded like buried somewhere beneath his frat-boy facade was someone who actually needed some help.

I've never been able to ignore other people, maybe because I'd been on the receiving end of being shunted aside too many times to count.

"Here's the deal." The words came tumbling out of my mouth before I could overthink them. "I'll become the first— hell, the *only* female friend you may ever have, and I won't have any ulterior motive for doing it. But whether or not you want to lie to everyone else at that hellhole we call high school, you do *not* get to lie to me. Try that on for size, hotshot."

I didn't give him a chance to respond. Instead, I bolted from the car before Spencer could take me up on the offer I couldn't believe I had extended.

And I didn't slow down until I had reached my bedroom, flopped on my bed, and muffled my shriek into a pillow.

Because that's what I do whenever it becomes clear that I'm out of my *freaking* mind!

Chapter 4

Prom is a tradition, but that doesn't necessarily mean it's one that needs to remain for future generations. People only recently stopped holding cheese-rolling competitions, which involved participants barreling at breakneck speed down a hill in the hope of being the first to snag the aforementioned dairy product.

But eventually people realized that it was probably better for everyone if they just ate the cheese instead of trying to tackle it first.

So why has nobody considered ditching prom?

—from "Ditching Tradition,"
by Vida Condon
Published by *The Smithsonian*

I had no intention of seeing Spencer King ever again. There was no reason for me to see him because: 1) he would never take me up on my offer, and 2) it was no longer even on the table. Maybe I could have detailed a longer list of reasons why pretending to date Spencer was such an epically bad idea if Melanie had picked up her fracking phone, but I'd been able to come up with enough of them on my own to realize I was in way over my head.

So . . . new plan. Avoidance was my watchword.

But I couldn't help wondering if maybe Spencer was interested in the offer, even though the more I thought about it the less sense it made. How could I be friends with someone I didn't even like? Friendship requires trust. Admiration. Esteem. *Something.*

Most of the time I spent around Spencer I wondered if he was a Cylon infiltrating high school so that he could see what life was like for the humans. That would explain the perfect golden boy looks and the way he seemed to skate over every problem that sprang up in his path.

Okay, so he had a pretty solid sense of humor when he wasn't acting like a total jerk. He didn't take himself too seriously, and since I could never seem to turn my brain off, I envied his ability to just hang out. There was no way Spencer King would remain awake at night recalling every uncomfortable social interaction he'd had over the course of the day and then systematically berating himself for each and every screwup.

He probably never gave any of his social faux pas a second thought.

That seemed a whole lot healthier than the complicated tangle of emotions I inevitably fought at two in the morning.

So maybe it wasn't entirely impossible for me to respect Spencer King, just incredibly unlikely.

Then again, it wasn't as unlikely as a Notable asking me to fake a relationship to tank his chances at prom king, and *that* had already happened. I rubbed my forehead wearily. As far as I was concerned, there wasn't enough sleep or coffee in the world to make any of this seem normal.

That's why instead of asking Melanie how it had gone with Dylan the day before, I couldn't even let her get beyond, "I owe you an apology."

Although that was partly because I saw Fake headed right toward me and I was flooded with a sense of foreboding. Yesterday she had pretty much ignored me. The day before I hadn't even been on her radar. But if Spencer actually took me up on that harebrained offer of friendship . . . every mean girl at Smith High School would be out for blood.

Specifically, *my* blood.

"An apology?!" I choked. "Oh, you owe me a whole lot more than that! You talked me into going to Mackenzie's house only to ditch me with *Spencer King!*"

But it didn't look like Melanie was picking up on the gravity of the situation. Why would she, though? The only reason Melanie wasn't already sitting at the Notable table with the rest of the absurdly attractive people there was because she cared about *me*. But the girl was still total Notable queen material.

Melanie could fly through unfriendly airspace whenever she pleased, but I would be shot down the second I came within range.

It was almost funny that I was just thinking about getting shot down when I spotted Spencer walking right toward me with the same relaxed, loping stride that revealed an innate sense of coordination I certainly hadn't gotten as a kid.

So naturally, I panicked.

"Cover for me!" I blurted out to Melanie as I booked it in the opposite direction. Maybe if I didn't actually speak to Spencer, he wouldn't try to hold me to my word. He would let the whole thing drop and I wouldn't have to look like I couldn't hack hanging out with the Notables.

Even though, let's be real: I couldn't hack it.

Not even slightly.

Unfortunately, running away from Spencer meant that I was moving toward Fake—and she didn't look happy to see me. Probably because I hadn't been able to keep my big mouth shut the day before and had accidentally made her look bad in front of Spencer.

Although to be fair, I thought she had made herself look bad.

Then again, in my experience, popular girls don't exactly want to admit their own missteps because it proves they are just as fallible as everyone else and shatters the myth they've spent a great amount of time and energy constructing. So it's a whole lot easier to persecute the geek as an example for anyone else who might be tempted to speak up. But of course our guidance counselors will be the first to assure incoming students that *nothing* bad ever happens in high school.

I searched for a way out and came up empty. Diving into the girl's bathroom might keep Spencer temporarily at bay, but it wouldn't help with the Notable problem that was flouncing confidently toward me.

Never underestimate a flounce. Ruffles can be incredibly misleading.

My glasses began slipping down the bridge of my nose, probably because of the perspiration that began to sheen my face. I could tell I was glowing red, although I had no intention of verifying that by looking at myself under the harsh glare of the bathroom lights. I'd learned long ago that if I wanted to feel even slightly good about myself, it was best to avoid the florescent bulbs that must have been created to highlight every wayward hair, blackhead, and pimple.

I had trouble imagining even Chelsea Halloway glancing at herself in those mirrors and leaving unscathed.

But the real reason I couldn't use it for my escape was because bathrooms are notorious for being the place where the worst possible stuff goes down in high school. Bathrooms, locker rooms, and cafeterias. The places where everyone is supposed to be able to peacefully coexist are the ones most fraught with danger.

Even if that danger is being on the receiving end of a pity-

ing glance that lingers too long on a round stomach and jig-
gly thighs, before catching the tail end of a cutting remark.

*"I'm amazed she can even fit her ass in a pair of pants,
aren't you? I feel sorry for the denim."*

*"If I ever start wearing baggy sweatshirts like that, please
burn them for me. She looks like she's a couple of imaginary
friends away from a mental institution."*

My face heated further as a wave of memories washed
over me. I fought for each and every breath as the distance
shortened between me and Steffani Larson, and I saw her
carefully eyelinered and mascaraed eyes narrow and her perfectly lip-glossed lips open to speak.

It was about to get nasty.

And there was nothing I could do to stop it. It had played
out too many times before for me to imagine that this time
something would magically change. Steffani would mock me,
I would freeze, people around us would laugh nervously to
break the tension and hope that whatever happened, Steffani
would never take them on that way.

Then I would do my best not to cry for the rest of the day.

Maybe I wasn't cut out to be the badass heroine who
could fly back with a snarky quip, but at least I'd become
skilled at postponing the waterworks.

I liked to think that counted for something.

Still, it was better to let Steffani say whatever it was that
she had planned than to let it simmer. Once she got the bile
out of her system, I would be relatively safe . . . until she
needed an outlet for whatever the hell problems life was
throwing at her. I was her stress relief.

But even intellectually identifying that this was just her
way of working out her issues didn't make it any easier to
keep my head up in the hallways.

Not when some small part of me wondered if everyone
else could be right.

"I don't want to be rude," Steffani announced the instant I

came within earshot. Even if I hadn't had hundreds of run-ins with her before, I still would have known that her words didn't bode well. Saying, "I don't want to be rude" or "no offense," is just a weak tactic used by petty people to distance themselves from the way they hurt people with their language.

Sure enough, the zinger lagged behind by only a millisecond. "But do you *always* wear sweatshirts? Is that some kind of cult thing? Or wait . . . do you have, like, religious objections to looking like a girl?"

I should've channeled my inner badass and blasted her.

"I don't want to be rude, but do you have, like, an objection to being a decent human being? Is that too hard for you?"

The words refused to come. They were lodged behind an enormous ball of emotion in my throat, one that left me wondering if it was possible to gag on an insult.

I stood frozen in the hallway as I watched it happen. There was nothing cute about my deer-in-headlights moment. The whole scene reminded me of the time my parents had driven us to Ashland, Oregon, to see some Shakespeare plays, and Bambi's cousin had rammed into the car at top speed. We weren't even moving at the time—just waiting at a freaking stop light.

That's what it felt like to see Steffani act all doe-eyed and innocent while she wreaked senseless havoc.

Only there was no repair service I could call to fix this kind of social situation. Melanie was nowhere in sight, and none of these bystanders had any intention of stepping forward. They were probably preoccupied trying to figure out how many points the Notable would score with that direct hit.

I felt someone walk up behind me and my already stiff body jolted forward. The only thing worse than being left dealing with Fake on my own was having some other Notable jerk join in the fun.

Someone like Alex Thompson would have no trouble picking up where Steffani Larson had left off.

I flinched when I felt a warm hand on my shoulder. Even with a layer of sweatshirt between me and the outside world, the touch felt too intrusive, too intimate.

The last thing I could handle was *anyone* trying to get close.

But the instinctive jolt didn't do anything to shake off the strange hand, and I couldn't bring myself to find out who the offending digits belonged to in case that would only make this whole situation worse. I wanted to squeeze my eyes shut and chant, "None of this is real," until the bell rang and everyone split for class.

"Hey, I was hoping to catch you."

That undeniably wry voice held a strain of laughter underneath, and I found my stomach unclenching slightly as I looked up into Spencer's gorgeous green eyes. Okay, so they were a little out of focus because once again my glasses had slipped down my nose. But even when his face was blurry, it still looked unreasonably good. All chiseled and defined in a way that nobody should actually look if they aren't secretly twenty-four-year-old actors pretending to be high school students on a network TV show.

"You were?" I asked stupidly, as I tried to find some subtle way not to lose my glasses. I probably should have purchased contacts and been done with it, but I kind of liked readjusting my frames. There was something comforting about it.

"Yep." Spencer leaned in closer, and even though I knew that his presence was *not* going to make this situation any better, I couldn't seem to get that message through to my racing pulse. I shifted so that my body fit against his side. His eyes widened momentarily, as if he hadn't expected me to respond in any way other than a hissed insult; then his mouth curved into a smile. "I had a great time with you yesterday, especially when we were alone. We're still on for tonight, right? I have hockey practice, but I'm all yours after that."

I didn't miss what he was implying with the emphasis on *I'm all yours*—and neither did anyone else.

Steffani looked shell-shocked. Her shiny bottom lip stuck out in an unflattering pout that made her look like a big-mouthed guppy bobbing around in a fish tank.

"You're hanging out with *her?*"

Spencer barely acknowledged Fake's existence with a quick glance before he refocused on me. It was strange being the center of such intensity. I hadn't noticed it before, but he always radiated energy; even when he was driving his car, there was an undeniable air of power and competency that surrounded him.

The fact that it was a really great car didn't hurt matters either.

"I don't know. Am I hanging out with you, Belle?" The way Spencer lingered on the nickname made it sound way too sexy to ever be applied to me.

"Um . . ."

I could feel the eyes of everyone in the hallway upon me and my hands began shaking even harder now. "Yes?"

Spencer nodded as if my agreement hadn't really been in question, as his hand trailed lightly across my back until his whole arm was slung across my shoulder. Such a small, casual gesture that Melanie made on a regular basis was now electrifying.

It felt like my skin was too tight to contain my racing heartbeat.

"But . . . what would you even do with her?" Steffani sounded appalled, and my stomach clenched again.

"Oh, there's plenty of things we can do." Spencer's voice contained a hint of something downright wicked as he squeezed my shoulder lightly and began walking—with me still pressed against his side—down the hallway. He raised his voice so that everyone lurking in the hallway would be sure to overhear. "The real question is what should we do *first.*"

And just like that, I was the geeky half of Smith High School's most unlikely couple.

Chapter 5

Salt and pepper. Cats and cardboard boxes.
Prom king and queen—some things just go together as a matched set. But recently, some of
the pairs that Smith High School has produced
are rather . . . uneven. Only one half of the couple has the kind of popularity to cinch a nomination. So what happens to the dangler? Will
they get a pity vote, or will Smith High School
remain true to the premise that we may all be
created equal—but not everyone is destined to
wear the crown?

from "Power Couples or Pity Couples?"
by Lisa Anne Montgomery
Published by *The Smithsonian*

It's amazing how quickly rumors can spread.
By the time Spencer released me so that I could walk the
rest of the way to my psychology class alone, the damage was
done. Everyone at Smith High School was whispering that
Spencer King was hooking up with that "Isodore-chick."
They didn't even bother getting my name right. Not that they

had any incentive to fact-check the gossip. Why would they bother themselves over trivial details like the truth when they could snicker in my general direction?

I didn't want to hear the whispers.

I knew that the stories most likely to spread were going to be the very worst of the bunch. Rumors that he was with me because I was seriously kinky in the bedroom. That I had agreed to do all of his schoolwork for him. Or maybe that one of his hockey buddies had dared him to get into my pants.

Whatever they came up with, they'd all believe that he was scraping the bottom of the barrel with me.

I wondered what they would say if I told everyone the truth; that the only thing I had offered was friendship.

Probably that they had known it all along. That *of course* he wouldn't actually be interested in having sex with me. Spencer King had standards, after all.

High school was such a lovely place.

Still, I kept my head down and focused on my classes for the rest of the day. I only had to make it through the next three years and then all of this crap would be relegated to entertaining anecdotes that I'd tell when in the presence of my college friends. And all of them would say supportive stuff like, "Are you *kidding* me? You're gorgeous, Izzie! Those kids must have been seriously twisted!"

And I would nod and then shrug and say something like, "Oh, high school, I've nearly blocked all of it out. You couldn't pay me enough to relive those years!"

Then the conversation would move on to something else, and future Isobel would fall asleep thinking of the exciting plans she had for the next day instead of obsessing about the past.

I just had to give time a chance to make these years seem less terrible. Maybe someday I'd be able to get all nostalgic about my lunches with Melanie, Jane, and Mackenzie.

Maybe . . . but I doubted it.

I didn't exactly have hours to kill dwelling on the emotional state of future Izzie when the entire school was trying to analyze my every move. If this was what it was like to be a Notable, they could keep their popularity. I certainly didn't want it.

I nearly burst out laughing when I remembered the way Spencer had tried to dangle the promise of notoriety like a carrot only the day before. Nobody in their right mind would *seek* this kind of scrutiny. Although at least nobody was repeating the rumors to my face.

Or they hadn't . . . yet.

It was only a matter of time before some girl in one of my classes tried to pump me for information under the guise of being "friendly." Then she'd probably act all offended if I brushed her off. If one of my friends actually wanted to discuss it with me, I'd be fine with that. . . . But someone who had never said more to me than, "Heyyyy . . . can I borrow a pen?" didn't deserve to know the details.

Not that I was in much of a position to share; I didn't have a clue what was going on. Spencer had said he wanted to hang out after his hockey practice, but that could have been entirely for Steffani Larson's behalf. Something to get the gossip mills whipped into a frenzy. It didn't actually mean that he had any intention of spending time with me.

He just wanted everyone to think that we'd be meeting up for a prearranged booty call.

My stomach flopped. I didn't want *this*. I hadn't thought the plan through very far, but these whispers certainly hadn't been part of it. Then again, I'd figured it would be enough of a stretch getting people to believe that he wanted to date me without adding in a sexual component.

What I hadn't factored into my calculations was that with Spencer King, everyone took sex as a given.

And now that those rumors included me, I wondered

whether Spencer's reputation had actually been earned. Sure, he'd had sex with girls at our school. That was common knowledge. But I had never heard him brag about it, certainly not with any kind of seriousness. He acted like it was all some kind of joke. So maybe he had adopted humor as a coping strategy to handle the scrutiny that was unnerving me. If his fellow classmates were going to whisper no matter what, maybe he'd simply chosen to raise one cynical eyebrow and smirk until someone else stepped into the spotlight.

It was undoubtedly more effective than adjusting glasses and wiping sweaty palms against the denim of worn jeans.

The weirdest part of the whole day was speculating on whether or not I should expect to see him at my house later that day. Whether I should warn my parents that their little girl would be receiving a gentleman caller whose interest rested solely in harnessing her geek power for his own nefarious purposes. Especially when I still didn't know if I even *wanted* his friendship.

Funny that I had absentmindedly accepted that befriending Spencer King would be great without considering the baggage included in the package deal. I had been too intrigued with the idea of setting myself apart. Too determined to leave Smith High School secure in the knowledge that I had done something memorable. That no matter what kind of glamorous life awaited Spencer, he'd always think of me fondly as a girl with integrity.

I wanted to leave an indelible mark that said, *Isobel Peters was here.*

But did that make me any different from anyone else at this fracking school?

For a girl who was supposed to have all the answers, I was sure coming up empty far too often. Or maybe I'd just been asking myself the wrong questions for a whole lot longer than I wanted to admit. Normally, I would've asked Melanie for advice, but I reached the school parking lot just in time to see her head toward Mackenzie's house. Apparently she hadn't cut things off with Dylan, which left me with a limited number of options. I could help Jane and Scott plot world domination from the headquarters of *The Smithsonian* or try to message Sam while she sat in detention for her most recent act of civil disobedience. But I wasn't sure I wanted to discuss Spencer with anyone, let alone two girls who had their thumbs pressed firmly against the pulse of Smith High School. There was no way they would let the rumors that Spencer and I had a clothing-optional arrangement die out on their own. And the last thing I needed was for a reporter and a rabble-rouser to get indignant on my behalf.

So I walked home and waited.

Of course, I told myself that I wasn't some pathetic girl who put her life on hold in case some boy decided to make a move. I legitimately wanted to spend my time rewatching the second season of *Battlestar Galactica,* and if I happened to think that Captain Lee Adama looked like an older, darker haired version of Spencer King . . . that was purely an intellectual observation. It didn't mean anything. Neither did the fact that I pressed pause when a shirtless Adama tried to kick a reporter out of the pilot's changing room.

That was just . . . research. For something.

I didn't know the details, but I had no doubt that someday it would come in handy.

I pulled out my notebook and started slogging through my math homework while Starbuck defended the galactic fleet on my mom's old laptop. It was soothing, actually. I had seen the show enough times for it to have the familiarity of an old friend, even though the suspenseful moments still sucked me in.

"Don't do it, Apollo!" I muttered, before I double-checked my last answer in the back of the textbook. "You don't want to go in there. Trust me, you don't . . . *go! RUN!*"

I was so riveted to the action onscreen that I ignored what might've been a light rap on my door. My dad was in his office downstairs, probably dealing with an endless amount of paperwork, but both my parents knew better than to knock quietly. It takes a whole lot more than that to break my concentration, with or without *Battlestar Galactica*. That's why they usually sent me a text when they wanted us to spend "quality time" together.

Or they would pound on my door until I responded.

My parents were great, but I didn't get why they had to make a big production out of cooking dinner as a family since it was part of the daily routine. My dad and I always took over the kitchen, while my mom set the table and avoided anything that was even remotely dangerous. We had banned her from helping when she accidentally created an oil fireball and then tried to douse it with water.

But even though my body instinctively tensed as it tried to warn my brain that I was no longer alone in the room, I didn't so much as glance over at the doorframe.

"RUN!"

"I had no idea you were a sports fan, Izzie."

I toppled out of my chair. I twisted to see who was intruding on my personal space and *then* my shoes tangled together as I tried to lurch to my feet. The next thing I knew, I was looking at the world from an entirely different perspective. Mostly because my face was smooshed against the carpeting.

"I'm . . . uh . . . not sports. Sci-fi. Hi."

Spencer's laugh reminded me of his walk—easy and relaxed.

"You want a hand?" he offered, as if belatedly remembering that it was probably his fault I had tripped in the first place.

"I want you to go back in time and call first," I groused as I debated taking the proffered help. His presence, in my *bedroom,* was a jolt to my system, but I couldn't see how I could refuse without looking rattled.

But the feel of his warm, calloused grip tugging me to my

feet made me feel a whole lot more off balance than when I'd landed on the floor.

"I didn't have your number. So, let me guess . . . you decided to try out Mackenzie's personal brand of yoga?"

I grinned back. It was impossible not to smile as I remembered Mackenzie's expression when she'd gone down for the count the day before. It also made me feel a whole lot less ridiculous for taking a tumble in my own bedroom. That kind of thing just . . . happens.

But not everyone was able to brush it off as easily as Spencer King.

"You're really good at that."

"I'm really good at a number of things. Want to be more specific?"

I rolled my eyes. "Putting people at ease . . . usually by acting like a jerk."

"I'm never a jerk. And if this is how you look when you're relaxed"—Spencer's laughter rang out in my room—"then you seriously need to loosen up. You're practically bracing yourself for a body check."

I gaped at him. "For a *what?*"

"Hockey term. Sorry." His smile widened, and there was another flash of pure mischief in his eyes. "You're kind of cute when you're embarrassed."

I froze. Maybe if I were some other girl—the type of girl who showed up to his Notable parties—I'd have known how to respond to a statement that was half-compliment, half . . . something else entirely, without inwardly panicking. I would have been able to say something flirty back.

You're not bad looking yourself, hotshot.

That wasn't something that would ever come out of my mouth. Not in this lifetime.

So instead of flirting, I . . . snorted. "Save the lines, Romeo. I never agreed to be more than your friend. *Comprende, amigo?*"

He nodded slowly, but his eyes were lit with something that looked suspiciously like excitement. My words of advice to Melanie came echoing back to me.

As long as you distract him with a bet or a dare—some kind of feat to prove his manliness—he'll probably forget you even exist.

My genius plan didn't work so well if the competitive boy in question thought that *I* was the challenge.

Especially when a small part of me—the stupid, optimistic part that went a little mushy when I noticed a couple who had probably been together for half a century—wasn't entirely sure it might not be fun to be caught.

Even if it only ended in heartbreak later.

Chapter 6

How that special someone asks you to prom sets the tone for everything. Does he go for something cute? Sweet? Whimsical? Or did he shrug and say, "Hey, I don't have anything better to do. Want to go?"

If you get that last kind of invite, feel free to wear the highest heels you can find, because you probably won't be dancing in them. You and your date are going to be the sideline couple.

—from "Preparing for Prom,"
by Lisa Anne Montgomery
Published by *The Smithsonian*

"I thought school went pretty well today—all things considered."

I stared at Spencer in disbelief. My brain did not want to compute all the possible interpretations of that sentence. Was he trying to needle me with his sarcasm? Did he actually think that was *funny*? Or was he so removed from the geek lifestyle that he had no idea just how royally he had screwed me over?

Every ounce of frustration that had built up from having spent an entire day with whispers dogging my footsteps blasted through my system and I felt my reserve . . . crack.

There was no holding me back.

"Yeah? Did you have a good day? Glad to hear it. I didn't. Funny, but I don't remember writing *have the entire school speculate on sex life* in my daily planner. Here, why don't you double-check." I grabbed my agenda and shoved it in his face.

"You have really tiny handwriting."

"And you have a really messed-up idea of friendship. Did you honestly think I wanted our farce to go that far? Here's a newsflash for you, hotshot: I didn't."

Spencer nodded, but one corner of his mouth was creeping upward. He was trying to smother his laughter. At me. I saw red—and it had nothing to do with my bedroom decor.

"What's so funny?" I snapped. "Fill me in. I could use a good joke."

"Sorry, it's just that you've called me 'hotshot' twice now. It . . . distracts me." He shook his head and his expression sobered. "I'm sorry if I overstepped. I saw you talking to Steffani and thought you could use some backup. The rest was pure impulse. That's it, I swear."

I looked at him skeptically. "You swear?"

"Yeah, I do. And my word is solid, ask anyone." He seemed to remember that I couldn't exactly call up his hockey buddies for verification, and tugged on the collar of his shirt as he tossed out an alternative. "Ask Logan or Mackenzie if you want."

"I'll pass, thanks."

"Because you trust me?"

I considered that longer than I probably should have. It was one of those questions that people ask when they expect the other person will tell them exactly what they want to hear. Kind of like when a friend asks if their new haircut makes them look like a ferret. What they want is a short, concise answer that leaves their worldview intact.

But did I actually trust the King of the Notables to be upfront with me?

Surprisingly . . . yes. I had heard girls crying in the bathroom because he had ended their relationships before they could even change their Facebook status to "it's complicated," but never that he had lied to them.

In fact, I distinctly remembered a rumor that Spencer laid out his rules of engagement before anything happened. That he never hooked up with anyone who had been drinking at his parties. That he never made promises he didn't keep.

And yet he still left a trail of pissed-off girls in his wake.

"I believe you were trying to help," I said at last. "But you didn't have to take it that far. You could have walked over without pretending there was something going on between us."

Spencer rubbed his temple, and it was only then that I noticed a red bruise that was only deepening in color on his jaw. "I thought you needed backup," he repeated. "Do you mind if I sit down? I got kind of banged up in hockey practice today."

"What happened? Did you get, uh . . . body checked?"

Spencer's eyes seemed to brighten with amusement as he looked at me, and I could feel my cheeks begin to flush. I quickly scooped up a pile of textbooks that were sprawled out across my bed and moved them to their rightful place on my desk as Spencer sat on the side of the bed and idly rubbed his knee. He winced briefly, but instantly tried to mask the pain.

"There was a skirmish on the ice. Patrick got in a lucky swing. Or two." Spencer folded his arms and you didn't have to be a body-language expert to tell that he was still pissed off that he had been caught with his guard down.

"Do you need frozen peas or something?" I jolted to my feet. "I could—"

"Don't worry about it. Although I should probably warn you, I think your dad wanted me to declare my intentions on the porch before speaking to you."

I rolled my eyes. "My parents can be a bit on the overprotective side." Understatement of the year. "But I'm surprised you didn't make up some story for my dad. You've already got the *entire* school whispering about us."

"Those girls were going to talk about us no matter what I said," Spencer informed me with perfect calm, as if being the focal point of the school's gossip didn't faze him at all. "All I did was make sure they know I'm the one doing the chasing."

I crossed my arms. "How is that supposed to be comforting?"

"Because if they thought you were pursuing me, they'd ridicule you nonstop," he said bluntly. A chill began to creep down my neck as I soaked in the truth of his words. "It's a shitty double standard, but I didn't want you to be diced to pieces for doing me a solid."

Is that going to be so much worse than what I faced every day already?

If my high school experience was a rollercoaster, it would probably be called "Crap Mountain" and involve a lot of gut-wrenchingly sharp twists and turns. It was a shitty experience, but at least it was a familiar ride. Even if the suckitude increased proportionally to the amount of time I spent at Smith High School, I could still make it out with my sanity more or less intact. But all of those calculations had been made before Spencer triggered a Mount Vesuvius–level explosion on my social life.

"I changed my mind." My chest clenched tighter until I felt like I couldn't breathe. "I can't do this."

Spencer nodded absentmindedly. He seemed preoccupied surveying my room; from the Einstein poster, to the autographed promo shot of the band ReadySet, to the rich red color of my bedroom walls. My parents had been skeptical of the color choice when I had first broached the idea, but when I promised to do all of the work myself, they had eventually caved.

I still had a worn tank top in the bottom dresser drawer that was speckled and splotched with crimson paint.

"Earth to Spencer!" I snapped. "I. Can't. Do. This."

"Yeah, I heard you the first time. I'm just not sure what there is to say. We've passed the point of return. Even if we said that I was joking earlier, I doubt anyone would believe it."

I sank down numbly on the bed next to Spencer, too overwhelmed with the dire reality of the situation to pay attention to the fact that our limbs were mere inches away from touching.

"What have I gotten myself into?" I murmured. "I must have lost my fracking mind when I suggested this."

"To be fair," Spencer said reasonably, "your reputation will probably get a boost now that people think we've gotten"—he seemed to rethink his choice of words when I glared at him—"closer."

"That's *not* the kind of reputation I wanted!"

He gently nudged my shoulder. "Lighten up, Belle. It's only high school."

"Easy for you to say. People aren't exactly insulting you on a daily basis. Why would they? You're *Spencer King*." I let the sarcasm roll heavy off my tongue but was surprised to feel him stiffen beside me before he cranked up the intensity of those piercing green eyes.

"Is Alex still bothering you?"

I instantly regretted saying anything. The last thing I needed was another rumble in the cafeteria. I'd much rather let the subject drop entirely.

"It doesn't matter," I said evasively.

Spencer nudged my shoulder again, but this time there was nothing gentle about it. "I thought we were going to be friends. That's the deal we both agreed to yesterday."

Yes, it was. But I'd already begun regretting the offer. Maybe

Spencer needed a girl in his life who didn't have an endgame, but the last thing *I* needed was an arrogant, annoying, absolutely impossible—

"Well, as your friend, I want to help. And I know how we can make everyone shut up."

I eyed him nervously. Spencer's smirk was nowhere to be seen, but that didn't mean he didn't have something entirely inappropriate in mind. With a guy like Spencer, you could never be too sure what he had in mind.

"C'mon, Belle. Live a little. What's the worst that could happen?"

I hoped I wasn't about to find out firsthand.

Chapter 7

Prom is one stupid dance that looks exactly like every other event our school throws. So why exactly is there so much pressure for the guys to do the asking? This isn't Elizabethan England, people. This isn't even *Downton Abbey*.

If you like someone, ask them!

And lower your expectations, because real life isn't a Disney movie.

—Anonymous letter to the editor
Published by *The Smithsonian*

"So, this plan of yours . . . does it have to start right *now?*"

Spencer glanced from me to the swirled silver bedspread he was sitting on and leaned back until most of his weight was resting on his forearms.

Maybe I had spent too much time watching *Battlestar Galactica,* because now I couldn't help noticing his arms looked all . . . sinewy and strong. And he was stretched across my bed, with a smile lifting his lips, looking like an invitation to sin.

My pulse kicked into high gear.

"Is there something else you'd rather do with me?" he asked evenly, and I lurched over to my desk and grabbed a chair.

"Yes, actually." I straddled the back of it, because that looked tough in the movies even though it wasn't comfortable in real life. Still, I rested my arms on the back of the chair and looked him dead in the eyes. "I want to know why you always crank the sex to eleven."

He grinned. "Sex? I don't remember offering. Looks like someone's got her mind in the gutter."

"And someone promised to tell me the truth whenever I asked for it," I said staunchly. "So, I'm going to ask you one last time: Why do you snow every girl within a three-mile radius?"

Any trace of a smile was wiped off his face. "I'm friendly. That's it."

I waved my hand to indicate the way he had taken over my bed. "So . . . this is just your way of being friendly?" I couldn't stop myself from laughing. "Yeah, I don't think so."

"Here's something for you to consider, Doc; just because people don't square up to your expectations, doesn't mean they're lying. I'm a friendly guy. And I'd rather be the life of the party than spend my time analyzing all the opportunities I'm missing."

That pulled me up short.

"You think I'm—"

"Hiding," Spencer finished for me. "I think that's easier for you than risking rejection."

Well . . . wow. Considering that *I* was the one who planned on being a psychologist, I should have evaluated that possibility ages ago. Then again, it's a whole lot easier to judge somebody else than it is to get an accurate read on yourself.

"I think you're playing a role," I told him, unable to keep the words bottled up. "I might fear the spotlight, but you've found a way to disappear in plain sight. All you have to do is act like the guy most likely to throw an epic bachelor party in Las Vegas."

He didn't flinch at the accusation. In fact, his mouth twisted sardonically. "That's *exactly* who I am, Isobel."

"I don't buy it."

He sat upright with a laugh. "You want to study me? Fine. You can even jot down notes as you go along. But don't try to save me, Belle. I'm not broken."

I flushed. "I'm not—"

"You wouldn't be the first to try." He stood and then winced before his hand flew up to his side as if to protect him from a blow that had already landed. "And you're a great girl. Really. I'm sorry this whole situation became more than you bargained for, but you're not going to change me. Isn't the first rule of treatment that you can only help someone who wants to be helped? Well, I'm not interested."

I raised my hands in the classic don't shoot position. "I'm not trying to fix you, hotshot!"

"Good." His stance loosened and he looked very much himself again. In control of the situation. "Then are you ready to go or what? I believe we've got a reputation to salvage."

I was following him out my bedroom door before it even occurred to me to object. "You're a lot smarter than you let on."

"Yeah?" There was a gleam in Spencer's eyes as he turned to look at me. "You're a lot more fun than you let on. Even when you're grilling me."

I had no idea how to respond to that twisted compliment, so I just nodded. Then I texted my dad that I might be late for dinner and booked it out of there before he could psychoanalyze Spencer himself. It was weird having a secret from my parents.

I've never told them every little detail about my life, but going anywhere with Spencer King felt like, well...a Notable occasion.

And I was doing my best to leave them in the dark.

Then again, they didn't know Alex Thompson had ridiculed me in the cafeteria either. There are some things my parents were probably better off not knowing.

Like how the ride home yesterday hadn't made it any less strange for me to sit in Spencer King's car.

In some ways, he was more of a mystery to me now. Yesterday, I had been fairly secure in my analysis of him.

The only thing I knew for sure now was that he was a whole lot more complicated than I'd wanted to believe.

"So where are we going?" I asked, trying to get some conversation going. I wasn't entirely sure whether that was a good plan either. It seemed like every time he spoke we wound up arguing. Which was why the glint of mischief in his eyes that seemed to brighten around me left me wondering if I'd *ever* understand him.

"It wouldn't be much of a surprise if I told you in advance."

"I've had enough surprises lately."

He raised an eyebrow. "You're having fun with this, admit it."

"Fun!" I spluttered. "Okay, we must have some seriously different definitions of that word. You know what's fun to me?"

"No idea," he said.

"Fun is eating pizza in sweatpants with a few friends. Fun is knowing that you can make a complete idiot out of yourself and nobody will ridicule you. Fun is... *Battlestar Galactica!*"

Spencer grinned. "I'll make you a deal then."

"Because the last deal we made has worked out so well for me," I interjected.

"If you follow my lead tonight, we'll try your thing tomorrow."

I stared at him in confusion, waiting to see his mouth quirk upward in the tell-tale sign that he was joking. "My *thing?*"

"Battleguard Galactricka."

"Battle*star* Galactica."

Spencer nodded complacently. "Exactly. That. I'll watch it with you. I'll even bring the pizza."

My mouth dropped open as I tried to imagine Spencer sprawled next to me in the living room watching the Cylons take over Caprica. As they would say on the show: No. Fracking. Way.

"I'd pay good money to see that," I said skeptically.

Spencer glanced over his shoulder and then slid into a parking space right outside the local Wells Fargo.

"Don't tell me you're planning a bank robbery. I draw the line at being an accessory to a felony."

Spencer burst out laughing. "Well, in that case—keep moving, Belle."

I didn't budge. "You've started calling me that a lot. Did you run out of options and decide to stick with the one nickname that suits me the least?"

Spencer didn't say a word as he took my hand.

And the sensation of feeling his palm sliding against my own before his fingers locked us together . . . yeah, it made speech impossible for me.

"I like the way it sounds. *Belle.*" He drew it out and I felt my knees go melty. It was so freaking unfair that all he had to do was say a girl's *name* and she would want to tangle both hands in his dirty blond hair, rise up on her toes, and let her lips communicate in an entirely different way.

Or at least that's what it was doing to me.

And I should have been immune. Clinical. Dispassionate.

Not inwardly thinking that it was a good thing he liked repeating my name because I was close to forgetting it as we walked down the street. I instinctively kept pace with him and somehow it began to feel . . . right.

Normal.

As if it totally made sense for the two of us to be holding hands in public because that's what happens when someone likes you and doesn't care who knows it.

My whole body felt like it was tingling by the time Spencer slowed his steps, and I pushed my glasses up haphazardly with my free hand as I glanced over to see what destination he had in mind for us.

The Yogurt Shack.

"Too late to back out now," Spencer whispered in my ear right before he pushed open the door, squeezed my hand, and walked me right into the belly of the beast.

Or at the very least the belly of the Notable crowd.

Same thing, if you ask me.

The frozen yogurt place wasn't all that special really. The walls were a cheerful shade of yellow that probably had some super perky name like "daisy bliss" or "lovin' lemon," and the radio top hits were blaring over the speaker system. It looked like your basic family-friendly dessert shop.

Unfortunately, it was also where the Notables flocked to gossip after school, which meant that walking inside was the equivalent of announcing, "Hear ye! Hear ye! I stand before you today to declare that these two students have forged the sacred bonds of a relationship."

Not exactly what I had in mind when I said that I wanted to, y'know, *kill* the rumors.

The opposite of it, actually.

"C'mon, babe. I want you to meet my teammates," Spencer said loudly enough for everyone to hear as he tugged me over to the Notable table.

Fake and Bake were perched next to each other on stools,

probably flirting with everyone willing to pay them attention. But now their smoky eye makeup made them look only more hostile as they gave me a painfully slow once-over. They didn't need to expend that much energy on it; I was wearing the exact same clothes I had chosen for school that morning. Comfortable jeans and a purple shirt that barely peeked out beneath my Doctor Who sweatshirt.

My geeky armor at its finest.

I saw Patrick turn to someone who would be perfectly cast as Neckless Jock #4 in the latest teen movie, before he mouthed, "Is this for real?"

No. No, it wasn't.

"I'm going to kill you," I murmured in his ear, knowing full well that he wouldn't take the threat any more seriously than Melanie or anyone else who deserved some payback. I'm just not a very intimidating person. I blame the glasses.

Spencer laughed, but it wasn't the rich, husky sound that I'd grown accustomed to after two days of verbal sparring. It was just another part of his performance piece.

So was the way he leaned in and lightly brushed his lips across my forehead.

It was a gesture that I'd received countless times from my parents when I was sick, and there was nothing revolutionary about the kiss. Except . . . this wasn't coming from my mom.

"Belle, meet everyone. Guys, this is my girlfriend, Isobel."

My stomach dropped two feet and I began to worry that my sweaty palm would slip right out of Spencer's grip.

"N-nice to meet you," I forced myself to say hesitantly.

I received a collection of nods, grunts, and unenthusiastic hey's from the guys, and pursed-lipped grimaces, which were supposed to be smiles, from the girls.

I felt welcomed all right.

About as much as a Time Lord facing down a Dalek.

"C'mon, let's get our order started, Belle," Spencer said, smoothly taking over as if his so-called friends weren't staring at him in confusion. He released my hand to grab a cup before he began working his way down a row of self-serve flavors.

"How does alpine vanilla sound?"

Right, as if *anything* sounded appetizing when I was stuck in restricted quarters with a pack of Notables. The last thing I wanted to do now was eat in their presence. The cafeteria was more than enough of a minefield for me to endure five days a week, thank you very much.

"Uh . . . good," I mumbled.

"You sure you don't want to try some first?" Spencer's eyes were gleaming mischievously as he dipped his index finger into the bowl; then moving faster than I thought someone so laid-back could go, he brushed my bottom lip with the icy treat.

I jumped back in shock, staring at Spencer incredulously as he . . . winked.

I spontaneously burst out laughing.

It was just . . . so ridiculous.

The fact that I was pretending to be dating Spencer King right under the noses of the Notables, despite the fact that he couldn't even act his age long enough to get a freaking frozen yogurt . . . I dissolved into a giggling mess.

"Need a bigger sample?" Spencer teased as he reached once more into the bowl. "Because I have plenty right here."

No way.

I scurried over to a yogurt dispenser at the far end of the store so that I would become a much more challenging target. I couldn't manage to lengthen the ten-foot gap between us because there was virtually no room to maneuver. Or hide. Or do much of anything except eat frozen yogurt and gossip. Still, the look on Spencer's face was downright predatory as he stalked forward.

"I'm going to get you, Belle."

I was breathless from laughter, anticipation, and a light

buzz of anxiety. "Oh yeah, hotshot?" I lifted my chin defiantly. "Let's see what you got."

I jerked down the yogurt lever at the same time that Spencer moved within striking distance. The cold came as a jolt as it molded against the palm of my hand and I instinctively threw it at Spencer.

It landed with a soft, yet satisfying, *whump* against his chest and began to trickle downward in a sticky mess. The Yogurt Shack instantly fell silent.

Well, not *completely* silent. It's not like I had the authority to instruct the employees to turn off the music or anything. Some unbearably bubbly pop star was still gushing about her boyfriend or . . . the guy she wanted to be her boyfriend? I wasn't exactly giving it my full attention.

That was completely engaged by Spencer. More specifically by the way the King of the Notables now looked as if he had been caught doing an imitation of Frosty the Snowman. He didn't say a word, and neither did anyone else in the place. They were probably too busy waiting with bated breath for the most epic dumping in the history of breakups.

But they didn't see the way Spencer's eyes practically crackled with amusement.

He dipped his finger across the frozen yogurt, lifted it to his own lips, and pasted a considering expression on his face as he slowly tasted it. "Nah, I think the alpine vanilla is better."

An uncomfortable-looking college kid in his early twenties walked over to us. "Um . . . I need to ask the two of you to leave."

"He started it!" I said, pointing at Spencer as he reached into his pocket and pulled out his wallet.

"It won't happen again," Spencer said confidently, as if he ran into trouble with management all the time. For all I knew, he did. "We'll be out of your hair in just a minute."

And then he proceeded to fill up his bowl with three

different types of frozen yogurt and a billion different toppings while I looked nervously from the Yogurt Shack guy to the Notables, who were still watching my every move.

Even with a yogurt glob on the front of his shirt, Spencer looked like a young, lighter haired Superman.

I nervously fingered my glasses before I remembered that my hand was still coated with frozen yogurt. I was pretty sure all I had managed to accomplish was smearing the sticky ice cream evidence onto one lens and the left side of my nose.

Spencer's grin widened when he turned back to me with his fully loaded dessert. He grabbed a napkin. "I can't take you anywhere," he said teasingly as he wiped at my face.

I batted his hand away. "Yeah, because *I'm* the one who's always causing trouble. Try again."

He leaned in even closer and murmured, "Admit it, you're having fun."

And then he laid a twenty-dollar bill down on the counter, took hold of my hand, and wrinkled his nose when he realized too late that it was the same one that had been clutching frozen yogurt only minutes earlier. He pulled me toward the door, pausing only to toss a casual "see you guys later" to his gaping friends.

"What was *that?*" I managed to say at last when he slowed down as we neared his car.

"I thought about it. Your plan for the night sounded better than mine. Do you want to order the pizza at my house or yours?"

I blinked up at him owlishly. "I'm never going to understand you."

"Nope." He handed me the frozen yogurt while he fumbled for one of the napkins that had come with it. "But imagine how much fun you're going to have trying."

I took a big spoonful, with a large chunk of Oreo, and tried to imagine sharing pizza and fro-yo with my parents constantly checking up on us.

No thank you.

"Your place," I decided as I slid into the passenger's seat. "But don't get any ideas, *friend*."

Except I didn't know whether those words were intended more for Spencer or myself.

Chapter 8

There are three obvious reasons why that special someone might not have issued a prom invite yet (although three days out is cutting it awfully close, don't you think?) and they are the following:

1. They are morally opposed to having fun. Just like the people who keep writing stupid letters to the editor. Maybe the person you like is one of them. (Although, trust me, you can do so much better.)
2. They are still trying to work up their nerve. Rejection is scary. So maybe the problem isn't that they don't like you back, but that they are uncertain of your affection.
3. They want to play the field.
    Let's be real: This close to the dance date, there are plenty of desperate singles to choose from, which doesn't mean you should lower your standards. Speaking of which . . . who knows why Spencer King is interested in Isobel Peters? Seriously. Who knows what is going on with that? I want details.

—from "Cutting It Close,"
by Lisa Anne Montgomery
Published by *The Smithsonian*

I had heard rumors about Spencer's house.

Melanie had mentioned there was a fountain and a small gazebo, which both perfectly complemented the Victorian architecture of the place. The effect was stunning. And sure, I'd heard snatches of conversation in the girl's bathroom about a hot tub behind the house that could comfortably seat half of the hockey team . . . and their girlfriends.

But it was one thing to get secondhand accounts and quite another to hear the gravel crunching under the tires right before Spencer pulled the car into an empty garage.

He unbuckled his seat belt and then glanced over at me, taking in the way I was tightly gripping the frozen yogurt carton.

"So . . . is there really a dungeon?" I asked.

He burst out laughing. "It's just a house, Belle. There's no party scheduled. There's probably nobody here. If that makes you uncomfortable, I can take you home right now. No pressure."

"Do you do this all the time?" I couldn't keep the thread of nervousness out of my voice.

"Bring girls to my house? Sure. More than once. But since you're my first girl period friend period—I guess not."

I forced myself to meet his eyes. "You still think we're friends?"

It wasn't the question I meant to ask. I was going to ask if it was weird for him bringing me over when it was so obvious that I didn't fit into his world. I had just thrown *frozen yogurt* at him. In public. In front of all of his hockey buddies. And my only regret was that I had missed his face and hit his chest instead.

But now that the question was out, I wouldn't have changed it for anything. I needed to know if a garden-variety platonic friendship was the only thing between us, because I wasn't sure how I felt anymore. If I had to categorize the medley of emotions, I'd say mostly confused, with an underlying current of attraction that didn't exactly scream, "Hey, buddy, ol' pal."

"I guess that depends," Spencer said thoughtfully. "Friends introduce friends to Battlesword Galactica, right?"

I laughed, which was probably his plan all along. And suddenly I had no trouble climbing out of Spencer's car, handing him the frozen yogurt I had put a decent-sized dent into during the car ride, and nudging him with my shoulder. "Let's go, then."

He opened the door with his foot, probably to avoid another yogurt-related mess, and then pushed open a bathroom door so that he could rinse off his hands. I followed suit, although I couldn't resist splashing him in the process.

"What was *that* for?"

I didn't bother responding. Instead, I bolted up the stairs before he could retaliate, grinning like a fool the whole way as every particle in my body became hyperaware of the threat of retaliation.

Spencer was right: I was having fun. Even though a tiny part of my brain, which always went off in preparation for an attack during a horror movie, was ringing an alarm. Not because I thought I was in any physical danger. Sure, I was alone in a freaking mansion with a boy I was still getting to know, but that didn't mean I was *afraid*.

Okay, that's a lie.

I *was* scared, but it was the normal level of anxiety I felt whenever it was dark outside and I wasn't home. The persistent voice in my head couldn't resist pointing out that this was a risk. That the majority of assaults were committed by someone known to the victim, so maybe trusting Spencer so far was a mistake.

But it was even more likely that I was using my knowledge of statistics to make a cowardly retreat look like a perfectly rational decision.

I had to remind myself that Spencer had offered to take me

home, that the only reason I was at his house was because we were getting to be *friends*. That even if he was interested in me in some other way (which he wasn't), I had made it clear I wouldn't be reciprocating those feelings.

Mostly.

I mean, *maybe* my eyes had lingered on the yogurt glob on his chest longer than I would've had it been, oh, I dunno . . . anyone else. But that was simply a hormonal response to visual stimulation. Spencer was the last person who would think it meant anything, especially given his willingness to chase anything in a skirt.

I was glad I had chosen to wear jeans.

"Nice place," I said, trying hard not to be overwhelmed as I reached the staircase landing and found myself standing in an enormous living room with an understated decor style that screamed of money. The walls were different shades of beige that were probably named "french vanilla" or "blanched almond" or something that sounded expensively delicious. There was something about standing in such an immaculate room that instantly made me feel a thousand times clumsier. My brain automatically started flicking through every item I could possibly destroy . . . and the price tags that were probably attached to them.

I could trip over my own feet and knock over the modern art sculpture on a nearby end table. Maybe Spencer would shoot me one of those devastatingly wicked smiles and somehow I'd become discombobulated enough that I'd drop the frozen yogurt container . . . right on their taupe-colored carpeting.

"Home sweet home," Spencer said dryly. Instead of slowing down, he passed me and headed down a hallway. I tagged behind him sheepishly, like a lost puppy . . . or, y'know, a sheep.

"So where are your parents?"

It seemed like a reasonable question to me, especially since one glance down at my cell phone showed that I had seven text messages waiting in my inbox, all of them from my mom and dad.

WHEN WILL YOU BE HOME?
WHO ARE YOU WITH? YOUR DAD SAID IT WAS A BOY!
IN THE FUTURE, WE WOULD APPRECIATE ADVANCE NOTICE.

That last text made me wince. Of course, they wanted time to properly vet anyone who might be spending time with me. I was lucky they didn't know anything about Spencer's reputation, or they might not have let me go at all.

I personally thought that would be taking the whole protective thing way too far.

IS MELANIE WITH YOU?
CALL US IF YOU PLAN TO STAY OUT LATER THAN 8:30 PM.
SCHOOL NIGHT RULES, ISOBEL. HOME NO LATER THAN 9:30.
STAY SAFE, HONEY. CALL US IF YOU NEED A RIDE.

It was sweet. A bit much sometimes, but I wouldn't have traded their concern for anything. Especially after receiving late-night phone calls from Melanie when it was painfully obvious that everything was not okay at her house. She wouldn't come out and say it, but I could hear the tension vibrating in her voice.

All I could do was keep her talking until the worst of the disappointment, the bone-aching frustration of watching her father slowly drink himself to death, had passed.

I would take a billion concerned text messages from my parents over Melanie's situation any day of the week. Even if that meant I had to tell them, *Be home by curfew. All good here. Love you!* while I tried not to accidentally bump into something that cost more than a semester at a private liberal arts college.

I wondered how Spencer managed to throw his parties in a house that looked like a museum showroom. If he liked living somewhere that had to include a regular cleaning service to maintain its air of stately elegance.

I wanted to know what he thought about *my* house.

Mentally filing all of those questions away for a later date, I pulled up short when Spencer opened the door to his bedroom, tossed his wallet on the dresser, and strolled into his walk-in closet. I stood frozen at the doorway like a freaking vampire waiting for permission before crossing the threshold, while I examined Spencer's room every bit as closely as he'd looked at mine.

It was a mess.

Okay, to be fair, it probably wouldn't have seemed so disorganized if the rest of the house hadn't looked like it was on the market to be sold. In fact, I had expected it to be a whole lot worse. I didn't see any half-naked girls tacked up on his walls, which didn't mean they weren't there somewhere . . . they just weren't visible from my vantage point. Maybe because the enormous windows that overlooked some trees and gave the barest glimpse of the gazebo cut into the available poster space.

Even without a tanned swimsuit model pouting back at us, the room was undeniably masculine. There was a dartboard to the left side of his desk and judging by the wayward holes in the wall around it, he had probably enjoyed more than a few rounds when he wasn't entirely sober. There were weights sitting on the other side of the desk and a beatup-looking pair of boxing gloves. I craned my neck, wondering if he had a bag hanging from the ceiling in my blind spot or if the King family would *never* keep large athletic equipment in a bedroom.

That was probably stored in their private home gym.

"Do you want me to—uh . . ." My words petered out as I watched Spencer grab a shirt from his dresser and in one smooth move yank off the yogurt-splattered one he'd been wearing. I sucked in my breath and wondered if he'd forgotten about me entirely. If he was so comfortable in his own space that he didn't care who witnessed this impromptu strip show.

Or if he was in the mood to drive every platonic thought out of my head.

It was working.

My mouth went dry as my brain began cataloguing every detail, like the way the low-slung waistband of his jeans perfectly showcased his abs. I half expected someone to yell, "And cut! That was a great take, Spencer. Now, I just want to film your smolder from a different angle. Think sexy." Not that Spencer would ever have to think sexy. The guy left a trail of pheromones in his wake, which was why, despite the fact that everyone knew he wasn't boyfriend material, he had no trouble with girls.

Unless . . . maybe this was a test?

I gulped nervously and then leaned against the doorjamb; the pose was more to ensure that my knees wouldn't start wobbling than because I thought it would make me look cool. "So, is this the part where I'm supposed to swoon?"

Spencer silently tugged a clean shirt over his head, tousling his hair in the process, before he tossed the wadded ball of cotton in his hand toward his laundry basket. It sailed right in, and I fought the urge to roll my eyes.

Spencer King, everyone. He shoots, he scores.

"I'd prefer it if you didn't. Hardwood floor, y'know? They're easy enough to clean, but not exactly the most comfortable surface to sprawl out on." He flashed a grin. "I would know."

"You're doing it again."

He sank down on his bed and waited with an exaggerated air of patience for me to finish that thought.

"The sex to eleven thing!"

He glanced at his watch. "It's not even seven-thirty. I

appreciate the vote of confidence on my stamina, but not even I can—"

"Is this supposed to *impress* me?" I demanded. "How does this usually work for you, Spencer? You bring a girl home, give her the grand tour, take her to your room, and . . . what? Raise your eyebrow at her until she strips?"

He made no attempt to hide his amusement. "I like that one. I'll have to keep it in mind for future reference. Do you think it's enough to raise just one eyebrow, or will clothes be removed twice as fast if I use them both?"

"Not funny," I ground out.

"Sure, it is. Almost as funny as the way you're staring at me as if I were the big bad wolf."

"I'm not entirely convinced you're not."

He shrugged and then stood, moving toward me with a predatory grace that didn't help change my opinion. Still, instead of invading my space the way he had back at Mackenzie's house, he paused with a little over an arm's length between us. "That's because you're as suspicious as you are smart." Spencer took one deliberate step closer and my breath caught in my throat as he raised his hand and . . .

Ruffled my hair as if I were a petulant five-year-old kid.

"Come on, *buddy*. We have a pizza to order."

Chapter 9

Ballots will be handed out tomorrow and the instructions are simple. Every class will vote for five male and five female nominees for prom court. The results will be tabulated by the student council and announced at the actual event. There have been rumors that perhaps this year there should be greater transparency in the voting process, but this reporter thinks that would kill the suspense.

So relax, everyone.

—from "Predictions for Prom,"
by Lisa Anne Montgomery
Published by *The Smithsonian*

I paused to stare at the family photos lining one of the hallways.

There were hardly any of Spencer.

I mean, sure, he was in all of the professionally taken family portraits, but nothing that felt remotely like *him* was up on the wall. Every hair was combed neatly in place, and his frozen smile was stiff as he stood next to his older brother

and an impeccably dressed, distinguished looking man I
assumed was his dad. The photo belonged in a presidential
library or an election campaign. I had no trouble picturing an
overworked intern creating a promo piece with it for Spencer's
older brother.

> *Brandon King knows the real meaning of
> family. A devoted son and brother, he works
> hard to keep his family's tradition of philan-
> thropy going strong. He asks himself every day,
> "What can I do to help my community?"*
> *It's time for the community to help itself by
> electing Brandon King for Congress.*

It wasn't hard to imagine Spencer being forced to hand out
pamphlets and shake hands with strangers. Okay, and he'd
probably flirt with some intern at the same time . . . or maybe a
politician's equally bored daughter, until they were discovered
together in a supply closet at the campaign headquarters. His
hair would be mussed and there'd probably be some tell-tale
lipstick stains smeared in a downward trail. And he'd be busted
with an enormous smile on his face.

Even a photo of him like that would be better than the row
of bland portraits. At least that would be honest. The lock-
jawed guy on the wall looked like Spencer's painfully boring
doppelgänger. The charismatic Notable next to me was really
good at messing with my head . . . and my nerves, but there
was still no doubt in my mind that he was infinitely more
interesting than anyone who would fit his family mold.

"Any insights now, Freud?" Spencer quipped. "Or do you
need to start all the way back with my baby pics to get a
major revelation?"

"Now that you mention it, that sounds like fun. I'd kind
of like to see for myself if you were born with a silver spoon
in your mouth."

Spencer laughed, but it wasn't the rich, throaty sound I'd become accustomed to hearing. This one sounded decidedly upper crust, like a stereotypical rich person's chuckle before they said something obnoxious like, *"Oh, how droll of you."*

"The spoon was sixteen-karat gold and passed down from generation to generation. The King family never does anything halfway."

I pursed my lips thoughtfully and then tried to steal a glance at him from the corner of my eye. I'm not sure why I bothered; without the aid of my glasses he looked like a decidedly blurry lump. But I didn't have to see him to sense the tension that suddenly filled the empty corridor.

"Do pizza toppings fall within the scope of the family motto? Because we *definitely* shouldn't skimp on those." I wanted to get him to smile and relax again. I wasn't sure if it was the subject of money or his family or . . . something else entirely that had him look ready to bolt, but I felt guilty for being nosy.

Our deal was that I could ask anything, but it was still rude to pry into parts of his life that were private.

It worked. Laughter danced in his eyes as he lightly tugged the sleeve of my jacket and led me into a new room; the term "entertainment center" didn't do it justice. There was a flat-screen TV, surrounded by leather couches, and in the middle of the room stood a regal-looking pool table. I half expected Spencer to open a secret compartment and offer me a glass of bourbon and a cigar.

"Definitely. We take pizza very seriously. What toppings do you like?"

"Everything except anchovies," I said without hesitation.

Spencer nodded, pulled out his phone, and gestured at the couch in a silent, *Well, what are you waiting for?* Coming from Fake or Bake, I would have flinched with embarrassment at my obvious display of uncertainty. Then again, the girls would have said something snotty.

Spend time with humans much, nerd? Apparently not.

Listen up, loser. You don't have to stand at attention until the food is delivered.

Alex Thompson would definitely have gone for the direct approach: *Yo, fat-ass. Down in front.*

I sank into the buttery soft leather of the couch and tried to block out the barrage of imaginary insults. Spencer *hadn't* meant the gesture that way. I knew he hadn't. The same way I knew that he hadn't meant anything with his slow, appreciative once-overs.

It was simply a reflex for him.

"Yes, I'd like a large pizza with anchovies. Lots of anchovies. Pile 'em on there for me, will you?"

I jerked upright in the sofa, or at least, I *tried* to move. I suspected it would take a harness, a crane, and maybe the help of a Navy SEAL team to tug me free from the couch.

"What?!"

Spencer's smile widened. "Payback for the frozen yogurt." He turned his attention back to his phone call. "Hi, I'd like to order a large pepperoni pizza with olives, tomatoes, and green peppers. No garlic, please." He pointedly raised an eyebrow at me, and I knew that he was thinking about the idiotic statement I'd made in his bedroom about girls stripping off their clothes for him.

I burst out laughing.

"Never going to happen," I mouthed slowly.

Spencer rattled off his address, ended the call, and then claimed the sofa cushion right next to me. "In the wise words of Justin Bieber . . ."

"Don't say it!" I instinctively lunged forward to cover his mouth with my hand.

Spencer did his best to evade me, but I had no intention of giving up easy and he began laughing himself as he tried to clearly enunciate, "I will never say—mmph!"

I tackled him.

It wasn't intentional. Not really. It just seemed like the fastest way to shut him up, and technically . . . it worked. Spencer stopped talking real quick.

His grin faded away and that intense look came back into his green eyes, the one that made me feel as if he could see every single inch of me. It both unnerved and excited me, especially now that I was acutely aware of the way my body was plastered against his. I knew he felt every curve of what my mom called my "generous" figure pushing him deeper into the cushions.

I tried to prop up some of my weight with my arms, but the movement didn't help the situation. Instead of putting distance between us, I'd somehow managed to awkwardly straddle his knees, and for a brief moment, I panicked. There was no trick I could use to appear slimmer. Sucking in my stomach wouldn't do anything to alter my weight.

But then I looked into Spencer's eyes and I forgot to care about my body mass index or the number on my bathroom scale. None of that could change the power—the sheer exhilaration—I felt as our limbs tangled and the heat between us sparked higher.

He wanted me.

The full force of that shook me to my core. It didn't matter that Spencer was probably interested in any girl who sprawled across him. That for him this might be nothing more than a normal Thursday night. That he might not even bother adding me to his list of high school conquests.

In that moment, I wanted him right back.

His pupils were dilated, his breathing was shallow, and then his gaze dipped briefly to my lips and rose back to my eyes in an unspoken question.

Are you going to kiss me?

Yes.

I didn't give myself time to think through all the possible repercussions so that I could reason myself out of making a mistake. And, yes, I knew it was going to be a mistake. I didn't doubt it for a second. Launching myself on top of Smith High School's biggest Lothario wasn't exactly the way I had daydreamed my first kiss would happen. I thought it would take place at Comic Con with some adorably nerdy guy who wore glasses and enjoyed discussing the nuances of political discourse as presented by the third season of *Battlestar Galactica.*

Not some . . . hotshot.

I was supposed to be smarter than this.

But apparently everyone, including myself, had been deceived about my level of intelligence, because I tilted my head slightly so that we wouldn't bonk noses and . . . kissed him.

It wasn't slow and the only thing sweet about it was the hint of alpine vanilla that still lingered. Neither of us was gentle either. My hands gripped his arms as our lips met in a heated battle that I suspected wouldn't have a winner. Or maybe it had two winners. Or a billion. I couldn't think straight and never before had that seemed more perfectly, gloriously right than in that moment, because my body was doing just fine with my brain off-line. There was no reason for me to overthink it. Not when I couldn't remember the last time I'd felt so alive.

I wasn't entirely sure I had *ever* felt so alive.

Spencer's hands gripped my waist and the world began tilting while I struggled to catch my breath before diving back in for more.

I wanted so much more.

And he seemed to be on the exact same page because his hands slid lower and gripped tighter right before the world tilted. My glasses slipped off entirely and I wasn't sure which direction was up, but that seemed irrelevant since our bodies were still pressed together.

"Belle." Spencer's voice was hoarse and held an urgent *I want to keep you pinned against me like this for a week* undercurrent that made my heart feel like it was humming, and not just because my nickname sounded thrilling coming from him, but it proved that Spencer knew he was kissing me.

Isobel Peters.

Smith High School's biggest geek. The girl most likely to be asked to fake a relationship with a hockey player in order to *lower* his social standing.

That thought silenced my stupid heart midway through its musical audition.

Instead of feeling sexy and strong and powerful and very *I am woman hear me roar,* I suddenly felt like I was spiraling out of control.

"Don't . . . stop," I managed to say as Spencer lightly nipped my neck and I choked back a moan.

He lifted his head to stare at me. "Was that a *don't stop, this feels so good* or—"

I tried to shove him away but only succeeded in nearly rolling off the edge of the couch, which probably would've been disastrous for my glasses had I landed on them. But I didn't tumble off because Spencer steadied me before he raised his hands as if he were following instructions from a cop.

"Okay, I guess I know the answer now." He raked one hand through his hair while I took a deep breath to compose myself and retrieve my glasses. "What's the problem here, Belle?"

Everything. The problem was everything. His golden boy looks and frat boy charm, and *incredible* kissing skills that temporarily had the power to turn me stupid—all of it was the problem.

But I couldn't tell him any of that.

I scooted back until I was as far away from Spencer as the couch would allow. "That was a mistake."

Spencer nodded slowly, his face impassive. "Okay. Want to be a bit more specific? Was the mistake sticking your tongue in my mouth or was it letting me grab your ass? Because, honey, you sure seemed to be enjoying all of it."

My cheeks flamed red. "That's not . . . I'm not . . . I'm not that type of girl!"

"You know, I've never liked that phrase. It's vague and judgmental, if you ask me. It's a shorthand way of distancing yourself from an imaginary slut without having the bad taste of the word in your mouth. So tell me, Belle, exactly what kind of girl are you?"

I gaped at him openmouthed and I wanted to be able to brush off his comment like it was nothing more than a mild irritant. Something vaguely annoying that was best ignored. Except not only was he absolutely right, but that particular observation? It was really smart.

Which only succeeded in rattling me even more.

I mean, I've always had to search for people who could keep up with me, who didn't care if I saw the world a little wonky, who forced me to reevaluate some things I might take for granted, because people like that were in short supply.

But I didn't want Spencer King to be one of them.

It would have been so much easier if he'd said something obnoxious like, "We both know you can't do any better than me, Isogeek." Then I could have stormed off in a huff before confiding all the details to Jane. And then, depending on how much his retort stung, I might've tried to plot some kind of revenge with Sam. Hell, if he had acted like a full-fledged Notable jerk, I'd have considered letting Sam put her most outrageous plan into action . . . even if that landed both of us in detention.

I knew how to respond to being mocked and belittled by Notables. At the very least, I knew how to keep the scoreboard in the single digits. No dramatic scenes. No tears. Not if I could help it.

Nothing that Fake and Bake had thrown at me had ever prepared me for this, though.

Because with Spencer meeting my gaze head-on, no games, no bullshit—just straight up asking me to spell out what I wanted—my chest felt so tight I couldn't breathe. I wanted to be the kind of girl who cut through all the high school mind games and didn't care what people said about her. The kind of girl who *never* worried about being in someone else's league because she was perfectly happy being herself.

The kind of girl who could tell the most popular guy in school, *I want to ask you random questions about your life between make-out sessions. And then I want to snuggle against you while I introduce you to the awesomeness that is* Battlestar Galactica. *But mostly I want you to choose me, not because you're hoping it will sabotage your chances for prom king, but because despite the weird way we started hanging out, we somehow sort of . . . click.*

I wasn't that girl, though.

"I'm not looking for anything serious with you," I said uncomfortably, as I tried not to notice that the temperature in his green eyes seemed to drop several degrees.

"Okay. So we keep it light. Pizza and movies. We can see where that goes."

"No, we can't. I'm not . . . look, Spencer. You're a nice guy and all—"

"Feel free to stop there."

I plowed on anyway. "You're just not my type, okay?"

It was quite possibly the biggest lie I'd ever told.

Chapter 10

Rumors are swirling that there may be a celebrity musical performance at this year's prom. ReadySet lead singer Timothy Goff has come out of the closet and is now openly dating Smith High School junior Corey O'Neal. But now the $200 question—literally, that's the going rate for candid photos of the rock star—is whether or not he will trade in the red carpet for a small-time event.

—from "ReadySet . . . Going to Prom?"
by Lisa Anne Montgomery
Published by *The Smithsonian*

"Well, this should be good. Why exactly am I not your type, Isobel? Let me guess, it's because I don't wear glasses or skinny ties, right?" He leaned back against the armrest of the sofa as if he didn't have a care in the world. As if our tongues hadn't been dueling only minutes earlier. As if he hadn't been affected in the slightest by the absurd amount of heat we had generated together.

Maybe all of that was true, and I was the only one with a

slight ache in my bottom lip where I suspected he had nipped me at some point. At least that's what I was guessing had happened. The details about that particular moment were a little fuzzy.

"It doesn't matter. I don't know why we're talking about this, since you don't even do girlfriends. That's not how you operate. You have hookups and flings and . . . whatever else you want to call them, but they aren't real relationships."

"I thought you weren't looking for anything serious with me." He crossed his arms and I couldn't help imagining how that gesture would look if the shirt went missing again. The tendons of his forearms tightened and I wanted that strength focused on me. Holding me up. Pinning me down.

Never letting me go.

"I'm not. And I'm not going to be writing your name in my notebooks surrounded by little cartoon hearts. Which should save you the trouble of coming up with a new *it's not you, it's me* speech to deliver this week. We're friends. Just friends. I won't be one of the crowd. Case closed."

That drew him up short. He paused to collect himself, and when he spoke his words were layered with a frost I hadn't heard in them before. "I enjoy joking and teasing and yeah, having sex. I'm not ashamed about any of it." He looked pointedly at me. "Can you say the same, Belle?"

"That's not my name and this isn't about me."

"Sure it is. I have no idea where you came up with that bullshit about being my friend, but that's not why you're here with me right now."

"Oh yeah?" The words came out defiant, but a small part of me—okay, a large part of me—really wanted to know where he was going with this. "Then why do you think I'm here?"

"Because you want to study me, observe me in my natural habitat. Ask pointed questions so you can categorize my flaws and use them as an excuse to keep your distance, because you're too afraid to actually connect with anyone *human*." He sat upright and crossed his arms across his chest. "But you couldn't say that outright because that would make you pathetic, right? Especially because you've got nothing to gain by sharing your endgame. It might even skew the study results. You couldn't let that happen."

"And you could have just told Fake and Bake that you weren't interested! You didn't have to concoct some elaborate scheme to sink your reputation, and to hell with the girl you take down with you in the process!"

"I really don't like the way you play doctor."

"Well, I don't like the way you play frat boy. So I guess we're even."

I hadn't expected that to shut him up. I thought he would raise an eyebrow and then make some quip about how fraternities were the training ground for the American political system. But he didn't, probably because we both knew that it was my shorthand way of calling him an arrogant, overprivileged jerk. Both of us fell silent and the room became thick with the words we had spoken, and even worse, the ones we had implied.

Spencer ran a hand through his hair in tense frustration, but nodded, "If that's what you think of me, I see why I'm not your type. You shouldn't have any problem keeping your mouth to yourself. Wouldn't want to become infected with frat boy."

I felt lower than scum.

"You're a gr—"

He laughed hoarsely. "I think we can both save the canned speeches. Although for future reference, if you're going to go with the whole *it's not you, it's me* thing, you should work on the delivery."

I stared at him and part of me was so close to telling him the truth. That it was, *absolutely, positively, unequivocally* him. That I couldn't handle the pressure of dating the most popular boy in school because sooner or later he would want to trade me in for a hotter model and my self-esteem would bottom out. That eventually one of his "friends" would make some nasty comment and he would laugh right along with the rest of them.

Fifteen points, guaranteed.

"What is it that you want, Spencer?" I asked instead. "Do you actually want to be with me?"

"I always want to be with a pretty girl."

My stomach plummeted and the tiny bit of hope I'd had that he would say, "Yeah, Belle. That's exactly what I want, because you're smart and funny and I happen to find you insanely hot," withered up and died. He was Spencer freaking King, the boy with the smirk and the charm set to stun. The guy who left the sex cranked up to eleven. And I was an idiot for ever thinking otherwise.

"Great. You go enjoy that, hotshot. Really, knock yourself out." I hauled myself up off the couch and headed right past the pool table. "See you around."

"Wait, what about the pizza and—"

"I think it's probably for the best if I don't stick around. But hey, look at it this way, now you can throw one of your famous parties without a buzzkill messing it up."

I heard his footsteps as he followed me down the hallway, but I didn't slow down. I needed to get out of this house with its stilted photos and a guy who made me question whether I knew the first thing about human interactions.

"Belle."

I needed to get away from him so that I could cry without thinking about my point score. I didn't even want to know what value the Notable crowd would assign this level of mortification.

My first kiss had been with a guy who was using me to tank his social standing.

I could practically see the points racking up with every

step I took as I passed the kitchen and unlocked his front door.

"Look, it's getting dark. I can drive you home. Just let me leave money on the porch for the pizza and I can—" I could hear the concern in his voice, but I knew if I so much as glanced over at him, it would be game over. My eyes would well up and he'd know how shaken I was by whatever it was we had started on the couch. Or maybe it had started in the Yogurt Shack . . . or during that car ride home from Mackenzie's house. The where didn't really matter anymore.

"Thanks, but I'd rather walk it."

"Yeah, well, I'd rather make sure you got home safely. If you don't want anything to do with me, that's fine. I can call Logan or—"

I ground to a halt. "Believe it or not, there are people *I* can call. People who don't care about the kind of car I drive, or the house I live in, or the type of parties I throw. And they like me exactly the way I am!"

I don't know why I shouted that last part. It wasn't as if he had ever implied that I needed a Cinderella-esque makeover. He knew better than to suggest that with a few pounds of makeup, a new wardrobe, some Photoshop, maybe a little airbrushing here or there, I could pass for a Notable.

That was the whole reason he had chosen me in the first place. No amount of trappings would ever allow me to crash his social strata.

Just to prove my point, I whipped out my cell phone and called Sam before I could talk myself out of dragging her into this mess. Not that it would bother Sam in the slightest to tangle with a Notable. That probably sounded to her like a lasting high school memory she'd enjoy reminiscing over someday.

"Isobel!" she answered cheerfully. "Great timing. What's your position on breaking and entering?"

"Um . . . I'm trying to keep my record clean. Listen, any chance you could give me a lift?"

I walked toward the street, refusing to glance at Spencer, even though I could feel his presence right behind me. I had seen enough horror movies that featured girls wandering outside at night—who were found brutally dismembered in the morning—to feel a twinge of relief that I wasn't alone. It had grown pretty dark while we were inside . . . making out.

I had to force myself to pay attention to the phone call, although the chill in the air didn't feel quite so cold anymore.

"Sure. I can be at your house in ten minutes. I'll see you—"

"I'm at Spencer King's." I blurted out the words, knowing that there was no subtle way to ease *that* into the conversation.

Her tone instantly became sober. "Are you okay, Isobel?"

Yet another question I had no idea how to answer. I was definitely on a losing streak and I had a feeling that I was in for the mother of all inquisitions when Sam showed up.

"Fine," I said, because it seemed like the right thing to say. It wasn't as if I could share any of the details with Spencer less than three feet away.

Well, since you asked, Sam. I'm starting to wonder if I've got a bizarre case of Stockholm syndrome. I know that technically Spencer King didn't kidnap me, but honestly, I have no idea why else I'd feel this kind of . . . attachment to him.

"Give me eight minutes to get there." Her words sounded muffled and I heard a thump that might've been a shoe or a protest sign; knowing Sam, they were equally probable. "I'm on my way."

"Do you need directions?" Worst-case scenario, I could always hand the phone over to Spencer.

"Nah, I know where he lives. I nearly protested one of his parents' fund-raisers, but—seven minutes!" she interrupted herself and disconnected.

Leaving me alone with Spencer.

Not that we hadn't been alone before, but walking with him at night felt way too personal. And . . . too tempting.

I shivered slightly as a cold breeze lifted the hair at the back of my neck. It would have been so simple to burrow into Spencer for warmth. So easy to pretend that I could do this lighthearted, casual fling thing too. That it wouldn't bother me in the slightest that his so-called friends would mock us behind our backs. Or to *my* face.

"She'll be here in a matter of minutes," I informed him with a calmness I didn't feel. Part of my brain must have stalled on the idea of initiating take two of our kissing experiment. Considering the explosive results we'd gotten from our first try, I wasn't entirely sure I'd be able to walk away from a second round. I wasn't sure I'd even want to leave. "You can go now."

"Not until your friend shows up." He moved forward as if he had nothing but time. "So, how do you want to play this tomorrow?"

I blinked, feeling at a disadvantage with the darkness and shadows partially concealing his face. "I don't know."

"Do you want to keep pretending to date me? Drop it entirely? Do you want to go to—"

"I. Have. No. Clue." I enunciated each word, just to make sure they'd sink in.

"Well, that clears things right up for me. Thanks, Belle."

"You want me to be clear?" I nearly choked on the last word. "Seriously? Because *I'm* the one with questionable motives here? I still don't have any idea why you want to avoid the stupid crown in the first place!"

Spencer crossed his arms, and again that ridiculously attractive tendon in his forearm tightened. The unfairness of it made me want to hate him. "My brother was prom king."

I pulled up short and then shifted so that I could get a good look at his face. The dim glow of the moon didn't do much to facilitate a close examination, but he didn't look like he was kidding. The patented Spencer King smirk was nowhere to be seen.

"Okayyy . . ." I said slowly. "What does that have to do with anything?"

"I don't want to follow in his footsteps. Ever. It's a slippery slope in my family. As soon as they start raising their expectations for me, they'll want to get me applying to Ivy League schools and interning for local politicians."

"Still not seeing the problem," I said. "I'm pretty sure prom king is a one-night deal. You don't actually have to rule the place . . . well, not any more than you already do. And I'm positive you could come up with hundreds of ways to disappoint them that don't include *me*."

He raked a hand through his hair, which appeared to have darkened to a burnished gold hue at night. "I repeat: It's a slippery slope. As for the rest . . . you just sort of happened."

"I happened?" I could feel my brow furrowing. "What does *that* mean?"

"It means, you happened. Don't overthink it."

"Right," I said sarcastically. "Because that's something I'm really great at doing. I just flip a switch and—"

"I want to be a firefighter," Spencer interrupted. "And the only way my parents are going to sign the forms for me to take the fire safety class next year is for them to believe I'm incapable of doing anything more impressive."

"Well, that's crazy—" I coughed and tried again. "I mean, speaking as your friend . . . I don't see why they'd have a problem with it. Firefighters are . . ." *Hot.* ". . . essential. They provide a vital service to the community. And you're obviously going to be great at it. So your parents should be thrilled."

It was kind of hard to tell with the darkness settling in, but I thought I saw his mouth curve into a smile. "What makes you so sure I'd be good at it?" he asked slowly.

I didn't try to stifle my snort of disbelief. "Oh, I dunno. You're athletic. Quick thinking. Loyal. And I have the feeling that you get whatever you go after. If you cared half this much about being captain of the hockey team, you'd be the one wearing the fancy jersey instead of Logan."

"It's not covered in sparkles, Belle. The only difference is the 'C' on it."

I shrugged. "Whatever. You get what I'm saying. The only one standing in your way is you. So own it."

He didn't say anything for a second, but when he spoke his voice had a rough quality to it that set my nerves to jittering. "Good advice. Think you'll take it yourself?"

I was spared trying to produce an answer because headlights cut through the darkness and Sam appeared. At least, I assumed it was Sam. I couldn't exactly make out her face since she was wearing a motorcycle helmet and riding a Vespa.

She pulled up to a stop in front of me, quickly climbed off the bike, and in one smooth move unlocked the seat and tossed me a spare helmet.

And before I could overanalyze this new potential for danger, I tugged off my glasses, pushed the helmet on, and slid behind her, all without saying a word. Unless "Eeeeek!" counted as a word when she gunned the motor and we took off into the night.

Leaving Spencer in our dust.

Chapter 11

Everyone at Mitch High School couldn't wait for prom to come . . . mostly because life would be so much simpler once it was over. They would be able to open the school newspaper without having their worth determined on the front page according to their relationship status. No longer would they walk the hallways in fear that any slight hiccup in their prom plans would land them in an editorial. . . .

—from "Mitch High School Confidential,"
by Jane Smith
Published by *The Wordsmith*

Turned out, Sam was every bit as fearless on the road as she was in the hallways of Smith High School.

I was probably safer getting a ride from Fake and Bake and the rest of the Notable crew. Taking Spencer up on his offer of a lift sounded incredibly appealing now that it was no longer an option. Sure, it would have been awkward sitting in the car with him, pretending to be fine despite everything that had happened between us, but I would've been physically safe. My body wouldn't have been in danger of being scraped off the side of the road.

I clutched my arms around Sam's stomach with all my strength as she sped up. If the plan was still to take me home, she was definitely taking a circuitous route. But I was too afraid of flying off the back of the Vespa to loosen my hold, flip up the visor of my helmet, and begin shouting directions.

Which left me stuck hoping that Sam's idea of a good night didn't include fleeing the state.

She slowed only when we pulled up to my old elementary school.

I doubted that Sam knew about my history with the location. There were five elementary schools in our town back then, and they had been shutting down one by one for as long as I could remember. The year I headed off to the Forest Grove Middle School, my fifth-grade class had participated in a pretty epic bake sale, but not even a few hundred gluten-free, organic pies could save the school. These days, I thought it was an art studio type space where locals could rent out rooms, but it could have been something else entirely. It had completely fallen off my radar over five years ago.

Now I wished I had paid more attention.

Sam stopped the Vespa and I lurched off on unsteady legs that steadied beneath me after a few seconds. My bones felt like they were rattling from the force of the vibration. Between my acrobatics on the couch with Spencer and the scooter ride with Sam . . . I was ready to collapse and sleep for a solid ten hours. Instead, I yanked off the helmet and stared at the slightly blurry mass that remained seated on the death machine.

"Okay, that was *terrifying!*" I jammed my glasses back on my nose, which revealed Sam's obvious amusement in high definition. "Are we even allowed to be here?"

Sam climbed off the Vespa in one easy movement and I felt a twinge of jealousy. She moved with so much confidence. All the time. It reminded me of . . . well, Spencer.

"As long as you contain the urge to graffiti something, we'll be just fine."

The idea of me vandalizing *anything* was ludicrous, but I wasn't entirely sure the same could be said for Sam.

I eyed her suspiciously. "You haven't actually—"

She merely smiled, and I knew she wasn't going to tell me anything. Instead, she would enjoy watching me squirm as I reached my own conclusions.

Unfortunately, that reminded me of Spencer too.

I shook my head, hoping that would clear it. I needed to snap out of this. Whatever feelings I had for Spencer, they couldn't go anywhere. The faster I squashed them, the better.

"Let's focus on you. So what were you doing with Spencer King? I've been hearing some rumors, but I didn't actually believe any of them."

There was no way I could keep all of the craziness a secret for long. At least not from Sam. She once told me that anything worth knowing at our high school inevitably reached detention. And if there was one person at our high school who knew the ins and outs of that world, it was Sam. I wouldn't be surprised if she listed detention as an extracurricular activity.

Although I suspected she would put a dramatic spin on the punishment.

Unreasonable Detention for Civic Disobedience.

Regardless, it was obviously time for me to set the record straight. Although that was much easier said than done. I was mixed up inside when I sat down on Spencer's couch, and that was before he had opened up about the firefighter thing. I couldn't even begin to process what his willingness to share that with me might mean.

"It's not what you think," I blurted out, and then winced at the cliché. *It's not what you think?* C'mon, Isobel. You can do better than that. "I mean, maybe it's what you think. I don't exactly know what you're thinking, but the rumors definitely aren't true."

"So you're *not* carrying his secret love child?" Sam gasped in mock outrage. "And I had all these baby names picked out for you guys! They were gender neutral and everything. How do you feel about *Kong*?"

"Kong?" I repeated. "As in the sound of someone getting bashed in the head?"

"As in *King Kong*. Or in this case, *Kong King*." She sent me one very self-satisfied smile. "Don't answer just yet. It'll grow on you."

I laughed. "No, it won't. And, no, I'm not having"—I blushed fiercely as I struggled to get the words out—"Spencer King's love child."

"Oh, okay. Then yeah, the rumors are wrong."

"We're . . . y'know—"

"Expecting?" she offered helpfully.

"Friends!"

Sam seemed to consider that as she perched on her Vespa. "Um . . . yeah, see that doesn't make as much sense to me. Are you sure about baby Kong?"

I shot her my best *I'm serious* look.

"I'm sorry! But come on. It's hard to picture you hanging out with Spencer King, unless there was something else going on beyond friendship."

I scowled, but part of me couldn't help wondering if she was right. It had fleetingly felt like friendship back at the Yogurt Shack. Strange how something so small, an event that couldn't have lasted over twenty minutes, now seemed like one of the most important moments of my life. Something I would look back on and think, *Yeah, that was when I realized . . .*

Something.

Too bad that epiphany wasn't forthcoming.

"He was going to watch *Battlestar Galactica* with me."
I'm not sure what I thought that would prove, but it seemed
relevant. As if by analyzing his willingness to watch one of
the most addictive television shows ever created in the same
room with me, we'd be able to determine whether his interest
was purely platonic.

"Oh. Well, in that case, it must be true love." Sam went
heavy on the sarcasm.

I didn't say a word because, despite the obvious snark, her
comment continued to reverberate in my head.

True love.

Truuueee love.

The words were so ridiculous, it felt like they should be
sung—belted out, at top volume—at some karaoke night.
I've never been able to take that kind of overly sentimental
crap seriously. Even if I did concede that I wanted to be in a
relationship, statistically speaking there were *thousands* of
people who would appreciate my personal brand of crazy.
Maybe by the time I left Smith High School in my rearview
mirror, the cooler, more confident version of myself would
have millions of romantic possibilities.

But I couldn't keep myself from remembering the way
Spencer had leaned toward me and said, *"What kind of girl
are you, Isobel?"*

The type who couldn't stop trying to categorize people by
"type" apparently.

"He's . . ." I didn't even know where to begin.

Enigmatic.

Interesting.

Out of my league.

"The father of your unborn baby?" Sam held up her hands
in surrender before she'd even finished the sentence. "I'm
kidding!"

"There's more to him than you think, okay?"

I thought I heard Sam mutter something like, *The bar has been set so low, he could trip over it,* but she pasted a forced smile on her face. "Okay. So you like this guy now?"

"We're friends," I said with a firmness that I didn't really feel.

"I doubt that." Sam gestured at the air between us. "*We* are friends. You can call me at"—she glanced at her watch— "nine o'clock and I'll pick you up. Whatever you have going on with this guy . . . I'm betting it's not that."

"Okay, but it took some time for you and me to become friends!" I protested. "It's not like it happened overnight. And there was never any, y'know . . ." I was so sick of desperately searching for the right words and coming up empty. "Romantic tension."

Sam glanced away. "That's not entirely true."

"So this thing with—wait, what?"

She shrugged and looked past my right shoulder as if she found the swing set that still remained from my elementary school days absolutely fascinating. "I . . . liked you. Right away."

"Sure, but you didn't *like* like me."

I wanted to blame the setting for the fact that I'd reverted back to a third-grade vocabulary.

"I did, actually." Sam's smile twisted. "You don't have to look so horrified. Lesbianism isn't catching."

"It's not—I'm—" I forcibly closed my gaping mouth. I'd always known that Sam was gay, but this . . . "Whoa."

"Well said, Keanu Reeves."

I wasn't sure what she was referring to, but it didn't seem like a good time to ask her to cite her pop culture reference.

"I'm honored," I said at last. "I think you're amazing, Sam. I'm, y'know . . . really flattered."

I winced at the last word. *Flattered?* That couldn't be the right thing to say when somebody put their heart on the line. But I couldn't come up with anything better.

"Sure. Flattered. It's okay, Isobel. I understand if you're freaking out." Sam crossed her arms.

I could feel my panic rising. "I'm not! I'm . . . look, I want us to stay friends! This isn't going to change that, right? Because high school sucks enough already and I'm not sure I could handle it without you."

Sam laughed and even if it was a little rougher than usual, it still sounded genuine. "Like I said, it's okay. I kind of guessed you didn't feel the same when you asked if I had a crush on Valerie McDobbs."

Right, I had forgotten about that. Partly because Sam had laughed it off and then suggested we see what Jane and Scott were doing. At the time, I had assumed she was just eager to suggest an article for *The Wordsmith* because she wanted to needle Lisa Anne.

Apparently not.

"Do you . . ." I had no idea how to phrase this question, so I tried to rip it off like a Band-Aid. Well, actually, I usually try to soak in the bathtub until my Band-Aids slough off on their own, but that wasn't exactly going to happen here. "Do you still . . . like me? Like that, I mean?"

"Past tense, Isobel. I got over it." She grinned wryly. "Believe it or not, you're not entirely irresistible."

The idea of me being even slightly irresistible was so ludicrous I had to laugh self-consciously.

"Trust me, you can do way better than me, Sam."

She snorted. "Well, that's obvious! I can find a girlfriend who isn't straight for starters!"

The sound of our laughter made the playground seem simultaneously more desolate and alive, and it made me wonder whether this spot had an imprint of my childhood on it. Maybe I was just being fanciful, but I could almost believe that the place was imbued with the sound of children's laughter.

Or maybe it was just growing late and I wanted to believe

whatever story would make the shadows poetic instead of menacing.

"I'd also rather date someone who isn't hopelessly in denial about a preexisting relationship."

My head jerked away from the swing set where my eyes had lingered. "I'm not—"

"Hopelessly in denial," Sam repeated forcefully. "Even though a blind man could pick up the tension between you two. He wouldn't need his eyes. He could just stand in the room and sense the intense vibrations you guys give off."

"Vibrations? I don't think so," I retorted weakly, as I shoved my glasses firmly up my nose. I never wanted to climb onto her contraption of death again, but if that meant a reprieve from this conversation, I was willing to risk life and limb.

"Fine. Waves of lust? Pulses of pheromones that fill the air? Throbbing—"

"You've made your point!" I didn't think it was possible for my cheeks to get any redder. If we had been back at Smith High School with the fierce florescent lighting bearing down on us, she would have seen just how embarrassed she was making me.

Sam nodded and dropped the joking facade. I wasn't sure how she could snap back into seriousness so quickly, but it made me feel like I was getting emotional whiplash. As if she had been barreling her Vespa down the street at top speed and then slammed on the brakes.

"My mom likes to tell me that I have nothing to fear, except fear itself. But I think that quote is full of crap. There's a whole lot to fear, Isobel. High school is terrifying. Anyone who says otherwise is a freaking liar. We're supposed to figure out who we are and we're supposed to make something of ourselves, but the truth is we're all faking it so hard you could cut the desperation with a knife."

I almost couldn't believe these words were coming from *Sam*. I'd always assumed that she was immune to the social minefield of Smith High School. Why would she elect to keep upsetting the administration and landing herself in detention if she actually wanted to fit in with the rest of the student body?

"You know who you are, Sam." It almost came out like an accusation.

She laughed, but there was a dark undercurrent to the sound. "Yeah, I know some of it. The basics, maybe. I can correctly fill out standardized test forms." Her voice dropped to a steady monotone. "Seventeen years old, Caucasian female, no arrest record, founder of the school LGBTQ club, and cofounder of the baking club. I can also recite my name, birth date, and social security number. That doesn't mean I know who I am beneath all of that garbage."

"It sure seems like you do," I mumbled.

"Yeah, well, I can fake it with the best of the Notables. But what you do have to fear is a life spent wondering what could have been if you'd been willing to fight for what you want."

She was right.

She was totally, completely, painfully right about everything . . . except maybe the Roosevelt quote. Because I suspected that deep down it was the fear of confrontation, the fear of losing to the Notables, the fear of making a colossal mistake, that was what kept me clinging to the shadows. It's what made me perfectly happy to be ignored for the next three years of my high school sentence.

I couldn't lie to Sam, not when she had me pegged. She wouldn't have believed a half-truth anyway.

"I'm not a fighter," I admitted. "I refuse to do anything that would land me in detention with you. I want to keep my academic record sparkly clean."

Sam shoved my arm good-naturedly. "Yeah, well, rumor has it you're really good at creative problem-solving tests. Maybe it's time for you to apply those techniques to your life." With her knuckles, she rapped the helmet I was still holding. "Let's take you home."

It was the best idea I'd heard all night.

Chapter 12

In the most recent issue of *The Wordsmith,*
Jane Smith not so subtly implied that the trials
and tribulations of Smith High School students'
love lives will be printed in this publication.
That couldn't be more untrue. Mostly because
the vast majority of you aren't nearly intriguing
enough.

But I still want to know why Spencer King
appears to be mooning over a certain freshman
girl. . . .

—from *"The Wordsmith* Lies about Your Love
Lives"
by Lisa Anne Montgomery
Published by *The Smithsonian*

I didn't exactly get my beauty sleep.
Sam's words reverberated around my head for hours and I
kept searching for a brilliant comeback, for some pithy line
that would make my cowardice look noble. I wasn't taking
the easy way out, simply exercising precaution. I wasn't

letting my fear stop me from living to the fullest, merely listening to my instincts.

And my gut was telling me that I had no business getting cozy with a Notable who would probably dump me with a text. A guy like Spencer King could probably manage it with less than three emoticons.

I didn't need that weighing down my life.

Except the rest of my body didn't seem to have gotten that memo, because when I wasn't stewing over Sam's rant, I was replaying every second I had spent on Spencer's couch. In slow motion. And there were a handful of memories I had stuck on repeat.

The feel of his hands tightening around my waist, of my fingers sinking into the softness of his hair . . . yeah, all those details haunted me well into the night. Well, into the *morning,* truthfully. And when I wasn't obsessing about our seven minutes in heaven, I was re-creating the intensity of his eyes as they lasered in on me when he asked if I was going to take my own advice.

Even spending an hour giving my parents a detailed account of the evening—well, minus a few events, of course—couldn't imbue me with a sense of normalcy. Usually their grilling put everything into perspective for me. Their intensity might make me roll my eyes, but I never doubted that they cared. The Notables could use me as the punch line for their jokes— none of it would change the way my parents saw me. That might not count for much, but it was enough for now.

Still, showing up to school the next day wasn't easy. Not when I had to ignore all the kids twisting in their seats to get a good look at me on the bus. Everyone was whispering, and I couldn't tell if they were speculating about my relationship with Spencer or if I was being paranoid. So I tried to distance myself from everything. To act like a sociologist studying an interesting ritual from some poorly documented tribe. Everyone on the bus deferred to someone higher up in the pecking order, until the person closest to Notable status—some jock whose family couldn't afford a set of wheels for him—smirked and then pointedly looked away from me.

I couldn't tell if that was because I was too far beneath his notice even to acknowledge with a withering comment or because he feared retribution in the form of Spencer King if he opened his mouth and the wrong words came out.

Either way, the attention twisted my stomach and made me want to hide deeper in the loose gray sweatshirt I was wearing. I closed my eyes, which only heightened the prickly sensation of being examined from all angles. It made me hyperaware of my body, specifically my breathing. Every time I thought about Spencer, it hitched. And every time I considered pretending that yesterday had never happened . . . it sputtered. As if it couldn't believe I was even considering that as a real possibility.

Maybe because it wasn't.

Not now that I thought I might have an answer to the most important question I'd been asked the day before.

So, I gritted my teeth and fumbled in the pocket of my sweatshirt for my wallet, as I disembarked from the bus and headed straight for my two least favorite people in the world: Fake and Bake—Ashley and Steffani—I mentally corrected myself. I was going to do this right because I refused to have any regrets.

Which meant treating others the way I wanted to be treated.

Even if they so didn't deserve it.

I forced myself to straighten my shoulders instead of slouching as I stood in line to buy tickets for prom. Ashley was in charge of the cash box, or at least she was in charge of sitting behind it and looking perfectly . . . perky. And judgmental. Both girls belonged in a teen magazine with price tags coming off every item of their clothes.

I took a deep breath. I could do this. All I had to do was stand in this stupid line and fork over twenty bucks. Then I could put phase two of my plan into action after school when I might be able to get some privacy. Five people ahead of me. Two of them were nuzzling each other and looking all doe-eyed and in love, which meant that I only had to wait for four purchases to be made. Assuming that it took no more than three minutes to complete each transaction, I should be free and clear—with time to spare—within the next twenty minutes.

I could survive being an object of curiosity for the Notables that long.

"Hey, you're in the wrong line, Fatty. You have to get your cookies from the cafeteria."

I flinched, even though I knew Alex Thompson would probably award himself five points for that small display of weakness.

"Stop, Alex," Ashley called out from the table.

Everyone turned to stare at her in amazement. She was the last person I had ever expected to defend me, and it looked like no one else at Smith High School saw that one coming either.

And then she smiled nastily.

"That's no way to treat a pregnant girl."

"She's not pregnant," Steffani giggled. "She would have to have sex for that to happen. And who would want to sleep with *her?*"

"Oh yeah? Then how come I can see her baby bump from here?"

Alex guffawed right into my ear and I totally froze up, just like I had the first time in the cafeteria. My palms went all sweaty and I began calculating how many points I would lose if I cut and run. If I sprinted toward the English building and didn't stop running until I was safely ensconced in the library.

But that'd be quitting and I wouldn't get what I wanted if I didn't fight for it.

So I cut the line.

I stalked right over to the desk with the huge sign that read PERFECT PROM in sparkly letters with little hearts bouncing around the words, and I slapped down the twenty.

"Two tickets please," I gritted out. And then I shoved up my glasses because even though I wanted to channel a total badass version of myself, I still needed to be able to see without squinting.

"I'm sorry," Steffani said coolly, "but prom is for upper-classmen only. Not for geeky freshmen."

"I'm taking a junior. Now give me the tickets."

"Well, that puts a new spin on 'putting out,' " Ashley said snidely. "Isn't the guy supposed to pay? I guess this is part of the bribe for taking you, huh? You know, I almost feel sorry for you."

My breath whooshed out of me as if I had been walloped right in the stomach.

She feels sorry for me.

For some reason, that's what did it. I leaned forward.

"You know what, Ashley? There are days when I feel sorry for myself. Days when I wake up and I look in the mirror and I feel like crap. And I hear people like you in my head telling me that I'm worthless. And there are days when I believe it." I paused for that to sink in before I continued. "Here's the thing: I may wage a daily war against my mirror, but I will *never* look back on high school and know that I intentionally made other people feel like crap. That's something you will have to live with. So . . . feel free to choke on your pity. I'm going to be just fine."

I inched the twenty across the table closer to her, noting the slack jaw with a fair amount of pride. Maybe she was shocked to hear the geek stand up for herself. Maybe she wasn't as heartless as she let on and my words would haunt her for years to come.

I didn't care anymore.

They didn't matter. Not to me. I hadn't been exaggerating when I had told Spencer that there were people who cared about me. Really freaking awesome people like Sam who liked me already. I had friends who didn't need me to change in order to earn their affection.

"Freak." Alex pitched his voice so that everyone within a fifteen-foot radius would hear.

I nodded as I scooped up the tickets Steffani had hesitantly laid out on the table. "Of course I'm a freak. Now ask me if I care?"

"I care."

I whirled around. I'd read that in combat situations, when soldiers were in a state of battle readiness, suddenly everything would intensify: colors, tastes, textures, even seemingly unimportant details. I had thought the adrenaline rush from facing down the Notables was already pumping as much adrenaline into my system as I had on reserve, but apparently the sight of Spencer stalking toward me activated some untapped reservoir.

Maybe some of that reaction was chemical. Spencer was unbelievably hot with a scowl twisting his face and his eyes flashing murder. So much for the good-time frat boy in training I had accused him of being. This guy wasn't about to crack open a six-pack or joke everyone into a good mood.

He looked like he was five seconds away from using Alex as practice for body-checking a hockey opponent to the ground.

And while I had no trouble imagining how I wanted a fierce battle for my honor to proceed (Hint: It somehow included Spencer losing his shirt and a much longer display of those fascinating tendons that I had spotted earlier), that wasn't the best move for any of us.

Plus, I was getting sick of other people trying to fight my battles for me.

"Hey!" I said, trying to cut Spencer off at the pass. "I have something for you."

He nodded brusquely but didn't take his eyes off Alex. "I thought Logan and I made it clear that you should keep your opinions to yourself. I'm happy to give you a reminder, though."

I darted between the boys, even though it forced me to turn my back on Alex. I was counting on him having the good sense not to provoke an already pissed-off Spencer, but it was never a good idea to depend on the intellect of an asshole. "That's not necessary."

"Move, Belle."

I felt a wave of relief at the ease with which my nickname slipped off his tongue. So maybe he didn't hate me for panicking after our kiss last night. Then again, it was entirely possible he was just a staunch defender for the geek population at our school. There was only one way to find out.

"Make me, Spencer."

That's when I stood up on tiptoe and flung my arms around his neck. I hoped it looked like a romantic gesture that deserved swelling music and the rest of the world to go slightly out of focus, instead of a desperate attempt to stop him from picking a fight with a football player. Spencer looked momentarily poleaxed, possibly because he never expected to feel my body pressed against his again. Then his lips tilted upward into a wry smile. "Now who is cranking the sex up to eleven?"

He was right.

I instantly released my hold and found myself wobbling back on my feet. Everyone was staring at us as if they expected Spencer to make some devastatingly snarky comment and it was just . . . too much. So I took a different page out of his playbook, grasped his wrist, and began pulling him away from the line for prom tickets. Past Ashley and Steffani, whom I could feel glaring fiercely at the back of my head, and away from the lurkers craning their necks to catch a glimpse of my train wreck of a fake relationship.

"Am I being taken aside for punishment?" Spencer's tone was light and easy, and if I hadn't spent all day yesterday getting to know the guy beneath the jokes, I would've believed that he felt nothing more than idle curiosity. "It's because I read the spoilers to *Battlestar Galactica,* right?"

I pulled up short. "You did *what?!*"

"I read the—"

I raised a hand. "Stop talking. I'm going to pretend you didn't just tell me that you single-handedly ruined one of the greatest television shows for yourself, because otherwise we might not be able to be friends."

Spencer raised that damn eyebrow, and even though it was probably an ingrained natural reaction—completely unrelated to my snarky comment the day before—I felt my cheeks start to redden. "So we're back to being friends, huh?"

I crossed my arms. "Yeah, I thought about it last night. I want to be your friend." I said it with the same firmness I had used with Alex Thompson only minutes earlier, but it was far less effective now. Maybe because my voice had a new husky quality to it that I'd never heard before coming from me.

Spencer stiffened. "Fine, then—"

"I want to be your friend," I repeated. "And I want to, um . . . get to know you better."

I watched his body loosen slightly, but his eyes didn't lose their hard, focused edge. "What does that mean, Belle? Spell it out for me. If you want me to tell you more of my deep dark secrets, then you're out of luck. I'm not into the whole tall, dark, and brooding thing."

I laughed uncomfortably and I briefly considered bailing. I could probably run to the nearest girls' bathroom without raising too many jeers from the crowd of students I hadn't been able to escape entirely. I could call Melanie for advice from the safety of a stall. She'd drop everything, knock on the door of the handicap toilet, perch on the railing, tuck a strand of her long black hair back behind an ear, and patiently hear me out.

But I was determined to test out my new problem-solving method, and that meant earning points instead of losing them. And giving Spencer an honest answer to the question he had asked me last night. That would earn a whopping one hundred points for me.

"I want to kiss you again." I avoided looking at his face in case that would make me lose my nerve. Instead, I focused my attention on the scraped sides of my battered sneakers. "And I still want to watch *Battlestar Galactica* with you—except this time, I plan on eating the pizza. But I'm not the kind of girl—" I stopped myself and tried again. "I'm still getting to know you, so . . . I want us to be friends who also make out." My eyes darted up to his face and my heart leaped when I saw the grin that was beginning to spread across it.

"You want to be my girlfriend."

"That's not—" I choked. "I mean . . . can we hold off on the labels?"

He placed a firm finger under my chin and lifted it so that I would have no choice but to get the full force of his laser green eyes. "You want to get to know me better."

"Yes," I agreed.

"You don't want me to be kissing anyone else, do you?"

My stomach plummeted painfully at the thought. I shook my head.

Spencer gestured to the tickets that were now seconds away from being mangled in one clenched hand. "Good. I'm guessing one of those is for me?"

"Um . . ." So much for my plan to do the actual asking. "Yeah."

"Okay. You totally want back on my couch," he crowed. "You're just dying for me to—"

I shoved him, but since he didn't budge or stop laughing, I decided I needed to try a nonverbal approach. One that had worked out pretty well the last time we had been alone. So I cut him off with a long, slow kiss.

The sensation of his lips against mine swamped me.

I didn't care who stood gawking and whispering at our public display of affection. Sure, Principal Taylor could effectively kill the mood by clearing his throat and telling us to get to class, but it no longer mattered to me what the general population of Smith High School thought about the bad boy and the geek getting caught up in a heated lip-lock.

Because it was just Spencer and me.

He gently nipped my lower lip and then grinned irresistibly as I let out a quiet gasp. "I'd love to go to prom with you. Although if you want . . ." His voice lowered as he kissed his way over to my left ear. "We could always leave early. You could teach me all about the Cylons."

"I've got a better idea."

Spencer smiled against my jaw. "So do I. Mackenzie's yoga moves looked like a whole lot of fun—"

I smacked his arm but couldn't contain the laughter spilling out of me. He was ridiculous, and way too sure of himself, and . . . I could hardly wait to be alone with him again.

"I was thinking you could teach me how to play pool."

"How about strip pool?" he suggested teasingly, before he sobered as he stared directly into my eyes. "What changed your mind, Belle? About us. You weren't exactly wanting pool lessons yesterday."

I had spent half the night wondering if I had lost my fracking mind. I had even double-checked the details of Stockholm syndrome to make sure I wasn't suffering from the actual condition. But the answer—the most honest answer I could provide—was that I liked him.

I even liked the way he joked about playing strip pool.

"It was time for me to fight for what I wanted," I said slowly. "And, um . . . that includes you, I guess. My turn, similar question. What is it that you see in me? We both know you don't need my geeky reputation anymore, so why—"

"Because you'd do anything for your friends, even if that means watching Disney movies with strangers." Spencer's voice lowered, became more intimate. "Because you're smart and funny, and you can hold your own in a frozen yogurt fight." Something in his eyes heated. "You also kiss like a slightly unhinged librarian. And speaking from experience, I happen to love the way you—"

Whatever he was about to say was interrupted by the warning bell, which left me wondering if he'd been about to insinuate something perfectly innocent. He might love the way I . . . smiled. Maybe he loved my laugh. Or maybe the two of us were equally eager to feel my body pressed against his, and he was imagining what it would be like with fewer barriers in the way.

He grinned, as if he could tell *exactly* where my mind had wandered. "I'll let you mull over all the possibilities, Belle."

Then he pressed a quick, hard kiss to my lips before he sauntered off in the direction of his first class. Leaving me bemused and flustered and . . . smiling like a fool as my body buzzed with anticipation. He liked me too. All of me, not just the parts that conveniently helped him thwart all Notable plans for prom.

The rest of the school could dismiss me as a geek, but in Spencer's eyes I was more than a Notable.

I was the Belle of the fracking ball.

And that was totally cool with me.

After

Chapter 1

The Mardi Gras theme that so many people bitterly complained about a week ago has now been replaced with "Hollywood Glamor" by the prom committee.

No word yet as to whether the change is meant to make some very famous performers feel right at home. . . .

—from "Smith High School Goes Hollywood," by Lisa Anne Montgomery Published by *The Smithsonian*

I used to envy the people who dated rock stars.

Not just rock stars; all of the Hollywood elite, the award-winning actors and screenwriters who showed up to red carpet events clad in designer everything. I thought life must be fun for their plus one, to know that they were *beyond* special to be desired by someone who could have their pick from a pool of over 80,000 screaming fans.

But I had never considered the logistics of dating a celebrity until I was stuck trying to steal a moment of privacy with my boyfriend while his new bodyguard, Darryl, loomed conspicuously beside us. It wasn't supposed to work that way. Evading the media attention was supposed to be sexy and glamorous and *really freaking hot.*

There was nothing sexy about looking over my shoulder for a homophobe with a gun every time I wanted to reach for my boyfriend's hand. Even if that was supposed to be Darryl's concern.

Yeah, tell that to my parents, who were still wading through last week's death threats.

"You okay, Corey?" Tim asked me, tossing an arm around my shoulder in a possessive move that never failed to make something inside me flip over with excitement. "You seem like you're a million miles away."

Who me? I'm totally not thinking about the fact that our faces are plastered across magazine covers in every supermarket across the nation—and the rest of the world. I always dreamed of having hundreds of thousands of people openly debating whether our relationship is an abomination to God on network television. Doesn't faze me at all.

I shrugged lightly as I searched for a plausible excuse. "Sorry. Mackenzie called me yesterday. Apparently her dad wants to be back in her life. Now that she's famous."

Tim stopped abruptly on the sidewalk, concern written all over his face. "Is she okay? Do you need to go see her or—" He ran a hand through his hair, mussing it in the process, which only made him look like more of a rock star. "Is there anything I can do?"

"No, she'll be fine," I reassured him, slipping my hand around his waist and wishing that Darryl would come up with some excuse to make himself scarce. "Mackenzie's not a pushover, and she knows we've got her back no matter what she decides to do."

Tim growled and I tugged my cardigan closer so that I could pretend my shiver was related to the Portland chill instead of the fact that I was head over heels crazy about my boyfriend.

My boyfriend.

It still didn't feel real.

Maybe because when he was first confronted about us, Tim had lied and told the world that he was as straight as the next guy . . . provided that the next guy wasn't, y'know, *gay*.

Nothing could bring me back to earth faster than that little reminder. Every now and then I would catch myself staring up at him, wondering how someone so thoughtful and confident about his musical abilities could ever have thought it was okay to throw me under the bus. Even knowing that he had bought a freaking billboard and wrote that he loved me on it didn't erase the past.

Not completely.

"I hate people like that," Tim snarled. I let my arm fall back to my side as we swiftly returned to the Portland Rose Garden. It had been my idea to take a walk while the concert crew did their thing. Now I was wondering if it would've been a better idea to have stayed in the backstage room with all of his bandmates.

Or if I should've suggested we book a hotel room together.

We both knew where our relationship was going. We'd been dating for months, and if he hadn't been working on his new album in Los Angeles while I tried not to turn into a congealed lump in Oregon, it probably would have happened already.

Unless there was something he wasn't telling me, which was becoming more and more probable to my way of thinking. I mean, we had been in the same state—the same city—for over three hours and all I had to show for it was a few measly kisses.

Okay, maybe they weren't exactly *measly*.

But they had all taken place in super public areas where

we couldn't exactly take it any further without risking arrest. And the last thing I wanted to explain to my attorney father was that I'd been hauled off to the slammer because of public indecency. I didn't care how many rainbow flag bumper stickers my parents put on their cars, there were some things they definitely didn't need to know about my personal life.

". . . looking for a payday. You wouldn't believe some of the emails I get." Tim rolled his eyes, and I forced myself to concentrate on him again. Maybe he'd been right to say I was a million miles away. "Hi, Tim! Remember me? My cousin Bradley played on a Little League team with you. Anyway, I have a band of my own now and we'd love to go on tour with you. I'm sure we'd bring ReadySet up to a whole new level."

He looked so adorably indignant, I couldn't hold back a laugh. "Maybe he thought Bradley made quite the impression on you." I pretended to be jealous as I tugged him against me. "Any details of those Little League games you want to share, Tim?"

"Bradley who? Never heard of him. I *do* know this other guy, though. Smart. Funny—" I felt his hand slip into my hair. It was at sheep-dog length because I hadn't gotten around to booking an appointment for a haircut. "Incredibly sexy . . ."

Even knowing that he had to be talking about me—because *hello,* how awkward would it be if he was describing anyone else that way—it was hard to believe. It's not that I thought I was an ogre or anything. The cardigan looked damn good on me in a clean-cut, Ivy League kind of way.

But I wasn't Hollywood-caliber hot. Nobody was going to start handing me modeling contracts or anything.

So I tried to play it off as a joke. "Really? Want to give me his number? Turns out, dating a rock star isn't everything it's cracked up to be in the press."

I wasn't entirely kidding, but Tim didn't pick up on that either.

"What if I told you it was about to become a whole lot easier?"

I blinked up at him. "I would say that I have no idea what you're talking about."

He grinned. "I've talked to the guys and they're willing to move to Portland." Tim winced a little. "Well, okay, Nick would rather we stay in L.A. for a while because his girlfriend, Holly, lives there, but the other guys are okay with spending more of our time here. I agreed we should do it on a temporary basis, but there's no way they won't agree to make it more permanent. The city is great. The people are nice. The traffic doesn't give us road rage. . . . I'm sure they will be recognizing themselves in episodes of *Portlandia* in no time. And I will be able to spend more time with you."

Tim had definitely managed to capture my full attention, but I was too stunned to know what to say. Part of me wanted to ask Darryl to give us some privacy, and then go somewhere I could kiss the hell out of my boyfriend. And part of me wanted to ask if he had thought this plan all the way through.

Because if he was doing this for me—moving to an entirely different city just because I was temporarily stuck there— that wasn't some cute romantic gesture I could reciprocate. It wasn't the same thing as getting flowers on Valentine's Day or having a song on their upcoming album dedicated to me. Those I could handle.

Those were thoughtful gestures that didn't take all that much from him.

But this?

This was *huge*. And if it didn't work out between us, then all of them—from their manager to their roadies—would probably resent me for being behind the move. And as crazy as I was about him, there were times when I wondered if I had bitten off more than I could chew.

I used to roll my eyes when characters on TV dramas said crap like, "We're just from two different worlds!" But there was more truth to it than I wanted to admit. He was L.A. and I was Portland. Something as small as a change in area code wasn't going to change that, especially since he wouldn't be leaving the madness behind.

His loyal fanbase would stalk his movements here too.

Tim looked at me expectantly, and I saw a shadow of fear pass over his face. "Well," he prompted. "Aren't you excited?

Yeah, I am. I'm absolutely thrilled at the idea of spending time alone with you. But, um . . . can you excuse me for a moment? I need to have a panic attack in the bathroom real quick.

I glanced over uncomfortably at Darryl. "Of course I am. But shouldn't we talk about it somewhere . . . more private?"

Tim dismissed that with a wave of his hand. "Darryl won't repeat anything we say. That's the beauty of confidentiality clauses."

I knew he expected me to grin or make some joke out of my need for privacy. Maybe something like, *Wow, for a guy who took so long coming out of the closet, you sure have no trouble putting it all out there now. Any other dirty laundry you'd like to air?*

Scratch that. He would never expect me to be that passive-aggressive. Maybe because on the rare occasions we were together, I spent most of it focusing on ways to steal just a little more time together. I'd offer to drive him to the airport because it would mean we could have a few more minutes together. We could pretend to be normal, as if we were just two guys who happened to like each other, instead of a Grammy award winner . . . and his ordinary high school boyfriend.

Funny how I was getting exactly what I'd been complaining about for weeks—a chance to spend some quality time with Timothy Goff—and now I just wanted to ask, *Are you sure? Because I don't want to inspire your next hit song called "My Biggest Mistake."*

"That's really . . . uh . . . great," I finished lamely.

"And since I convinced the guys that we should spend some time after the concert tonight getting to know Portland, we're going to be sticking around for a while. Which is why I was thinking . . ."

I wasn't entirely sure I was ready to hear another one of his genius plans, except Tim looked so pleased with himself, I couldn't disappoint him. So I smiled encouragingly while I noted with a sinking heart that we were only a handful of blocks away from the concert hall. In a matter of minutes he would disappear with Darryl, not to be seen for the next twelve hours . . . unless something unexpected changed his schedule.

"Well, how do you feel about prom?"

I stared at him in shock. "I don't really have many feelings on the subject. It always seemed pretty cheesy to me. I mean, maybe it's great for girls if they actually get to have that Hollywood moment when they have a spotlight following them down a staircase and right into the conveniently open arms of their one true love or whatever. But most girls don't actually get that. And since I *definitely* wouldn't—"

"I wouldn't be so sure about that, Corey. I agreed to perform with the guys at your prom."

My mouth fell open and I didn't even care that I looked like a koi fish trying to suck food flakes on the surface of the water.

"*You* are going to my prom." I said the words slowly, hoping they would make more sense that way.

"Nick and Chris will be with me. We'll play a quick set and then join you for the full high school experience. It's no big deal."

"I . . . you know it might be held in the gym, right? Which means the whole place could stink of feet. Are you sure you want to go?" I conveniently failed to mention that the Left-bank Annex had already been rented, because . . . hey, the King family could still decide to pull their donation.

"Well, when you put it that way, how could I resist?" Tim elbowed me lightly in the stomach, so it was more of a love tap than anything else. "Don't you want to go to prom with me?"

I did. I really did.

But what I wanted even more was to skip that stupid thing entirely, check into a hotel, and lock the door on the rest of the world for the next sixteen hours.

Too bad life didn't work that way—even when you were dating a rock star.

Chapter 2

It has now been confirmed that the acclaimed
rock band ReadySet will be playing at this year's
prom!
We just became the envy of every high school
in America.

—from "ReadySet . . . Performing at Prom!"
by Lisa Anne Montgomery
Published by *The Smithsonian*

"So . . . Tim's thinking of moving the band to Portland."
I half expected Mackenzie to leap out of her chair
and cheer when I told her the news about Tim, the hearing of
everyone in the cafeteria be damned. I hoped she wouldn't
try to hug me, because knowing Mackenzie, she would
probably trip herself over one of the chair legs and then slide
across the table toward me, knocking over trays of food in
the process.

"*Seriously?* That's *awesome!*" Mackenzie beamed at me.
"That would be so great for you guys! And we could all get
together. On a regular basis. And actually *do* things." A
thoughtful gleam entered her eyes. "I might even be able to

collaborate on another song with them. Maybe. Do not mention that to Tim, though, or he will never give it up. Then again . . . I'm willing to say whatever it takes to convince them to move here."

I cracked up. Mackenzie's enthusiasm was infectious, which was kind of why I'd waited to tell her in person. If anyone could convince me that the drama was all in my head, it was Mackenzie and Jane.

Not that *anyone* would tell me this was bad news.

Because who in their right mind wouldn't be thrilled to have their rock star boyfriend uproot his life just so that the relationship could stop being long-distance?

"Yeah, well, it gets better—"

Mackenzie's smile quirked up. "Yes, it really does."

"Focus, Mackenzie. Tim is going to prom. With . . . uh, us." I had no idea what our prom plans were now. Before Tim had decided to crash the event, I'd assumed that I would chip in for a limo and ride there with Mackenzie, Logan, Jane and her boyfriend, Scott, and whoever else felt like joining in. I'd thought it would be a stress-free evening, because I didn't need to impress anyone there.

Now I would probably spend most of the night trying to come up with ways to leave Darryl in the lurch.

Mackenzie squirmed happily in her seat. "You're going to prom together? That makes it official. This is going to be the best night ever! Bar none."

Logan grinned down at her. "You sure about that, Mack? I have some pretty fond memories from last Thursday. . . ."

She flushed and I looked aside and fought the urge to start whistling to myself.

"Okay, so it'll be the best night that I can talk about in public, then," Mackenzie amended sheepishly. "My point is that it'll be great."

I rolled my eyes. "C'mon, this is high school we're talking about—there's no way you can put all the upperclassmen in a room and expect everything to work out perfectly. Speaking of which"—I winked at her—"have you practiced your shocked expression when you're nominated prom queen?"

"Don't even joke about that!" Mackenzie hissed. Then she pitched her voice louder. *"I'm not going to be prom queen!"*

Logan laughed. "Mack is convinced she'd trip in front of everyone."

I had no trouble picturing that at all.

She jabbed her boyfriend in the arm. "I will happily dance with you before and after your crowning moment. But if you, in any way, try to get me up on that stage with you, Thursday will become a distant memory, Logan."

"I seriously doubt that, Mack."

"A very distant memory."

I laughed and surveyed the cafeteria, hoping to see Jane's familiar red mop of hair somewhere. Ever since she had taken on creating a fiction paper for the school, most of her lunches were spent staring at a computer screen fiddling with layout issues. There was no sign of her and since I didn't see a certain green-eyed camera-wielding menace, I assumed Scott was working on it with her.

But my sweep of the cafeteria did bring something else to my attention.

"Is that *Isobel Peters?*" I said in disbelief as I pointed to the Notable table. The one that was usually reserved for Fake and Bake and the rest of that ilk. "Please tell me it's not opposite day. That's the only explanation I can think of at the moment."

Mackenzie shot me a mock glare. "C'mon, Corey. No need to be snarky."

I nearly choked on a sip of my soda. "You're kidding me, right? I love the girl, but she is *not* Notable material any more than you or I—holy crap! Spencer is sitting down next to her. I repeat, *Spencer King is sitting next to Isobel!*"

"Thanks for the play-by-play," Logan said dryly. "We do have eyes."

"Okay, then does one of you want to explain this to me?" I rose out of my seat, only to hesitate. "Does she need rescuing, do you think?"

I watched as Spencer stole one of Isobel's fries. She smiled up at him as her hand darted out and she nabbed two of his. I sat back down. Well, that answered one of my questions . . . more or less.

"Oh, she *definitely* needs a big, strong man like you to save her from the guy stealing her french fries," Mackenzie said sarcastically. "The scoundrel!"

"I'm not exactly puny," I pointed out. Not that Mackenzie was listening.

"The knave!"

Logan grinned. "The rascal?"

Mackenzie burst out laughing. "Yes! I love it. Spencer King: The Rascal." She spread her hands as if she were envisioning the words on a billboard.

"Okay, I get your point. I just didn't realize they were, y'know, *together.*"

I barely managed to refrain from pointing out that nobody at Smith High School would have expected the two of them to pair up. Then again, I was starting to think that prom was messing with everyone's minds. Maybe that explained why my boyfriend was willing to suddenly throw away the life he had built for himself in the City of Angels . . . for me.

Logan shrugged. "I'm not sure they're official yet."

I was on my feet in an instant. "If he's messing with her, I'm going to—"

Mackenzie cut me off, which was probably for the best because I had no idea how to finish that statement. Beat him up? Unlikely. I'm not exactly the strongest guy at school. Jane could probably take me in a fight, thanks to all her self-defense classes. So attacking a hockey player was an idea destined for failure.

But I couldn't sit back and watch Smith High School crush someone else simply because they were a little bit different. Not after countless days of being shoved against lockers after P.E. simply for trying to change my clothes.

And okay, I didn't think Spencer would physically hurt Isobel. But if he didn't care about her—if he was simply using the geek as a bit of entertainment—that would ache a whole lot worse than any bruise.

I would know. I'd been on the receiving end of both kinds of hazing ever since I came out of the closet my freshman year. Then again, I wasn't sure if it really counted as "coming out" if someone else yells that you're gay during the busiest lunch peak in the cafeteria.

I'd never forgiven Alex for that, but I doubted it kept him up at night.

"Chill. He's not going to hurt her."

I raised a skeptical eyebrow. "And you know this how, exactly?"

"Because I saw the way he looked at her when they came over to my house a week ago. Trust me, he wasn't trying to make her the punch line for a joke."

Logan glanced up at that. "Uh, speaking of that day . . . did you happen to notice anything else?"

Mackenzie smiled sneakily. "You mean the fact that Melanie is now dating my little brother? Yeah, I picked up on that." She elbowed Logan in the stomach. "Thanks for the heads-up on that one, by the way!"

"Hey, I have no interest in getting involved with your brother's love life. Zero. Nada. None."

Mackenzie nodded. "I'm just glad he has something else to focus on besides . . . it's good he's keeping busy right now."

It hurt to hear Mackenzie's voice change the moment she

thought about her father. There was a hesitant, uncertain quality to it, as if she was completely lost and trying to decide whether or not to stop a stranger to ask for directions.

The last time I had seen her this confused, she was thrust into Internet fame as America's Most Awkward Girl. In some ways, I wondered if that had been easier. At least she had known that her fifteen minutes of fame wouldn't last forever, but this . . . yeah, she was always going to be stuck with her dad.

The real question was whether or not she wanted him to be a part of her life.

"You okay, Mackenzie?" I asked quietly. "You know that if you need to talk about any of this—"

I trailed off, leaving the *you can always call me* part unspoken when she smiled at me and shook her head, as if trying to rouse herself. "I'm fine. Really. It's weird having him around, asking questions about my life, that sort of thing. I don't know what his endgame is yet."

"Does there have to be an endgame?" Logan asked.

Mackenzie and I stared at him in disbelief. "If he shows up after almost a decade of being parental non grata, then yeah, there has to be an endgame," I answered for her.

"Maybe he wants to make up for it now."

"Maybe he's trying to cash in now that he thinks his daughter is rolling in money."

"But I'm not!" Mackenzie protested. "I didn't post that stupid video, so it's not like I'm reaping any of the profits."

"Yeah, but that doesn't stop people from believing you're flush now." Logan shrugged. "Plus, you got a nice chunk of change from the song you did with ReadySet."

"Which means that I might be able to pay for a year of a private liberal arts college if I get a *phenomenal* scholarship. I'm in no position to start giving my estranged father a handout."

I couldn't resist rolling my eyes. "Perception, Mackenzie. It's all about perception."

She should have learned that by now. After all, she was the one who had been taken in by the idea of dating Patrick Bradford, only to realize that the reality of the guy did *not* live up to her vision of him.

He was almost as bad as Alex, in my opinion. And, no, he didn't intentionally knock into me in hallways, but he also didn't say a word while he watched it happen. Alex was a homophobe and a bully, no question about it. And he wasn't subtle about his prejudices.

Patrick, on the other hand, was the kind of person who would weigh the possible outcome of taking action before he would so much as lift a finger. He knew that telling Alex to knock it off was the right thing to do—but that if he spoke up, he might get teased about being my boyfriend.

In Patrick's mind, that provided enough of an incentive to keep his mouth shut.

"My perception of the situation is that if my dad is looking for a pay day, he'll find out soon enough that there isn't one coming and he'll leave."

"And you're okay with that?" I didn't believe it for a second. Mackenzie could talk a good game about being fine without her dad, but it had to sting like hell.

She bit her lip. "No, I'm not even remotely okay with it, but it's not within my control. If that's what happens . . . I'll deal." Mackenzie smiled, but it didn't quite reach her eyes. "It won't be the first time he has disappeared on me."

Logan rested his hand on her knee and I felt a wave of jealousy rush through me at the gesture. It was such a small display of solidarity and yet it spoke volumes.

Or maybe what spoke volumes was that I couldn't picture my boyfriend doing the same.

"I'm not going anywhere, Mack."

It would have been such a sweet moment—if Alex Thompson hadn't chosen that instant to make a guest appearance.

Chapter 3

Not everyone fully supports having Grammy award–winning rock band ReadySet perform at the Smith High School prom, especially after the band's lead singer publicly came out as gay. Some members of the community have reached out to the school board to voice their concern. . . .

—from "ReadySet . . . Riot!"
by Lisa Anne Montgomery
Published by *The Smithsonian*

"Well, if it isn't The Gay Who Stole Prom. Ruin any other traditions lately?"

I knew that whatever Alex said would be dripping with disdain and contempt, but I hadn't expected it to be so cryptic. The majority of his insults were straightforward. I'd grown accustomed to hearing him say that any guy who showed interest in me would be disappointed to discover that I wasn't a girl.

I'd hoped that the threat of having my parents press charges of harassment if he didn't leave me alone would force him to back off. It wouldn't stop him entirely, of course.

There would still be whispers, dark looks, and snide comments in the boy's locker room. I'd still be avoiding the school bathroom just to make sure nobody decided to assert his manliness by shoving me around.

But I had thought he might at least stop harassing me in the cafeteria.

I was wrong.

Logan and Mackenzie were both on their feet before Alex had even finished his sentence. I wasn't sure what they thought they were going to do; fight him, maybe? Kind of ironic considering that they had looked at me as if I were nuts when I'd stood up only moments before.

There was no point getting riled around Alex. He wanted the attention, and if there was something—or someone—he feared, I hadn't seen any sign of it.

"Want to get to the point, Alex?" I pretended to yawn. "Or do you want to keep misquoting Doctor Seuss at me?"

"Shut it, freak. Thanks to you and your little boyfriend, prom might not even be on anymore."

"Right." I snapped my fingers. "I nearly forgot; I'm going to be getting my gay germs all over the school dance! Which means you're going to be stuck lusting after me from afar. That's got to be rough for you."

Alex lunged forward, but Logan stepped between us. "You should reconsider, man."

"Yeah? Well, your little fairy friend should have reconsidered before inviting his boyfriend to the prom and making us a national laughingstock."

"You can taunt me in a box. You can taunt me with a fox. You can taunt me here or there . . ." I singsonged.

"And you can go straight to hell. But first you should tell the crowd outside that you're not going to prom!" Alex snarled. "Tell the school board while you're at it. Otherwise, they're going to cancel it entirely, just to be politically correct."

"Oh, man, there's nothing worse than being politically correct," Mackenzie said sarcastically. "The next thing you know bullies like you will actually have to face consequences for their actions." I could tell that Mackenzie wanted to say a whole lot more, but Jane's entrance cut her off at the pass.

"Corey, good, you're here. You need to go to Principal Taylor's office." Jane barely spared anybody else a glance. "I'll go with you."

I rubbed my eyes tiredly and tried to imagine how life had been only a few months ago. Before I started dating a rock star. Before my friends were famous. Before . . . any of it.

Maybe I'd been this exhausted back then, but that sure wasn't the way I remembered it now. Okay, so Alex Thompson had always been in my face—that wasn't exactly new. Still, at least before my life had gone all supernova, it was contained to the two of us.

Now all of my friends had been dragged into this mess.

"I'm not going anywhere," I said stubbornly, even as Jane rolled her eyes and muttered something about being stuck with guys who were too freaking thickheaded for their own good.

"Look, I'm betting your parents will be here any minute, which means you can either talk to them here—in front of everyone—or you can wait in Principal Taylor's office. That seems way more convenient to me. Especially if your dad threatens him with a lawsuit. . . ."

Both of my parents were lawyers. My mom focused on contract law and my dad filed malpractice suits, but they were never too busy to firmly discuss legalities with anyone they thought was in the wrong. They would never admit to threatening or intimidating others with the threat of a court date, but that didn't stop them from utilizing everything in their arsenal when it came to me.

Parents first, lawyers second.

If they were superheroes, that probably would have been the slogan they adopted.

There were times that seriously came in handy, and other times when I needed them to back off and let me handle things on my own. I'm pretty sure they still saw me as a five-year-old in train pajamas, or maybe it went further back to the "It's a Boy!" announcement they sent out to everyone they'd ever met.

Either way, as soon as they showed up, I would be whisked out of here and taken home where I would be safe. Except it was hard to feel safe with a whole bunch of photographers camped out on my lawn, ready to scream questions at me. Ready to do almost anything if it would get them a reaction they could splash across the front page of a gossip magazine.

**Hitting Rock Bottom! ReadySet lead singer
Timothy Goff's boyfriend loses it! More on pg. 26**

And this time the article wouldn't be lying. I was hitting rock freaking bottom all on my own.

"I think I'll save them the drive," I told Jane as I calmly collected my stuff and tossed the leftovers from my lunch into the trash. Food didn't sound appetizing anymore. "Catch you guys later."

It was almost alarming how easy it was for me to pretend to be fine.

My boyfriend was the rock star, but I was the one most likely to get an Oscar for Best Dramatic Performance. Hopefully, for a brilliant portrayal of James Dean, since that was usually whom I tried to channel when Alex Thompson got in my face.

James wouldn't flinch in the face of a bully.

So I sauntered out of the cafeteria, past all the gaping faces of my fellow students, and headed straight to the parking lot.

My friends weren't going to let me deal with whatever they thought might be waiting for me alone. All of them were way too protective of me to be content simply watching my retreat.

"I'm fine," I insisted as Jane and Mackenzie moved to flank me. I guess it could have been worse: I could have been stuck with Darryl watching my every move.

On the off chance that whatever I was about to face made me crumble, I wanted it to be around people I could trust.

"Sure, you are." Mackenzie nodded, but I could tell she was only trying to pacify me. "I was just about to tell Jane your good news."

I had no idea what she was talking about, but Mackenzie didn't wait for me to ask.

"Tim invited him to prom."

The forced cheerfulness in Mackenzie's voice made me want to gag. Only minutes earlier she had genuinely been happy for me. Now she was just trying to keep me distracted.

"I sort of knew that already," Jane said. "It's all over the Internet."

That shouldn't have come as a shock—everything else about my life was out there for the public to see. But there was still something about having it confirmed, knowing without a shadow of a doubt that a good chunk of the world was talking about my stupid high school dance . . . it gnawed at me.

Or maybe it was the fact that everyone thought Tim had asked me to the dance, but instead of getting an extra-large fortune cookie invitation or even waiting for *me* to extend the invite, he had decided to inform me of his plans as an afterthought.

Sure, he was a world-famous lead singer of a chart-topping rock band.

That didn't mean he couldn't have *asked* instead of assuming that my answer went without saying. The really scary part, the thought that made my stomach tighten and twist, was that I wasn't sure what I would have said if he'd given me the option.

Hey, love. Do you think we could skip my school dance and hole up somewhere alone? We could play dirty Scrabble together. And then maybe we could do something else for a few hours. . . .

The truth was that I didn't much care what we did as long as it was private.

It didn't look like I'd be getting anything that even remotely resembled privacy for a long time, though—if ever. As I rounded the corner and began walking along the concrete sidewalk that provided a straight shot to the parking lot, I could dimly hear Mackenzie and Jane discussing me, but most of my attention was claimed by the effort of putting one foot in front of the other.

"What did you read online?" Mackenzie asked curiously.

Jane shrugged next to me. "Something about how everyone at Smith High School is looking forward to an unforgettable prom with ReadySet headlining the event. They also speculated on whether or not the school was ready to handle hosting an event on this scale."

I forced myself to remain calm. "They managed it last year just fine."

"Sure, but that was before . . . well, look, ReadySet has a pretty, uh, intense fanbase. The local chapter will definitely try to crash. And last year there wasn't a crowd of screaming, crying tweenage girls who would do just about anything to get an autograph from any of the guys."

It was strange thinking that once upon a time I hadn't been all that different from them.

I had wanted Timothy Goff because he was hot and talented and because I had this image of him in my head. There was no doubt in my mind that we would hit it off if he ever got to know the real me. Even when he was in the closet, I was convinced that our personalities would mesh well. That we could hang out in his Hollywood mansion for hours without it ever getting weird between us.

We could laugh together about how everyone else put him up on a pedestal, but he'd know that I'd never do that to him.

Except maybe I'd been just like everyone else—falling in love with the image on magazine covers instead of the real man.

"I bet Lisa Anne fed them part of the story," Jane snarled. "I feel the urge to write a strong opinion piece coming on. Maybe something about the morality of leaking conjecture about the private lives of students under the guise of 'news.' "

I couldn't stop myself from smiling. There was just something about seeing the petite redhead ready to take on the world for me that made everything a little bit better. My life was still a royal mess, but the one thing I didn't have to wonder was whether or not my friends were really in my corner.

"Um . . . I don't think one article is going to do it," Mackenzie murmured in horror as we drew close enough to the cars to see the crowd that had amassed ever since those pop culture pieces had been posted online. The local news station was present with their pathetic excuse for journalists, holding microphones, ready to shove people aside to get a sound bite.

There were onlookers who had paused in the hope of seeing some kind of spectacle firsthand. I could understand the impulse. It was like slowing to check out a car accident on the side of the road. It wasn't like Forest Grove, Oregon, was a thrilling place to live. If you were hoping to find excitement, you usually had to make it yourself. The journalists were annoying, and the strangers snapping photos on their phones of me weren't much better, but I could deal with them. I could force myself to smile as I climbed into my car. Worst-case scenario, I could call the cops to make sure none of the paparazzi attempted to barricade the parking lot until I gave them more of a reaction.

The people who twisted my stomach were the ones holding enormous signs.

GOD HATES GAYS!

HOMO SEX IS SIN.

HOMO IS A THREAT TO NATIONAL SECURITY!

ADAM AND EVE—NOT ADAM AND STEVE.

HOMO GO HOME!

Some of the signs quoted Bible verses on the back, and some just had flames licking the words just in case I hadn't already picked up on the threat of an eternity in hell for being myself. And even though I knew that for every line forbidding homosexuality in the Bible, I could pull out an equally ridiculous rule about stoning women to death, and wearing garments from two different types of material, and eating a shrimp cocktail—hell, even *cheeseburgers* were technically against the rules—that didn't make it any less personal.

It didn't make me feel any less sick inside.

Oh sure, it was easy to laugh some of it off when I could see George Takei taking on the homophobes online. But there were so many of them. So many signs. So many hallways filled with whispers and cutting words that I was legally obligated to walk while I pretended to be deaf to the insults.

And even though everyone kept promising that it would get better once I graduated from Smith High School and left small-town Oregon behind in my rearview mirror, it was hard to believe. Especially when I saw middle-aged men holding signs that said they thought I'd be better off dead. That my very existence was a scourge to the earth.

Jane instinctively stepped in front of me.

I'm not sure what she thought that would accomplish, considering that she's a solid foot shorter than I am. Maybe her self-defense classes would be enough if she was in a one-on-one scuffle with a single cameraman, but not against a full-fledged *mob*.

"Go wait for your parents, Corey," she hissed. "Mackenzie and I can call the cops and keep them at bay here."

But it was too late for that—the paparazzi had already seen me.

Chapter 4

Rumors are circulating that ReadySet's notoriety might lead the school board to pull the plug on prom. However, this would be an unprecedented move by the administration. One that also hasn't been substantiated by any of my sources.

So don't start asking for refunds on your prom tickets yet, people!

—from "Cancelling Prom?"
by Lisa Anne Montgomery
Published by *The Smithsonian*

I sprinted for my car with my heart lodged firmly in my throat.

I couldn't shake the feeling that this must be what it was like for a rabbit when a pack of bloodhounds locked in on the scent of fear. I wanted to tell myself that it was stupid to be afraid. That the worst that could happen with all those cameras rolling was that I'd be forced to shove strangers away from me. And then I would be stuck explaining to my parents, the school board, and anyone else who would listen that, *No, I do not have violent tendencies.*

But the truth was that the cameras and the microphones couldn't stop a bullet.

And it would only take one crazy with a firearm to make it a very different news story.

I unlocked the driver's door, climbed inside with my head down, and mumbled, "No comment," until those two words slurred together into something else entirely. Neither of the girls was close enough to notice. Instead, Jane and Mackenzie were doing their best to distract the paparazzi by taking some of the heat themselves. I knew it couldn't have been easy for either of them to get involved with that level of craziness. Not when they had worked so hard to regain a semblance of normalcy in their lives after their own experiences with the press.

But if Tim was serious about crashing prom and moving to Portland, all of us would have to adjust to receiving this level of scrutiny.

My breathing hitched, so I rested my forehead against the steering wheel until it steadied. I could handle being photographed freaking out in my car. I didn't like it—but I could cope.

But if I barfed on the dashboard, the tabloids would mock me forever.

I tried to distract myself by focusing on the fuzzy blue steering wheel cover that Jane had given me as a birthday present. It tufted and clumped in places, and I was willing to bet that within another month or two large patches of it would wind up caught in the lint tray of the dryer. Still, it was almost peaceful to sit there and imagine all the places the blue fibers could explore by clinging to my jacket.

These reporters weren't all that different from the fuzz.

Except the steering wheel case didn't have an agenda. It didn't invade my privacy or try to interrogate me about my personal life. And no amount of lint would ever prevent me from leaving a parking lot by boxing in my car.

But if you could overlook those tiny, insignificant little details . . . yeah, they were practically identical. Cut from the same cloth.

It was a weak pun, but it gave me a reason to smile as I waited to hear the sirens of my approaching police escort. At this point, I was kind of surprised that the nearby station hadn't placed a patrol car nearby to keep watch over the school at all times. It wasn't like this was the first time the media had gotten out of control. Maybe they were simply waiting for my parents to either start homeschooling me or to ship me off somewhere. Either way, the local precinct would probably be happy.

And . . . I might be too. There were times when starting over somewhere else sounded nice. I would miss Mackenzie and Jane, of course. But the same could not be said for the majority of the Notables who ranged the hallways, especially Alex Thompson.

Although now that I knew Tim planned on relocating the band to Portland . . . well, that changed everything. I winced as I tried to imagine telling Tim that my living arrangements had changed.

Hey, babe. So you know how you decided to switch zip codes for me because you were sick of the whole long-distance relationship thing? Well . . . I've decided to leave. It's not you. Okay, it is you. It's the paparazzi you bring everywhere with you. So, um . . . good luck in Oregon!

If Tim's diehard ReadySet fans heard even the barest whisper of a rumor about that conversation, I wouldn't only have to worry about death threats coming from the homophobic sign holders of the world. Groupies would be sending me thousands of threats for breaking his heart.

That wasn't simply idle speculation on my part either.

When Tim had come out of the closet and confirmed to

the nation that he wanted to date me, I'd been inundated with messages that said, *If you hurt him, I will end you.*

And those were on the sane end of the spectrum when it came to the letters.

The weird ones included requests for pictures of Tim's feet, or at the very least, that I pass on their cell phone number so he'd know exactly what he was missing by dating me.

Oh, and there was one that simply said, *I want your face.*

I wasn't sure if that was meant to be a threat or a request for a plastic surgeon, but it definitely creeped me out.

My breathing stabilized, even as restless anxiety began to well up inside of me. And the longer I sat motionless in the car, the more I wondered if Alex had lied. Given the way he enjoyed bullying people, I wouldn't put it past him to make some prom-related hiccup seem like a sign of the apocalypse.

But the media wouldn't have flocked here if there wasn't a story to cover.

There was no way I'd be able to move my car until the police made their guest appearance, so I decided to check out the Internet headlines Jane had mentioned only minutes ago.

There was no way the rumors could be worse on the page than all the possibilities that whirled around my head.

I was wrong.

Timothy Goff Opens up about Plans for Prom

ReadySet lead singer, Timothy Goff, isn't going to let anyone keep him from attending that special dance with his new boyfriend, Corey O'Neal. "I never experienced a prom of my own," Goff admitted. "I was busy pursuing my career in music. So I'm really looking forward to discovering what I missed with Corey."

But this might be one party that won't pull out the red carpet for Timothy Goff.

Smith High School policy states that while their upperclassmen students are allowed to bring dates who do not attend that school, they do reserve the right to bar guests if they have reason to believe they might pose a threat to the student body.

Smith High School principal John Taylor declined to answer questions but did make the following statement, "Smith High School takes the safety of all its students very seriously. The school board needs to determine whether it is appropriate to allow a legal adult to attend a dance where minors are present."

Many outspoken LGBTQ activists are calling this simply a screen intended to obscure blatant discrimination based on Goff's sexual orientation.

"For years people have drawn an unfounded correlation between homosexuality and pedophilia," said one advocate who prefers to remain anonymous. "The idea that Timothy Goff poses a risk to the safety of minors is blatant homophobia."

My disbelief as I stared at the tiny screen of my cell phone was soon eclipsed by rage. The very notion that Tim would *ever* hurt anyone made my hands shake with fury. I knew from firsthand experience that he wasn't as perfect as some people thought—he could be thoughtless and ambitious, and he believed that he could bring everyone around to his way of thinking eventually—but he also possessed a bone-deep core of integrity. My life would have been so much easier if he was a danger to random high school students.

Because then I would be able to tell him that I wasn't cut out for life in the spotlight without the breath-stealing certainty that breaking up with him would be one of my biggest regrets. I could move on without hating myself for bailing the second the "for better" part of our relationship took a turn for the worse.

Not that I ever pictured marriage for us.

Mostly.

Still, my insecurities didn't make it acceptable for my high school to act as if he had appeared on a special celebrity episode of *To Catch a Predator*—and not as the host. So there was a *slight* age gap between us. Nobody would blink twice over a junior bringing a freshman to the dance . . . if they were straight. Okay, and as long as the guy was older than the girl; otherwise, she would be on the receiving end of snide cradle-robber comments.

Apparently the idea of having two boys show up together was out of the question. Too risky. It might even give impressionable students the idea that it's okay to be gay, or transgender, or asexual, or whatever felt most like them—and the school couldn't be seen doing anything that controversial. Oh no. It was a much better idea to pretend that teenagers were incapable of understanding the consequences of their actions whenever their opinions differed from the perspective of the administration. The school could even claim that according to science our brains weren't developed enough for us to *really* see the delicate nature of the situation.

It was discrimination, plain and simple.

Except there was nothing clear-cut about my reaction to it. Anger, obviously. Indignation, mostly on Tim's behalf. And yet there was a tiny part of me that was almost . . . relieved.

Because if the school administration forbade Tim's attendance, then I could go with my friends. I could pretend to be normal for a night. I wouldn't be the center of whispers and controversy. No screaming or crying fans would try to bulldoze a path through me in order to reach Tim.

I could experience a thoroughly typical prom without being the jerk who asked his boyfriend to stay home. Tim might've been fine letting the world document our every move, but it actually made me miss the privacy we'd had when he was in the closet.

At least people hadn't openly speculated about my sex life in the tabloids back then.

My phone vibrated and I nearly tossed it onto the back seat without so much as glancing down to identify the caller. The whole *if I don't see it, it never happened* knee-jerk reaction was a childish one that I probably should have outgrown, but lately the impulse had only grown stronger.

I had always been willing to pull the covers up over my head and keep repeating, *The monsters are not in the closet. I repeat, there are no monsters in the closet,* until I could almost believe it.

Speaking of coming out of the closet . . .

I glanced down at the phone and wasn't surprised to see Tim's face looking back at me. I had snapped that particular picture when Mackenzie and I had joined the band for an impromptu trip to Los Angeles. Tim looked exhausted in a wrinkled shirt that he had picked up off the floor and tugged on without even a moment's consideration. There was a coffee stain on the bottom left side that wasn't visible in the photo but that made me smile because *I* knew it was there.

That's also why I refused to change the photo even when Tim had gotten a glimpse of it and wrinkled his face in distaste. He didn't look like America's hottest rock star, and that smile wasn't meant to make thousands of tweenage girls buy out his concerts.

It was a private look meant just for me.

I answered the call. "Hey, Tim, are you—"

"I'm fine," he said before I could even finish the question. "I'm headed over to you now. Are you home or at school?"

I glanced at the paparazzi still swarming my car. "I'm sort of stuck in between."

Which described my life in more ways than one.

"Okay, I just scheduled a meeting with Principal Taylor. Your parents are on their way, right? It never hurts to have a lawyer or two present."

"Funny, most people would not agree with you," I quipped weakly.

"Most people also aren't going to press charges of sexual discrimination against a high school. I'm not opposed to their legal advice." He sounded so focused and determined— if he'd been discussing how much he wanted to spend some alone time with me, it would have raised the hairs on the back of my neck. Too bad lawsuits didn't get my heart pounding.

"Are you sure you want to do that?" There was a burst of static over the phone and I wasn't entirely sure he heard me. "Maybe we could just, y'know . . . stay home? And by 'home' I mean go to a hotel room?"

"See . . . Taylor . . . Soon . . . Bye!"

Great. So that was a big fat no to the hotel room plan and a huge new complication to add to my life.

Because apparently my high school life wasn't crazy enough already.

Chapter 5

Even though former queen bee Chelsea Halloway now goes to school in Portland, leaving Smith High School behind in her rearview mirror, our administration must not have gotten the memo. Her name is on the voting ballot for prom queen. This is a joke, right?

—from "Chelsea for . . . *Prom Queen?*"
by Lisa Anne Montgomery
Published by *The Smithsonian*

I debated driving off into the sunset by myself. All I had to do was press the horn and start backing up my car. If the paparazzi didn't move out of my way . . . well, the consequences wouldn't necessarily weigh on my conscience for very long. They knew the risks when they swarmed me. If they refused to consider my safety, I wasn't going to become overly invested in theirs.

But instead of bolting, I watched the police start flashing their badges as they pushed the press far enough back that I could open my car door without getting a microphone to the face. They escorted me to Principal Taylor's office, hustling me inside past all the gawking students and away from the sympathy radiating from Mackenzie and Jane.

I was a little too distracted by my armed guard and my upcoming face-off with my school principal to do more than wave halfheartedly at my friends. I knew they wouldn't take it personally. Not when I also had a pissed-off rock star and two outraged parents to reassure. Still, it was hard to refrain from snidely pointing out that Principal Taylor's office had become my own personal homeroom. I probably spent more hours bouncing between this office and the guidance counselor's room than all the other students at Smith High School *combined*.

Exempting Sam, of course.

That girl managed to get more face time with every member of the administration than their spouses probably achieved. So comparing our track records was like listening to a hoarder protest that his home wasn't a health hazard . . . yet. Maybe it was true, but the bar was set so low most people could trip over it.

The beleaguered administrative assistant, Sally Murphy, gave me a little finger-wave when I walked into the office and offered a smile that looked strained around her eyes. "Hi, sweetie. He's expecting you."

I nodded, then paused with my hand on the door handle. "I've got it from here, guys," I told the police officers. "But thanks for the assist."

"No problem, kid. We'll wait out here for you."

Yeah, I wasn't surprised that the bearded man with the slight paunch was already moving around the coffee table and heading straight for Ms. Murphy's desk. His partner seemed perfectly content grabbing a copy of *People* magazine and settling in to wait. By the time they frog-marched me away from school, he'd probably be caught up on all the most salacious rumors about me.

I strove for an air of nonchalance as I opened the door.

"Principal Taylor, we've got to stop meeting like this," I said, instantly noting that Principal Taylor looked every bit as exhausted as his administrative assistant. There was no way he could've been prepared to take the helm at Smith High School this year. I could picture him on a golf course with his friends, bragging about his plan to ease into retirement.

Instead, he had been saddled with America's Most Awkward Girl and her misfit group of friends. It almost made me pity the homophobic jerk.

Almost.

"Hi, Corey," he said. "I'm sure your parents will be here any minute. Would you care to take a seat before—"

The door jerked open and Tim strode in, looking every inch the rock star who graced the covers of magazines. His hair was sexily disheveled, as if he had raked his hands through it a few times.

"Thanks for making time in your schedule to see me, Mr. Taylor," he said smoothly. "I'm so glad we're getting this taken care of right away."

"As I was just saying to Corey"—Principal Taylor gestured at me and Tim spun around and shot me a sizzling smile that had adrenaline racing through my system—"we should really wait for his parents to arrive."

Tim glanced disdainfully at the mountain of paperwork stacked on the nearby chairs. Or maybe it was the empty bag of potato chips crumpled on the ground that earned his disgust.

It was kind of funny coming from a guy who could live in squalor for weeks at a time on a tour bus. But if it was a ploy to distract Principal Taylor into tidying up while he mouthed, *"Are you okay?"* to me, it worked.

I nodded, unable to put into words everything I was feeling.

Confusion. Stress. Panic. Nervous anticipation. A tingly rush of excitement at his presence.

There was no way to admit any of that in front of Principal Taylor without being forced to hear his not-so-subtle recommendation for homeschooling. Again. That would make his job so much easier. Then he wouldn't have to think about . . . oh, I dunno, hiding his blatant homophobia from the public eye.

No gay, no problem.

And okay, it wasn't like I was the only member of the LGBTQ club on campus. Just the one most likely to make national headlines.

The anger that had surged through me in the cafeteria reignited.

"Shouldn't we have the rest of the school board on speaker phone?" I suggested. "That way we can get a clear ruling right now."

Principal Taylor paused in his halfhearted cleaning efforts to adjust his tie. "I don't think that's necessary yet."

Maybe he picked up on my barely leashed outrage, but Tim crossed the room to stand at my side. "So . . . this might not improve your parent's impression of me, Corey."

I laughed in spite of myself. "You've already met them and they *loved* you."

"Yeah, but that was before I landed their son in the principal's office."

I grinned, slipping my hand into his, as I tried to ignore the way Principal Taylor flinched at even that small display of affection. "Don't forget about all the paparazzi that swarmed my school. Or the death threats that have been mailed to my house. Or the—"

Tim winced. "Okay, I've got it. Feel free to stop any-time now."

"They *loved* you." I lowered my voice and leaned in so that I could murmur the last part in his ear. "Almost as much as I do."

I pulled back a little to see if he had caught on to the fact that I wasn't joking. I wasn't tossing out the "L" word just to calm his nerves. I meant it. Absolutely.

That was one of the few parts of our relationship that I didn't question.

Whether or not I could handle the fame and the intense public scrutiny and the *huge* life decisions he was making . . . Yeah, those questions kept me up at night. But when I closed my eyes, I always wanted him to be right next to me when I opened them.

Tim squeezed my hand and for a moment I could almost pretend that we were alone.

Until Principal Taylor cleared his throat. "Ahem . . . would either of you like some water? There's some right next to the—" His face momentarily relaxed with relief when my parents picked that moment to enter the room. He was probably afraid that Tim and I would start kissing. In his office. And *then* what would he do?

Perform a religious ceremony with a priest, a clove of garlic, and some holy water to rid the room of its gay vibes, probably.

"Would someone please explain why our son has been banned from attending his own prom?" I half expected frost to issue from my dad as he pinned Principal Taylor with an arctic glare.

I enjoyed watching the relief melt right off Mr. Taylor's face and the fear of my parents slide into place instead.

"Um . . . well, I can understand why you're upset, but Corey hasn't been banned from prom. He's free to attend with all of our other students."

My mom looked at him suspiciously. "Then why were we hounded by reporters?"

"Me," Tim said simply, before he released my hand. "They're here for me. They want to know why I can't accompany my *boyfriend* to his school dance." He glared at Principal Taylor as if daring him to take issue with our relationship.

Apparently, Mr. Taylor hadn't become a high school principal without developing a sense of self-preservation. He carefully chose his words. "It's against Smith High School policy to allow unenrolled individuals to attend functions intended for our students."

I rolled my eyes. "Chelsea Halloway doesn't go to this school anymore and she's been nominated for *prom court.* Want to explain to me how she meets those rules of yours?"

Mr. Taylor cleared his throat. "Chelsea only recently changed school districts after spending three years as a student here. We consider that an extenuating circumstance."

"Well, my boyfriend is a rock star who never got to attend a prom of his own," I snapped. "That seems like an extenuating circumstance to me."

"Easy, tiger," Tim murmured in my ear, but when I looked at him in disbelief, his smile hitched up a little on the left.

"Smith High School policy also does not support the presence of, ahem, *older* individuals."

My dad's eyes narrowed. "A three-year age gap hardly qualifies Timothy for a senior citizen discount. Unless . . . is there something you'd care to tell us, Tim? Are you secretly in your mid-forties?"

"No, sir." Tim struggled not to laugh.

"Well, then, I don't see a problem."

Principal Taylor sucked in a deep breath. "Smith High School policy—"

My mom crossed her arms. "I seriously doubt that no Smith High School student has ever brought a date from a different high school."

"Yes, but Mr. Goff is *not* another student," Mr. Taylor

snapped. "He is a twenty-one-year-old adult who has no business attending a high school function!"

The room fell sickeningly silent as we absorbed his words. Tim instinctively took a step away from me, his shoulders rigid.

My mom's lips thinned. "It's *not* your place to judge my son's relationship. And if you prohibit either one of these boys from attending your school function, you will be slapped with a discrimination suit faster than you can say, *I'm not homophobic.*"

"But I'm not homophobic!" Principal Taylor protested indignantly.

My mom smiled coldly. "That wasn't very convincing. Don't worry, I'm sure you just need to practice saying it. That lie will come tripping off your tongue in no time."

"This has nothing to do with Mr. Goff's, um . . . with his—"

"He's gay," my dad said simply. "So is our son. And you can deny it all you like, but if Corey was a straight girl, this never would have reached your attention. You just don't want to get a reputation for being soft on gays."

"Yes, it's much better to ride hard on gays," Tim managed to say with a straight face. Everyone stared at him in disbelief. "Too soon?"

"Um . . . *yeah.* Way too soon!"

He shrugged. "Just trying to lighten the mood. None of us wants a lawsuit."

"I wouldn't be so sure of that," my mom retorted.

"Prom would be over by the time we even filed the lawsuit. So I'm hoping we can come up with some kind of arrangement that works for everyone."

Principal Taylor nodded vigorously, probably because he was picturing the kind of high-power attorneys that a celebrity like Timothy Goff could afford. "What do you have in mind?"

"Considering that my band was approached by the Smith High School prom committee, I'm assuming that the student body still wants me to perform."

Yeah, that is a pretty safe assumption considering that his last U.S. tour had sold out in a matter of minutes—eighteen of them, to be precise.

"I was also under the impression that there was no age restrictions for the performers. So Corey and I will arrive together, I will play with my band, and then we will go. No Smith High School regulations will be broken, and I will get to enjoy prom with my boyfriend. We all leave happy."

I had to admit, as far as compromises went . . . it wasn't the worst idea.

At least Tim would be able to go to the stupid event without any lawyers having to file briefs or take deposition statements or any of that crap. We would be able to attend my high school prom together—almost.

Since I still wasn't entirely sure *I* even wanted to go to the dance, having my boyfriend negotiate the terms of my attendance with my high school principal was . . . kind of weird. Especially because now I was even more locked into showing up. I could hardly have my boyfriend go through all of this trouble just to suggest that we do something else entirely.

"That sounds manageable to me." Principal Taylor adjusted his tie once more. "I will be sure to update the school board and tell them that we've resolved the issue."

"Great." Tim glanced down at his watch and winced. "Corey, I've got soundcheck in an hour at the Rose Garden. But I'll see you on Friday. I'll be the one with the limo and the corsage." He did a demented half wave to my parents so he wouldn't have to exchange any hugs in my principal's office, and tugged open the door.

Darryl was there in an instant.

Of course. We couldn't even discuss prom together without

having Tim's security guard lurking right outside. Then again, there were two police officers hanging around the waiting room so that they could see me safely back to my car.

"Friday," Tim repeated, shooting me one last sizzling look before he made his exit.

I could hardly wait.

Chapter 6

Now that Spencer King is dating freshman Isobel Peters (*Seriously. A freshman. Someone must be reaching for low-hanging fruit.*), it appears that this year there won't be one power couple for prom—unless Patrick Bradford and his new lady love, Steffani Larson, win over the student body.

Hey, it could happen. Considering the sudden geeky addition to Spencer's life . . . crazier things have happened.

—from "Predicting Prom"
by Lisa Anne Montgomery
Published by *The Smithsonian*

"Are you out of your *freaking* mind? You don't even like Chelsea Halloway!"

Mackenzie glanced up at me sheepishly from her bedroom floor. "Wow, Corey. Way to give me a heads-up. You know there is this thing called knocking. Maybe you've heard of it?"

"There are also these places called mental institutions.

Girls who create posters for their boyfriend's ex-girlfriends should probably live there."

She tried to wipe her hands off on her jeans, but succeeded only in sending glitter flying everywhere. "It's not that weird."

"*Chelsea Halloway for Prom Queen,*" I read aloud. "Seriously, Mackenzie? You can't post these up at school."

Mackenzie shook her head. "No way. I've put too much time and effort and . . . *glitter* into these things not to use them. And I have a very small window of opportunity here. Just because I got Chelsea's name on the prom ballot doesn't mean anyone will actually vote for her."

Careful to avoid any airborne sparkles, I sat cross-legged and checked out her work. The signs looked like they had been created by a well-intentioned preschooler, but I decided to keep that thought to myself.

"Want to tell me why you're campaigning for a girl who single-handedly made your life a living hell for three years?"

Mackenzie rolled her eyes. "You're exaggerating. Chelsea didn't even know I existed for most of that time. And now that she's going to a different high school and has a new boyfriend and y'know—"

"Isn't trying to convince Logan to dump you?" I suggested.

Mackenzie winced. "Right. Well, now that she's not doing *that* anymore, we're actually almost . . . friends."

"Bullshit." I crossed my arms and waited for the truth to come bubbling out of her. Mackenzie has never been particularly good at keeping her own secrets, especially around me.

"Okay, 'friends' might be overstating it a little. We aren't enemies, though."

"And for that she gets campaign posters?" I tapped one of the glittery signs for emphasis. "I don't think so."

"Who else do you think is a contender for the crown?" Mackenzie demanded. "If Fake or Bake wins, one of them will only become more obnoxious—if that's even possible. And if by some fluke, I get a pity nomination because of the whole YouTube thing . . . that's even *worse!*"

"I don't know why you're so against the idea," I said honestly. "I think you'd make a great monarch. Long live, Mackenzie." I pretended to raise a goblet of wine. "Queen of the Geeks!"

Mackenzie laughed. "Thanks, but no thanks. Did you know there is a special dance for the king and queen? Seriously. They rule the dance floor while everyone else gawks at them. That's way too much pressure for me. I'd much rather dance with Logan when nobody is paying any attention to my moves."

I could understand that. If I thought I could avoid all the openmouthed stares by creating a few posters, I'd be coated from head to toe in glitter too. Although I suspected that the decoration on my posters wouldn't look disturbingly like a cross between an octopus and a unicorn.

I picked up a glue bottle to test that theory.

"Do you, uh . . . ever wish you weren't dating Logan?" I asked nonchalantly, as if that were a perfectly normal question. "If the two of you weren't a couple, you wouldn't have to be dealing with all of *this*." My gesture nearly splattered glue everywhere.

"Sure."

I jerked my head up as I searched her familiar brown eyes for any sign that she was messing with me.

"Seriously?"

Mackenzie laughed. "*Of course,* I do! Every time someone gives me a slow once-over and then shakes their head because they still can't figure out what Logan could possibly see in me . . . that hurts. And yeah, my life would be a whole lot simpler without him. I'd have more time for my homework, that's for sure." She glanced ruefully at a stack of textbooks that were piled precariously on top of her desk. "It would be easier to catch up with Jane. Although now that she's busy running *The Wordsmith* and dating Scott, that might be wishful thinking."

"So then why don't you do it?" I sprinkled some pink glitter onto the petals of the flower I had outlined in glue. It wasn't half bad.

Mackenzie looked at me like I'd lost my freaking mind. "Off the top of my head? Because he makes me laugh and he doesn't care that I'm America's Most Awkward Girl. He wants to be with *me*, even when I make a complete idiot out of myself in front of his ex-girlfriend . . . even when I'm a total wreck after seeing my dad. And I don't want to change him either. Not his dyslexia, or his popularity, or even his past with Chelsea freaking Halloway." She glanced away from the rose taking shape on my poster and then glared at what I assumed was a horribly misshapen heart on hers. "Don't you feel that way about Tim?"

"Tim never dated Chelsea freaking Halloway," I said evasively. "I'm pretty sure he'd have mentioned her by now if he did."

Mackenzie laughed. "Probably. Although the two of them would have the most insanely beautiful children the world has ever seen."

I had no trouble picturing a little toddler with Chelsea's huge blue eyes and Tim's thick jet-black hair. Fast forward a few years and the kid would probably be ruling the preschool through sheer force of will—when not crawling the red carpet, of course.

"Okay, so I will never suggest using her as a surrogate," I said, pretending to really have to think it through. "I can live with that."

Mackenzie nodded. "The human race thanks you. But seriously . . . how are things with Tim?"

I began creating a long stem for the rose and then added thorns. Lots and lots of thorns. "In the wise words of Facebook: It's complicated."

"Yeah? Well, why don't you talk and we'll try to uncomplicate it."

That was the reason I had driven to Mackenzie's house, but now I wasn't sure I wanted to speak. Hanging out with one of my best friends was comforting. Just the two of us. It was so easy to pretend that nothing had changed.

"I don't know, Mackenzie!" The words tumbled out in a rush. "I have no freaking clue, okay? Is that what you wanted to hear? Tim just *does* things and then he expects me to get onboard with them. I kept telling myself the problem was that we were long-distance or that we could never get alone time together . . . but I think it's me. Or maybe it's *him*. I don't know anymore."

"Wow," Mackenzie said. "Okay. Here's a crazy idea: Have you tried talking to him about this?"

I squirted way too much glue onto one of the posters, leaving a goopy mess that rivaled Mackenzie's ugliest attempts at flowers. "When *exactly* do you think I should bring it up?" I growled sarcastically. "Right after he said he wanted to uproot the band to Portland for me? Or maybe in the principal's office when he negotiated our prom experience in front of my parents. I know, I should totally bring all of this up at prom. Nothing like getting into a huge fight in front of the *entire* school."

"Are you so sure you'd get into a huge fight?" Mackenzie asked tentatively. "He loves you, Corey. There's got to be a way to work this out."

"Do you know how to call off the paparazzi constantly hounding us? Because if you do, I'm all ears."

Mackenzie grabbed my hand, preventing me from sprinkling blue glitter on the blob and forcing me to meet her eyes. I instantly wished I hadn't glanced up, because the concern in them was almost too much for me.

"If you can't handle the rock star lifestyle, there is no shame in that," Mackenzie said quietly. "Not everyone is cut out for a life in the spotlight. Trust me, I get it. Just like not everyone can handle a relationship with someone in the military. It doesn't mean you don't love him."

"I thought love was supposed to triumph over everything."

Mackenzie nodded, but her smile twisted with sympathy at the bitter words. "Yeah, but that doesn't mean the timing can't suck."

I rubbed my face absentmindedly with my hand, realizing too late that I'd just coated myself in glitter. "God, I can't believe I'm acting like this! Remember when we mocked kids who thought they met the love of their life in high school? When exactly did I become one of those idiots?"

Mackenzie laughed. "Hey, right there with you. Sometimes I still glance at Logan and think, *Um . . . sorry. When exactly did he fall for me? Can someone explain how that happened?*" She gestured at the posters sprawled out at our feet. "I'm making prom posters for *Chelsea Halloway!* I think it's safe to say that nothing has turned out the way I expected."

"You really think you'll be together with Logan in college?" I felt like a jerk for even asking the question, for putting voice to a fear that probably crept in whenever she poured over college brochures.

She shrugged. "I hope so. But even if we're not . . . it won't change the way I feel about him right now. That's enough for me."

I laughed hoarsely. "Okay, who are you and what have you done to my geeky best friend?"

Mackenzie grinned, dipped her finger in a thick puddle of glue, and swiped the tip of her nose with it. "How's that? Recognize me now?"

"Nope, but I think you're getting closer."

She nodded and released red glitter, except instead of coating the tip of her nose, she accidentally breathed some of it in. "Oh crap. Bad life decision. Very bad life decision!" Mackenzie managed to say as her nostrils flared wildly. "You don't have to laugh quite that hard at me, you jerk!"

But I did.

"I love you, Mackenzie."

She looked like an elementary school kid who had gotten a bit overenthusiastic with a Valentine's Day project, but she accepted my statement with a nod.

"I love you too. Always have, always will. Now, will you *please* help me finish these stupid posters?"

Yeah, that I could handle.

Chapter 7

Nominating the prom court has never been so contentious at Smith High School! In years past, it was accepted that students would simply vote for their friends. Now the school is covered with posters for members of the junior class—one of whom doesn't even go to this school!

—from "Courting the Vote,"
by Lisa Anne Montgomery
Published by *The Smithsonian*

I agreed to drive Mackenzie back to school in the dead of night.

Well, okay, it was more like eleven o'clock by the time we got there, but it felt a whole lot later. Maybe because we had spent hours bedazzling every inch of the posters. They still looked like the work of amateurs to me, but I was hoping that would win over the "nonconformist" kids at our school.

I didn't really see anything nonconformist about wearing lots of black and trying to out-indie their friends by listening exclusively to bands they had found from low-budget movie soundtracks. But it was entirely possible that they would be the swing vote that determined who'd get the crown.

Which meant that it was essential we kept our identities a secret. Mackenzie's plan would only work if voting for Chelsea seemed like an obscure prank that the out-crowd was pulling on the current batch of Notables. So even though Smith High School was pretty much the last place on earth I wanted to be on a Thursday night—or ever for that matter—I patiently taped a sign that read, CHELSEA HALLOWAY MIGHT NOT DESTROY YOU . . . BUT WHY TAKE THE CHANCE? to the outside of the cafeteria.

"Are you sure about this one, Mackenzie?" I asked, trying to keep the skepticism out of my voice.

Mackenzie admired our handiwork. "Definitely. I think it strikes just the right amount of fear."

"I thought you were against underhanded tactics."

Mackenzie shrugged. "If there's one thing I've learned from politics, it's never to underestimate the power of blowing a valid concern way out of proportion. And when it comes to Chelsea . . . they should be afraid. Very afraid."

I burst out laughing. "Well, it's definitely more original than the fliers Patrick and Steffani handed out yesterday. Did you know they were dating? I only found out when I saw them acting all couple-y by the ticket booth." I gestured at the glossy poster of the Notables that was taped only inches away from Mackenzie's creation. "Maybe I should make a little addition?"

Mackenzie crossed her arms and examined Patrick's pearly-white smile as if she were in a modern art museum trying to make sense out of a particularly bizarre exhibit. "What do you have in mind?"

"We could always adjust their tag line," I suggested. "*Let's Make Prom Better Together* seems like faulty advertising to me. Let's Make Prom *Bitchier* Together, on the other hand—"

She shook her head regretfully. "As lovely as that sounds, I want to beat them in a fair fight."

I shrugged. Maybe my willingness to draw a mustache on Steffani's upper lip meant that my moral compass was skewed. But after all the crap those two Notables had put my friends through, I didn't really care. As far as I was concerned, the jerks had it coming. "Your call, Mackenzie. But keep in mind that prom voting will begin"—I glanced down at my watch—"nine hours from now."

"I doubt anyone is buying into their Abercrombie and Fitch ad campaign. So I am way more curious about the money trail."

"The *what?*"

Mackenzie pointed at Steffani's face. "This picture has obviously been retouched, airbrushed, and professionally Photoshopped. Considering that they weren't even dating two days ago, that's a pretty tall order for a photographer. Jane told me that Scott was impressed with the quick turnaround. So how exactly did they afford it?"

I couldn't stop myself from rolling my eyes. "They're *Notables,* Mackenzie. I'm sure their parents agreed to foot the bill."

She didn't stop staring at the poster as she considered my explanation. "I don't think their parents are loaded. Remember when Patrick accused me of being a gold digger for liking Logan instead of him?"

"Yeah, because when I think of you, 'gold digger' is totally the first adjective that comes to mind," I scoffed. "That guy is an idiot."

"No debate here. But if his parents would pay for a huge expenditure like this, why would he ever consider money as a factor?"

That was Mackenzie; always trying to find a reasonable explanation for everything. Even when the answer couldn't be any more obvious.

"You hurt his manly pride." I thumped my chest with a closed fist. "We're a whole lot more sensitive than we like to let on."

Mackenzie rolled her eyes. "I refuse to dignify any of that with a response."

I grinned. "You're overthinking this. Patrick wanted to get back at you for turning him down. That simple."

"I guess . . ." Mackenzie looked far from certain. "It's weird that he's trying this hard to be voted prom king, though, right?"

I burst out laughing. *"You are trying even harder to get Chelsea Halloway elected prom queen!"*

"Yeah, but that's different."

"Newsflash, Mackenzie: Not everyone lives in fear of big social events. Some people even look forward to them." I pointed at the smarmy smile on Patrick's face. "Case in point."

"What about you, Corey? Do you want to be crowned prom king?" The laughter on Mackenzie's face vanished when I didn't immediately answer. "Holy crap. That honestly didn't occur to me until right this second. I am the worst friend ever." She grabbed my arm and began pulling me toward the deserted parking lot. "If we go back to my place right now, we can make half a dozen posters for you before school starts. I can also—"

"Wow, Mackenzie. Calm down, okay? I don't want to be crowned prom king."

She stared up at me intently, searching for any sign that I might be lying. "Are you sure about that, Corey?"

I pictured the big romantic scene featured in most high school movies, the majority of which involved a staircase, a spotlight, and a stunning ballgown. The dress didn't do anything for me, but the thought of that one perfect moment— yeah, I wanted it. I could picture it too. Having my name called out . . . climbing the stairs onto the podium . . . spotting a beaming Tim standing right next to Mackenzie and Jane. And yeah, in real life, I'd probably hear Alex Thompson snarl, *Who voted for the homo?* while everyone else pretended not to notice.

But what really sucked was knowing that even if I landed the crown, I wouldn't be allowed to dance with my boyfriend.

I shuddered. "Positive. Now can we please get out of here? This place gives me the creeps."

Mackenzie glanced around the empty school and a mischievous twinkle sparkled in her eyes. "Do you think it's haunted by the ghosts of unhappy high school students?" She raised her arms and altered her voice to make it sound more otherworldly. "Corrreeeey! I am coommming for yooooouuuu!"

I knew it was stupid, but I scrambled to put more space between us as I headed for the car. "Very funny, Mackenzie."

"Whoooo issss thisssss Mackenziieeee?"

"I hate you right now."

"Ammm I offfennnding yooooour mannnnnly pride?" Her voice cracked with laughter on the "manly," but that only made it sound creepier.

I briefly considered lying, but decided to go with the truth. "Absolutely. If you keep this up, you'll be finding your own ride home."

"Okay." Mackenzie instantly dropped her arms back to her sides. "Would now be a good time to mention that I'm thinking of dipping into my college fund for a car?"

I raised an eyebrow. "What does that have to do with anything?"

"I was kind of hoping I could practice my driving. In your car. What do you think, buddy?"

I burst out laughing. "Never going to happen. Not until you can tell your left from your right without thinking about it for fifteen minutes."

"I'm not *that* bad."

I pretended to seriously consider the request. "True, you're worse."

She shifted back into her zombie pose and I gave up on all pretense of manliness by sprinting for my car as Mackenzie snickered at my retreat. I couldn't shake the feeling that someday I'd think back to my time in high school and this chilly night, dodging my best friend while we acted like complete idiots, would be one of the few memories I'd recall without fighting the urge to cringe.

The real question was whether prom would make that list too.

Chapter 8

Okay, we get it already! Some delusional, artistically challenged people at Smith High School want Chelsea Halloway to be crowned queen. It's not going to happen.
So get over it!

—from "No Way, Chelsea!"
by Lisa Anne Montgomery
Published by *The Smithsonian Online Edition*

"Oh, Chelsea is going to *love* this."
I glanced from last night's handiwork to the amused expression on Jane's face as she whipped out her cell phone and snapped a photo. "She swears that she has nothing to do with it, but she might just be covering her tracks so I'm not tempted to slip it into the school paper."

That was part of the reason Mackenzie and I had decided to keep our mouths shut. If some crazy gun-wielding maniac came at me, I could easily imagine Jane shoving me to the ground and taking the bullet. But secret keeping wasn't exactly her forte. And ever since she had created the school's fiction paper, *The Wordsmith,* I began pinpointing the real-life inspiration behind her stories.

It was best for everyone if the creator of Chelsea's posters remained a mystery.

"It's definitely . . . something," I said lamely.

Jane was too distracted by an incoming text to notice my uncharacteristically bland response. "Chelsea says she'll see me tonight at prom. Apparently she's bringing Houston with her." A wide smile spread across her whole face. "Is it wrong to hope that she has a showdown with Fake and Bake there?"

"Nope, I think we should make a betting pool too."

Jane snorted. "What idiot wouldn't put their money on Chelsea? Just because she doesn't go here anymore doesn't mean she's any less"—Jane flapped her hands as she searched for the right adjective—"Chelsea-ish. Speaking of prom . . . are you going with Tim? All I've heard are rumors."

I hoped that any second now the bell would ring and I'd have an excuse to leave all prom-related questions unanswered.

No such luck.

"The guys have agreed to perform at prom. That's all I know." I shrugged, but the tension in my shoulders made the movement stiff.

Jane looked worried. "Well, the cops have created a barricade to prevent the press from mobbing you here. Hopefully there will be added security at the prom too."

I ruffled her mop of red hair. "I'm going to be fine, Jane."

She instinctively rose up on tiptoe and pulled me into a hug. "I know. I'm just sorry you have to deal with all of this craziness." We both heard the distinctive click of a camera, and Jane automatically released me and stepped back. "This is *not* a moment you need to capture, Scott."

Her boyfriend merely grinned. "I disagree, Grammar Girl. It's definitely a Hallmark card waiting to happen."

She groaned and shot me an apologetic, *I'm sorry my boyfriend is bothering you* look.

"Corey might not appreciate having you take his photo without any warning, Scott. Especially since the paparazzi are all waiting in the parking lot for him to make his exit."

And wasn't that just going to be a blast for everyone. I still couldn't believe I'd managed to sneak away to Mackenzie's house unnoticed yesterday. I was willing to bet that the only reason I'd managed to get a temporary reprieve from being in the public eye was because everyone expected me to make it to the Rose Garden for Tim's show.

After all, what kind of boyfriend doesn't show up to watch his partner deliver an amazing performance to a stadium full of people?

The kind who was too busy putting glitter onto prom court campaign posters, apparently.

"Sorry," Scott said, as if it hadn't really occurred to him that either of us would object. "But the shot was too good to pass up. I'll send you a copy later."

The bell rang before I got the chance to tell him, *Thanks, but I've seen more than enough pictures of myself lately—usually plastered on magazine covers. I'm going to pass.*

"Catch you later, Corey." Jane slipped her hand into Scott's right before both of them strolled toward their English class. I couldn't move. I stared transfixed at their retreating figures.

They made it look so . . . easy.

The handholding, the way they looked at each other with their emotions right on the surface for anyone to see—all of it was totally out in the open.

No hiding. No fear.

No shame.

I wanted that kind of freedom with Tim. To walk down the hallways of my high school, or a street, or even to go to a freaking ice skating rink without having our every move scrutinized. Mackenzie's words from the night before haunted me.

If you can't handle the rock star lifestyle, there is no shame in that.

It doesn't mean you don't love him.

Some freshman kid I'd never met snapped a photo of me on his phone before he turned and walked away. He didn't even acknowledge me with so much as a nod. It was as if I ceased to exist once he had the picture.

"And a Merrrry Christmas to you!" I hollered after him, just because it felt good to yell something. "*Have a Happy freaking Hanukkah!*"

"Um . . . I'm pretty sure you're either really late or ridiculously early for that." I twisted around and saw Isobel smiling at me. "But don't let that stop you." She pitched her voice louder. "*Enjoy Kwanzaa while you're at it, jerk!*"

I burst out laughing, which was probably her plan from the beginning. "Want me to walk you to class?" she offered, before nervously shoving her glasses higher up her nose. "I was already planning on tracking you down. I've got a question for you."

"Okay, let's hear it."

She nibbled on her bottom lip as we began to move with a tide of other students. "Well . . . how big a deal is this whole prom thing? I bought tickets before I really considered the dress code."

"You do realize that being gay doesn't automatically make me fascinated with fashion, right?"

Isobel burst out laughing. "Of course! That's why I'm not asking everyone in the gay/straight alliance to fill out a questionnaire. I'm asking *you*. Now . . . some people wear sneakers, right?"

I stared at her. "Nobody wears sneakers."

"But . . . let's say, *hypothetically* that someone were to wear them, would that be, y'know, terrible?"

"Terrible? Compared to what, exactly? Famine?" I fought a losing battle with my laughter and Isobel's mouth quirked up into a self-deprecating grin.

"Definitely famine. I'm thinking sneakers are better than sex trafficking . . . hate crimes . . . sitting next to Fake and Ba—Ashely and Steffani—at the Notable table. All of the above, really."

"How can you even joke about sharing a meal with those two!" I went heavy on the sarcasm. "They can ruin anyone's appetite."

"So . . . what do you think? About the sneakers," Isobel prompted when I looked at her blankly. "Do I have to wear heels or not?"

Her expression was deadly serious, which made no sense because I had never once seen her express any interest in dressing up. To be fair, most of my friends looked at makeovers as the worst fate in the world. Mackenzie had blanched when I'd tried to update her wardrobe, and Jane had inched toward the exit when she received a similar treatment. But Isobel was in a whole other league; she practically *lived* in her sweatshirts.

And I couldn't shake the feeling that if she wore anything else, she'd spend the majority of her time adjusting her glasses and trying to convince herself that she hadn't made a huge mistake.

"I don't think you need my advice, Isobel."

"I kind of want to surprise Spencer." She lowered her voice as if there was something excruciatingly embarrassing about that confession. "We're not really dating. I mean, okay . . . we're kind of dating. Maybe."

"Well, that clears things right up," I said dryly.

"We're friends who . . . okay, we really like making out." She squirmed uncomfortably. "No judgment, please."

I raised my hands defensively. "Hey, no judgment here! I think it's great. And for what it's worth, I don't think you need heels."

"Really?" Isobel looked so relieved I tried my best to silence my inner fashion critic.

"Absolutely. You might want to consider finding a cute pair of flats . . . but if sneakers make *you* feel confident, who cares what anyone else thinks? Be yourself."

Isobel looked relieved. "Okay. Thanks, Corey. I'm not sure what to expect."

I smiled back at her. "You're probably going to be one of only a handful of freshman there. Mackenzie and Logan will be doing their whole *I can't take my eyes off of you* thing, while Jane and Scott sniff out a story for *The Smithsonian*. So if at any point you find yourself needing some backup, count me in."

"Thanks, Corey." She lifted her chin proudly. "I doubt either of us will need it, but the same offer goes for you. I'll see you later, okay?"

She disappeared inside a classroom and the rest of my day passed without any surprises.

Mostly, I sat in uncomfortably hard plastic chairs while I pretended to listen to lectures, although I managed a jaunty wave for the paparazzi waiting outside to swarm me despite the police barricade before I drove home. I pulled right into the garage where my parents used to park before my personal life became breaking news, and headed for my room. I could have called Mackenzie and sought refuge at her place again, but I'd probably be stuck listening while she tutored Logan in American history.

Even knowing that Mackenzie *wanted* me to throw the vote to Chelsea, I'd still felt kind of disloyal selecting her for prom queen during second period. Not that any of it should matter, considering that this wasn't even our senior prom.

But nobody had objected to having the school's attention focused on a bunch of juniors. The only explanation I could come up with to explain the absence of Notable seniors was that Chelsea had managed to scare them into silence during her reign at Smith High School. And then the older students had failed to fill the power vacuum in Chelsea's absence as quickly as Fake and Bake.

I didn't want to discuss any of that with my friends, though.

Not who they thought would get the crown, not what they should wear—none of it. I didn't even want to speculate on whether we were all setting ourselves up for disappointment by creating unrealistic expectations. All of that conversation required an emotional energy that I just didn't have to spare.

So I set my cell phone on silent before tossing it onto a pile of homework on my desk. And just to be sure I didn't obsess over who was calling—or more importantly, who was *not* calling—I cranked up my music and spent some quality time staring at my ceiling.

If you can't handle the rock star lifestyle . . .

Telling the Mackenzie in my head to shut up was even less effective than saying it to the actual girl. I could picture her glaring at me hotly before ordering me to figure out my problem and get over it.

I tried to find a solution, but every time I even considered breaking up with Tim, it felt like I couldn't breathe. I was suffocating right there on the bed. It hurt. This wasn't a sting or a pang—it was a bone-deep *ache* that I couldn't push away. And believe me, I tried. I rehashed every time I'd been stuck waiting for him to finish greeting a swarm of fans. Every time we were interrupted during a meal, a walk . . . a kiss. Every time I saw my face plastered in a magazine with the caption *Rock Star Relationship on the Rocks?* and wondered if there was something they knew that I didn't.

I replayed in slow, excruciating detail how I had felt when our relationship was first leaked to the press and Tim had denied the whole thing.

How he had thrown me under the bus.

And the stupid part was that it still didn't hurt enough to make me walk away.

Not when I also remembered the rough desperation in his apology, the audible catch in his throat when he said that he'd understand if it was too much to forgive. That he missed me. That he wanted me back. That he was crazy about me and would happily shout it from the nearest Hollywood mansion, if I would please, *please,* give him a second chance.

I rubbed my jaw and imagined staking my claim somewhere on his gorgeous body. Maybe a love bite right above his heart. I grinned as I pictured the slightly stunned expression I wanted on his face as I kissed my way down his neck . . . if we were ever to get a moment of privacy.

Making out with my boyfriend wouldn't be nearly as much fun with Darryl stationed at the door.

Groaning in self-disgust, I gave in to the temptation to check my phone for missed calls.

I had two text messages waiting for me.

HEY, COREY, I AM STUCK IN MEETINGS WITH
THE GUYS. I WILL CALL YOU LATER.

It never failed to amuse me the level of care and attention Tim put into even the shortest text messages. He never abbreviated words, even when he was in a hurry to get somewhere. I'd even seen him squint at his screen while being mobbed by fans, because he felt the need to make sure every apostrophe was in the right place.

The second text was more to the point.

I LOVE YOU.

My stomach sank with guilt. I couldn't bring myself to type the words back to him. Not when Mackenzie's voice still resounded far too clearly in my head.

If you can't handle the rock star lifestyle ... it doesn't mean you don't love him.

I wasn't entirely sure I believed her.

So instead I wrote, I CAN'T WAIT TO SEE YOU AT PROM! and hoped that the exclamation point would sell the enthusiasm that I hadn't been able to muster. But that would change. As soon as I put on my suit, I would definitely get into the spirit of things.

Of course, I would.

Except it didn't happen.

Not even when I received a series of frantic texts from Mackenzie, although I grinned as the tone of the messages swiftly changed from pleading to threatening.

GET OVER HERE, COREY. NOW.

JUST BECAUSE I'VE NEVER KILLED A MAN

DOESN'T MEAN I CAN'T!

It felt good to be needed. Too bad I instantly regretted agreeing to give my help when Mackenzie flung open her door, took one look at me, and said, "Oh, thank God," before she dragged me inside. I tried to stall in the hallway.

"Um . . . what's going on here?"

"See for yourself." Mackenzie grimaced. "And then please work your magic and make it stop."

She didn't release her grip on my suit jacket until I had passed the threshold to her bedroom.

It looked like her closet had exploded. There were dresses and skirts dangling off nearly every surface, and in the midst of the wreckage sat Isobel Peters, looking completely unruffled in a pair of dingy Converse sneakers. The only other person in the room who looked equally calm was Dylan, and

I suspected that was because he cared even less about prom than I did.

"I'm not going to let you do this, Izzie," Melanie said, as she rifled through another one of Mackenzie's drawers. "You are *not* wearing sneakers and jeans to prom."

"Corey said I should do it."

Melanie shot me a withering glare. "Well, that shows what he knows!"

"Hey," I said defensively. "Let's keep me out of this, okay?"

Dylan mouthed, *"Welcome to hell,"* at me, but the cat that ate the canary smile on his face betrayed that he was loving every second of this. It wasn't exactly hard to pinpoint that the source of his amusement was the same freshman girl who looked ready to bite my head off.

"You are going to have a great time, Izzie," Melanie said fiercely. "You are going to have the best prom ever documented in the *history* of proms!"

I glanced over at Mackenzie. "You're the history geek. Is there a written account of every prom stored somewhere? This is the first I've heard of it."

Mackenzie grinned. "Oh yeah, the History of Prom goes *waaay* back. Legend has it that the best one occurred in 1968 in No Name, Colorado."

"You're both hilarious." Melanie kept rifling through the few items still hanging in Mackenzie's closet. "We have less than an hour before Logan and Spencer show up. So, will you *please* help me help her?"

"I'm fine going like this, Mel. I promise."

Melanie crossed her arms. "I do *not* want you feeling out of place while you watch from the sidelines."

Isobel laughed. "Um . . . Mel? Story of my life."

"You deserve the very best of everything." The ferocity in Melanie's voice made it clear she had no intention of backing down. It might have taken her months to work up the courage to date Dylan, but her aggressive side had no trouble taking center stage around Isobel.

"Right now, I want to enjoy the very best in comfortable footwear," Isobel said dryly. "Why don't you help Mackenzie instead? Or maybe Corey needs . . . something?"

Melanie snorted. "Corey looks like he jumped off the pages of *GQ* in that suit."

Which was the whole reason I had bought it in the first place. Tim had invited me to a red carpet event in L.A., so I had gone out and made sure the suit fit me *perfectly*. I wasn't going to give anyone an excuse to toss me onto a Worst Dressed list. Not that it had mattered. There had been some kind of scheduling conflict or something—I hadn't listened too closely after Tim said, 'I'm so sorry, Corey. There's no way I can make it . . .' "

"And Mackenzie will get a double take from Logan in that blue dress," Melanie continued. "So you can't distract me with them, Izzie!"

Isobel sighed. "I'll make you a deal, Mel. If at any point I find myself wishing I had taken your advice, you can pick my outfit next year. I'll even let you take me dress shopping."

"Deal!" Mackenzie grabbed a handful of blouses off the floor and shoved them in Melanie's arms. "Agree to her terms, Melanie."

"Fine, Izzie. But that *includes* footwear!"

"No heels higher than two inches."

Melanie blew out an exasperated huff but nodded in agreement.

"Good," Mackenzie said with heartfelt relief. "Maybe while we're gone you could"—she gestured at her room— "make it look less like my room was tossed in a drug bust?"

There was no response from Melanie, probably because she'd been distracted the second Dylan moved to the closet and snagged a handful of hangers.

"Melanie?"

"Uh-huh . . ." she mumbled. "Drug bust. Sure. No problem."

Mackenzie grinned, probably fighting the urge to pull her little brother and his girlfriend into a big group hug. So I distracted her by checking my phone.

"The guys should be here soon, right?"

Isobel nodded. "Spencer talked Logan into ditching the limo idea. I guess he wanted more freedom in case the two of us, uh, decide to leave early." She blushed slightly. "He said they'd be here around seven. Although he also mentioned something about going out for dinner, so I'm not sure when we'll actually get to the dance. What about you?" She twisted toward the door with a sudden jolt of excitement. "Wait. Is Timothy Goff going to meet you *here?*"

"No, he couldn't get out of a meeting. So . . . I'll just see him there!" I tried to keep my voice upbeat, but I knew I wasn't fooling Mackenzie. I wasn't fooling myself either.

There had been a small part of me that had hoped we could walk into the dance together. That we'd be able to enter the rented-out ballroom space like every other high school couple.

But once again, I'd been sidelined.

And now I didn't even have the consolation prize of a limo ride with my friends.

The doorbell rang, so I pasted on a big smile and went to open the door.

Then I stepped aside so I could watch the reactions of the guys at the door to two of the smartest, nicest . . . geekiest girls I'd ever met.

Chapter 9

It should go without saying, but there is definitely a right and wrong way to dress for prom.

For girls: Dresses. Long, short, slinky, sophisticated . . . just make sure it covers all the essentials, please. And wear heels.

For boys: No jeans. No sneakers. No sweatpants.

Let's all try to exceed expectations, shall we?

—from "Dressed to Impress,"
by Lisa Anne Montgomery
Published by *The Smithsonian Online Edition*

Logan looked like he'd been Tasered.

He was momentarily slack-jawed as he stared at Mackenzie, who for once didn't trip over her own feet. "You look . . . um . . ."

Mackenzie grinned up at him cheekily and then adjusted the bodice of the dress, which really didn't need any straightening. "That good, huh?"

Logan pulled her up against him. "Definitely."

Whatever Mackenzie was going to say was cut off as Isobel emerged from the bedroom and locked eyes on Spencer. After the whole va-va-voom moment Mackenzie had had with Logan, I wasn't sure what to expect. For half a second I was worried Spencer would ruin the whole night by saying something like, "Um . . . I can wait for you to change," but then I realized his smile hadn't wavered an inch.

"Hey, Belle."

"Hey, hotshot. Nice corsage."

Spencer glanced down at his wrist as if he had completely forgotten the flowers. "Well, since you did the inviting, I thought it was only fair that I get to keep the flowers."

"Oh, absolutely." Isobel took hold of his hand and began tugging him toward the exit. "Well, it's been fun, everyone, but I think Spencer owes me a slice of pizza."

"Extra anchovies, if anyone is interested." Spencer dodged a playful mock punch. "No takers? Excellent. See you later."

Pausing only for a brief wave good-bye, Isobel and Spencer raced toward his car and the last I heard was her chortling, "I beat you! I won fair and square, hotshot!" before they climbed inside and drove away.

"I guess the sneakers were a good call, then." Melanie shook her head as if that would help her process what she had just witnessed. "Looks like you were right, Corey."

"That shouldn't come as a surprise," I said haughtily, knowing that it would get a laugh out of Mackenzie.

"And on that note . . . we're off too."

"Hold up, Mackenzie." Dylan pulled out a camera. "Mom's working a late shift tonight, so she made me promise. Get into formation."

"Why don't we leave the photography to Scott? I'm sure he'll be taking photos at prom. . . ."

"Not good enough. Say cheese, Mackenzie."

She managed a pretty frozen-looking smile, but that

changed when Logan gripped her waist and dipped her into a dramatic kiss.

Dylan snapped a few photos before he started to get uncomfortable. "Could you hold off on making out with my sister? Please. This is . . . just . . . no."

Logan straightened, but still kept Mackenzie pressed flush against him. Dylan might have had a problem with it, but Mackenzie certainly didn't. She was absolutely glowing, and it had nothing to do with her outfit.

"Okay, so *now* we're leaving," Logan said smoothly as he held open the door for Mackenzie. I wasn't sure if she was weak-kneed from that kiss or if the heels just brought out her clumsy side, but she took one step and nearly fell on her face.

"See you at the dance, Corey," she managed to say as if she had planned to trip all along.

And then it was just me—standing in the hallway of Mackenzie's house—playing the role of third wheel for a couple who definitely wanted me gone.

"Good seeing you, Corey." Dylan clapped me on the back as he escorted me to the porch. "Have a great night."

Melanie's eyes were lit with excitement and I couldn't hide a smile of my own. "You too."

Dylan shut the door in my face, but I could still hear Melanie protest, "*Dylan!* You can't just throw him—"

The sudden silence left no question in my mind that they wouldn't be discussing me for the rest of the night. They were so freaking cute together that I smiled as I climbed into my car, although the grin faded as I drove aimlessly around Forest Grove. The dance wouldn't begin for another hour, but I couldn't bring myself to go out to eat. I didn't want to sit alone in my well-tailored suit and pretend that I enjoyed the isolation.

Table for one, please. Oh yes, I do have a date. He just can't be seen in public with me at the event.

So I killed some time winding around the residential areas

and glancing in the rearview mirror to check that I didn't have anyone tailing the car. I assumed the press was too busy following Tim to spare much attention for me, but I had been wrong on that count before. Which was why I drove into Portland and passed the Leftbank Annex without even trying to find a parking space. Sure enough, there was a crowd of paparazzi staking out the entrance and they didn't appear to be enjoying their conversation with the bouncer on duty. Or maybe it was Darryl, it was kind of hard for me to tell for sure.

One thing was clear, I'd be safe once I got inside—or at least as safe as I could be in a place where jerks like Alex Thompson planned on making an appearance. So I drove into the attached parking lot and braced myself for the inevitable.

"Over here, Corey!"

"Are you meeting Timothy Goff?"

"What designer are you wearing, Corey?"

I ducked my head and tried to push past them, but it was a whole lot harder to maneuver than it looks in magazines. Never again would I mock the whole *maybe if I put my hand in front of my face you'll just go away* approach. Because I was seconds away from barreling straight ahead, and damn the consequences.

The security guard was swearing a blue streak, the paparazzi were muscling their way toward me, and just when I began to seriously consider making a hasty retreat—texting Tim to say, *Hey, I think this is one high school ritual I'd rather sit out. Have fun for me!*—I saw a flash of sparkly hot pink and a hand reached out of nowhere, grabbed onto my suit, and yanked me forward.

I blinked, desperately trying to adjust to the dim lighting despite the Technicolor circles that danced before me from the camera flashes.

It was Sam.

She was wearing an enormous poofy ballgown that stopped abruptly around her calf, highlighting a seriously kickass pair of combat boots and a sash with lettering I couldn't quite read. Sam's eyelids were coated with so much glittering gold eye shadow that for a second I wasn't entirely sure if my eyes were still playing tricks on me or if her lips were really stained a dark vermillion hue.

Nobody else at Smith High School could ever have pulled off that look.

"*CHARGE!*" Sam hollered, probably fulfilling a lifelong dream of hers in the process as the two of us forced our way to the door. The bouncer opened the doors and practically shoved us inside.

Not that I could blame him. There was no way he was being paid enough to make up for the inconvenience of keeping a horde of paparazzi at bay. And to the best of my knowledge, the screaming ReadySet fans had yet to make an appearance. They were hard to ignore, screeching at decibels that made everyone within a fifty-foot radius—dogs included— want to turn tail and run.

My knees locked up of their own accord about five feet from the door and I leaned against the wall while I tried to reclaim my sense of equilibrium. The dancing spots were still messing up my vision, and as they cleared I realized that my entrance hadn't gone unobserved.

All the upperclassman at Smith High School were staring at me in disbelief.

Yeah, when I pictured making a splash at my first prom, it was never as the kid who couldn't stop shaking, sweating, or gasping for air after a ten-minute altercation with some celebrity gossip hunters.

Although having Sam standing right next to me definitely helped. Half of the people who snickered as they glanced at me shut the hell up when they looked at her.

I made a quick mental note never to underestimate the power of combat boots.

"Thanks, Sam. I really appreciate your—" I interrupted myself when I caught a good look at her sash. "Does that say *Condom Queen?*"

" 'Condom Fairy Godmother' wouldn't fit," Sam told me by way of explanation. When she didn't see even the smallest spark of understanding in my eyes, she pulled out a wand and waved it at me. "Bibbidi-bobbidi-boo! Safe, consensual sex for you!"

She opened the clasp on a rather large handbag and flourished a long string of condoms. With one easy motion, she ripped two of them off and tucked them into my suit pocket.

"You're welcome."

"Um . . . are you for real with this?"

"As real as an unplanned pregnancy." Sam's face twisted. "Okay, so that's not something you need to worry about. But that doesn't mean there aren't STDs and—"

"Oh, will you look at that." I took a hurried step back and glanced around at the students milling around. "People. Other people who are not discussing this. I think I should go say hello to them."

"Real as . . . oh, hello, Principal Taylor. Good to see you. I assume you didn't storm over here just to admire my sash."

Had it been anyone else, I would've doubled back to provide some moral support. But there was no doubt in my mind that Principal Taylor would be the one walking away with a killer headache.

"Your sash violates the school dress code, Samantha."

"Interesting. You know who else is in violation? Ashley McGrady and Steffani Larson. They are *definitely* showing more cleavage than the school dress code allows. So I will stand here and wait while you discuss it with them."

Shaking my head with a mixture of disbelief and pure admiration, I moved past the photobooth and the ridiculously long line of eager-looking couples and headed straight for my boyfriend. I couldn't see him, but I knew exactly where he was standing.

Tim was never all that difficult to locate; I simply had to look for the biggest, loudest . . . shrillest group of girls in the room.

"Ohmigod, ohmigod, ohmigod!"

"I love you, Tim!"

"I listened to your song, "To Get Her/Together" about a *thousand* times when I was breaking up with my boyfriend. I don't know how I would have gotten through it without you."

"Can you sign my back?"

I pushed my way through the flock of his female admirers until there was nothing between us. Well, nothing except the full attention of a room full of high school students and faculty members . . . not to mention the fact that we were one Instagram photo away from the eyes of the nation.

"Hey, handsome." Tim's eyes gleamed and for one moment everything was absolutely perfect. All those hours I had spent agonizing over our relationship now seemed unbelievably stupid—downright pathetic, even—because Tim? Yeah, he was amazing.

"Hey, yourself." I couldn't resist reaching out and brushing some imaginary lint off his shoulder. "Fancy seeing you here. You sure you wouldn't rather crash a rapper's party or something?"

"Yeah . . . I debated with myself for a while. It was either this or a poker night with Jay-Z, but he's busy with Blue Ivy so . . . no dice."

I laughed. "I'm glad you chose me."

Tim didn't so much as blink. "Always."

"Well, if it isn't our second favorite Oregonian," ReadySet drummer, Dominic Wyatt, called out. "It's been too long, Corey. Hey, have you seen Mackenzie?"

"Not since she left for the dance. Why?"

Nick's smile looked more than a little devilish. "We were thinking she could—"

"Say hello," Tim finished for him. "Chris mentioned something about getting girl advice."

That was the first I'd heard of their bass guitarist needing any kind of help with girls. The guy had way too many interested fans trying to catch his eye already. Unless there was something else going on that I hadn't heard about yet . . .

"*I love you, Chris!*"

I spun around, curious to see if I could recognize his not-secret admirer or if she would be lost in a sea of dresses. It was a game I sometimes played. I would imagine what kind of girl—or guy, on occasion—would do the *I love you* screech. But either my Spidey senses had gone offline or the universe was having way too much fun playing a joke on me because the last person I expected to find wheedling attention from a rock star was Lisa Anne Montgomery.

That didn't seem to fit with her Ivy League aspirations and her disdainful articles for *The Smithsonian*.

But just because she was capable of geeking out around a celebrity didn't mean I had to like her now.

"Well, later for you, Corey. We've got a crowd to appease." Chris tapped the mic and grinned when even that little gesture was met with a shriek from four dozen girls. "Hey, Portland! It's good to see you again. I know this is a very special night, so we thought we'd start you off with this little number."

As they launched into one of their first chart-topping hits . . . Tim never took his eyes off me.

Which suited me just fine.

Chapter 10

Prom is supposed to bring out the best in people, but it often has the opposite effect . . . So watch yourself.

—from "Keep Your Promises," by Lisa Anne Montgomery Published by *The Smithsonian*

There's not a whole lot to do at a school dance.

I mean, you basically have three options: you can dance with a group of friends, you can stand around the edges of the room and compliment people on wearing something you've never seen them in before, or you can eat.

And after being bumped and jostled by all of Smith High School's diehard ReadySet fans for an hour, I was more than ready to take a huge step back. All the way to the buffet table, in fact.

Say what you will about the overblown expectations and the petty backstabbing that surrounds a glorified high school assembly, the crab dip was addictive.

Plus, it gave me a pretty good view of all my friends, without the discomfort of being tossed in as a third wheel.

Mackenzie whispered something in Logan's ear as they swayed back and forth in one of the less crowded areas of the dance floor. No doubt they had deliberately chosen that location to prevent even a royal klutz like Mackenzie from twisting an ankle in her heels. Isobel and Spencer weren't dancing together, but I'd never seen her look happier . . . especially when he took the corsage off his wrist and slipped it onto hers. Even if she did wrinkle her nose and say something that made him burst out laughing.

Jane and Scott were both obviously working the event—I was convinced that she had a notepad and a dozen pens in her clutch instead of makeup, and he was armed with his ever-present camera. But the two of them kept exchanging these looks across the room that made it obvious they were looking forward to ditching prom early. I doubted they would have bothered to attend if they didn't have a good excuse to avoid the dance floor.

Meanwhile, I ate to pass the time.

I was debating the merits of a second cookie when Jane gave a little yelp and moved past me in a blur of black satin, then pulled up short and crossed her arms with feigned nonchalance.

"About time you showed up. I see how it is now. You go spend a little time in Cambodia and suddenly you're too good for us."

Chelsea Halloway flashed a stunningly perfect smile that I'd never seen on her face during her reign at Smith High School. She looked radiant in a knee-length gold dress that brought out the burnished undertones of her long blond hair.

"I'm sorry, have we met?" Chelsea pursed her lips thoughtfully. "You remind me a little of this girl I used to know, but . . ."

Jane pulled her into a hug. "Shut up, Chelsea."

"Make me, geek."

A guy in an ill-fitting suit with floppy dark hair shifted

uncomfortably next to the girls. "Well, this is fun. Okay, give me a task, please. Someone. Anyone. Anything."

Chelsea raised an eyebrow devilishly. "Anything, you say? Interesting . . . I might have a few ideas."

Tall, dark, and geeky turned to Jane for help. "Hey, Jane, would you mind repeating that last thing you said?"

Jane grinned. "Shut up, Chelsea?"

"Perfect. Thanks. Feel free to say that whenever you want. Really."

Chelsea stuck her tongue out at him and I nearly did a double take at the sight of the Notable queen acting like, well . . . a geek. Then she turned to me.

"Oh hey, Corey! Have you met my boyfriend, Nashville?"

He grimaced as he held out a hand for me to shake. "Houston."

"But he loves it when people call him Tallahassee. Or better yet—"

"Jane?" Houston interrupted.

"I'm on it," Jane said dutifully. "Shut up, Chelsea."

"Okay, we obviously have some catching up to do, right after I dance with Atlanta." Chelsea pulled Houston into the fray before he had an opportunity to protest. Although when she hijacked one of his arms and did a little twirl, he grinned down at her instead of making an escape.

"I still can't believe Chelsea's dating a college guy like *Houston*." Jane slipped her arm around my waist. "I was starting to worry that she'd pine after Logan forever."

Chelsea did a little shimmy and then burst out giggling as Houston tried to leave the dance floor. He was all rumpled edges to her polished sheen, but the contrast made them look *right* together somehow.

It wasn't fair.

Chelsea could bring her *college-aged* boyfriend to a school dance—where she was no longer even *enrolled*—but my boyfriend couldn't be seen even holding my hand. And if I were to mention it to Principal Taylor, the only thing I'd accomplish would be ruining their night. I couldn't do it.

But the injustice of the whole situation had my stomach tied in knots.

"Hey, all you Portland people! Is everyone having a good time tonight?"

I couldn't bring myself to cheer in response to Tim's question. Then again, I didn't have to make a sound because the ReadySet cheer section was all over it; hooting, hollering, screaming themselves hoarse . . . the works.

"Well, we've had a great time with you tonight, but we think it's time for you to meet your prom king and queen!"

His last few words were nearly drowned out by my classmates, and Tim had to wait for everyone to settle down a little before he continued.

"So, without further ado, here's . . . Principal Taylor!"

I clenched my hands into tight fists as my classmates dutifully cheered for a man who thought that everyone was entitled to the full high school experience . . . unless they were gay.

Principal Taylor cleared his throat into the microphone. "Um . . . thank you, Mr. Goff. I'd like to remind all of you that underage drinking jeopardizes your life and everyone around you. Be smart, stay safe, and we'll all make it out of here alive."

He paused awkwardly, probably because he had planned on leaving an opening for laughter and applause. It didn't happen.

"Um . . ." He floundered, ripping open an envelope as if he were at the Academy Awards. "Your junior prom king is . . . Logan Beckett!"

I wolf-whistled as the hockey captain made his way over to the stage and accepted the crown with a good-natured shrug and a smile, but I was far more curious to see how Patrick would take this blow to the ego. I couldn't find him in the sea of sequins and suits, so I began hunting for Steffani instead. Her sparkly silver number was pretty hard to miss, especially because it included a slit that ran all the way up to mid-thigh. Sure enough, I spotted Patrick glowering right next to her *Dancing with the Stars*–worthy outfit. Judging by the viselike grip Steffani had on his hand, Patrick didn't have much choice in the matter.

I began moving toward them. There was no doubt in my mind that the only people who would hassle Mackenzie if she won were standing in that little clump. I didn't slow down until there was only one rather tall girl separating me from the worst of the Notable crowd.

"And your junior prom queen is . . ."

Mr. Taylor fumbled with the sheet of paper in his hands and I glanced over at Mackenzie in time to see her start inching toward the exit.

"Chelsea Halloway!"

Everyone went nuts.

"She doesn't even go here anymore!" Steffani wailed while Mackenzie cheered for all she was worth.

"Way to go, Chelsea!"

"God, she gets *everything* she wants. It's so unfair!"

"We love you, girl!"

Chelsea didn't seem to hear any of it. She sauntered elegantly on her three-inch heels to where her king was already standing, and accepted the tiara with a grace that nobody else could have pulled off. Mackenzie had been right all along: Some girls were just born to be prom queens, and Chelsea Halloway was one of them.

I couldn't make out what Steffani said to Patrick, but even though she had lowered her voice, it was obvious she was almost overcome with fury. Hoping her anger would consume her focus, I crept forward to eavesdrop.

Okay, so maybe I should have minded my own business.

Maybe I should have relished the moment and watched

along with the rest of the high school as two seniors were crowned with a whole lot less enthusiasm from the crowd. Chelsea and Logan had upstaged the seniors. Again. All eyes were riveted on the pair of them when both couples claimed the floor for the honorary first dance.

But a full-fledged Notable freak-out was too entertaining to resist.

"I told you!" Steffani hissed at Patrick. *"The only way to beat Chelsea is to get your hands dirty! But you had to go wimp out on me!"*

"Hey, I did not wimp out! I'm just not as desperate for attention as you are."

So . . . that relationship definitely wasn't going to last the night.

Steffani laughed coldly. *"I'm* desperate? Me? That's a good one. I'm not the one who anonymously posted a YouTube video because I was worried other people wouldn't like it."

"Back off, Steffani," he growled.

"Or what? You'll try and share my embarrassing moments with the world? Good luck with that, Patrick. I'm not a freak like Mackenzie Wellesley."

I stood frozen in place, unable to think or breathe or . . . do just about anything beyond feeling a layer of ice begin encasing my heart.

Patrick Bradford had been the one to humiliate Mackenzie.

He had intentionally posted that video to exploit her moment of embarrassment for social capital. And I really, truly, honestly didn't care that he hadn't intended for it to go viral. It didn't make a difference if he had planned to share it with five people or five billion.

There was no way I was going to let him get away with hurting my best friend.

Chapter 11

If you're not good at public speaking, please
don't try to prove yourself wrong at a big event.
It's going to be embarrassing for you and
painful for everyone else to watch.

—from "Preaching at Prom,"
by Lisa Anne Montgomery
Published by *The Smithsonian Online Edition*

It was strange watching Chelsea dance with Logan.
Together they were an undeniable power couple; all that
confidence and poise and freakishly great genetics combined
to make them every bit as golden as Chelsea's dress. They
looked completely at ease with each other too. Considering
that they were exes, I would have expected tension or
awkwardness or . . . *something*. Instead, the Notable queen
grinned up at Logan before he dipped her with the same
move he'd used on Mackenzie only a few hours earlier—
although this time he kept his mouth to himself.

I studied Mackenzie closely just to make sure she was okay
with all of this. It was one thing to create posters for your
former arch-nemesis and something entirely different to

watch your boyfriend whirling his stunningly beautiful ex-girlfriend around the dance floor. But Mackenzie was beaming at them as if the whole thing had been her idea.

Which I guess was the truth.

So instead of detouring over to her, I headed straight for the stage as soon as the special dance for the prom court ended. It was slow going because I had to squeeze between couples who had no intention of leaving any space between each other—or anyone else, for that matter.

"Hey, Houston, what do you think of my new accessory?" Chelsea posed jokingly in front of her boyfriend.

"I always knew you were a princess."

"Yeah, but you rarely meant it as a compliment," she pointed out.

I didn't hear his response because a sliver of space opened up in front of me and I seized the opportunity to move forward. Tim was halfway through a new song he had co-written with Nick in L.A. by the time I reached the stage. There was no way I could cut him off mid-performance, so I stood right next to Darryl while I waited for them to finish.

Tim could tell that something was wrong.

He cocked his head slightly to the side and began scanning my surroundings, obviously trying to identify the threat to my well-being so that he could eliminate it. Or at the very least get Darryl to take care of the situation.

His concern should have made me feel all warm inside, but I still felt cold. Numb with a seething hatred that had seized me the instant I had overheard what Patrick had released online.

I didn't bank the fury in my eyes as I waited for the final notes to make my move.

"Uh . . . Corey O'Neal, everyone!" Tim said lamely, by way of introduction as I climbed up the steps onto the stage. He leaned over to my ear and whispered, "Are you okay, Corey?"

I nodded jerkily, took a deep breath, and then spoke clearly into the mic.

"Hey, everyone! I know that we've already crowned our prom king and queen, but there are actually a few other people I think we need to recognize for their contributions tonight. So let's put our hands together and give Lisa Anne Montgomery a big round of applause for being the worst, most condescending journalist *The Smithsonian* has ever seen. Well done, Lisa Anne."

Everyone—the students, the handful of faculty members and parents who were acting as chaperones—all of them stared at me in shock. It would have been funny to see that many well-dressed people with their mouths hanging open if I hadn't been spitting mad and nowhere near finished.

"Congratulations, Alex Thompson. Your rampant homophobia pushed you over the edge in the very competitive category of Smith High School's biggest bully."

I could see Principal Taylor desperately trying to signal for someone to cut my mic, so I spoke even faster.

"Ashley McGrady and Steffani Larson have tied for the female equivalent of that award. It really was impossible to choose between you two ladies."

The shock was starting to wear off and I could see more than one adult begin pushing their way through the crowd to reach me.

"The honor of Smith High School's Worst Person Award goes to our very own Patrick Bradford. Congratulations, Patrick; you showed a complete lack of basic human decency when you deliberately tried to humiliate Mackenzie Wellesley with a YouTube video. She's a million times better on her worst days than you'll ever be on your best. And here to escort me to the door is the man who decided I couldn't attend prom with my date because of my sexual orientation. Let's hear it for Principal Taylor!"

"He's really coming up here, Corey!" Tim grabbed my

hand and pulled me across the stage in an attempt to put space between one seriously pissed off school principal and his boyfriend. *"Let's go!"*

I paused only to drop the mic.

Then I maneuvered my way through the crowd with Tim two steps ahead of me.

I'm not sure who started the slow-clap, but the room went from a heavily weighted silence to a resounding beat. It didn't take long for the other ReadySet boys to get in on the action. Nick pounded away on the drum set and Chris began chanting, "Cor-ey! Cor-ey!" into my abandoned microphone.

The amazing part was how quickly the students who had silently watched Alex Thompson push me and my friends around in the cafeteria joined in.

All it took was hearing we had the support of a rock band and suddenly they were all fervently anti-bully.

Go figure.

I wasn't really going to complain, though; especially since they sprang aside so that Tim and I could make a clean getaway. Maybe that was because they didn't want to risk upsetting the scowling Darryl, who was trailing right behind us. Darryl definitely would have been incentive enough for me to scurry away. Still, Tim and I were both breathing a little roughly by the time we reached the enormous doors that kept the reporters at bay. There was no time to strategize the next leg of our daring escape.

So for once we didn't even try.

Tim yanked open the door and forged onward toward the parking lot. But I twisted at the last second so that I could snag one last glance at the chaos I was leaving in my wake. I had a feeling that someday I would describe to my grandchildren the way the hundreds of red and silver balloons caught the glare from the paparazzi's flash photography. The twinkle lights wrapped around the support beams that glowed in cheery contrast to the absolutely livid expression of the school administrator who was still in full pursuit . . .

Then I left it all behind me as I followed Tim into the heart of the press.

"What's the rush, Timothy?"

"Are you being chased because you're gay?"

"How was your night?"

"Over here, Timothy!"

Tim never slowed down, even when we reached his sports car. He pulled his key fob from his pocket, unlocked it with a beep, and barely waited for me to climb in before he revved the motor as a warning to all the tabloid vultures to keep their distance. He didn't waste any time telling me to get in, or buckle up, or hold on, or any of those other clichés that get tossed around in every Hollywood car chase sequence. Instead, Tim focused his attention on putting as many miles as possible between us and everyone else in the world.

As we sped out of the parking lot and onto one of Portland's many one-way streets, I released a victorious war cry that had been hiding in some dark corner of my chest.

"Did you see that?" I lowered the car window so that the wind could whip through my hair. So that the very air could share in my exhilaration. "That felt . . . *amazing!*"

Tim nodded, but he kept his gaze locked firmly on the road ahead of us. "It was definitely something."

"Something *awesome,*" I amended. "I wish I had done that years ago."

"Did you really have to do it tonight? At prom?" Tim's voice was calm and steady, but I heard the reproof in it. "You couldn't have waited to go public with all of that?"

I couldn't believe he even needed to ask. "When would *you* have done it, Tim? A school assembly? During an interview with Ellen? When do you think the timing would be right to publicly call out the bullies who have made my life a living hell?"

He considered that for a moment before speaking. "I'm not trying to judge you, Corey. I know what you did took a lot of courage. But I wish we could have enjoyed prom without a confrontation."

I twisted in the plush leather seat so that I could get a good look at Tim. "I don't get why you care so much about this one stupid dance. It's *high school*, okay? You can dress it up however you want; it's still going to be a disappointment. Because for most of us, that sums up the whole high school experience."

"I guess I wanted more for us." Tim's voice was stiff, and the exhilaration I'd practically been swimming in only moments before evaporated like water on the sidewalk during a heat wave in Los Angeles.

"Could you pull over? Or drive to a hotel where we can really talk? There are . . ." I nearly lost my nerve, but I forced myself to spit out the rest of the words. "There are some things we need to discuss."

If you can't handle the rock star lifestyle . . . it doesn't mean that you don't love him.

The only way to move forward was to clear the air. I briefly wished I was back at prom, facing down a crowd that couldn't quite decide whether they wanted to treat me like a hero or lynch me on the spot.

Telling the truth in front of everyone hadn't been easy.

But it was nothing compared to the conversation I was about to have with my boyfriend.

Chapter 12

Looks like Lisa Anne Montgomery was right
again: Smith High School students will be whispering
about that prom for years to come. . . .

—from "Prom and Prejudice,"
by Jane Smith
Published by *The Smithsonian Online Edition*

Tim and I didn't speak during the rest of the drive, even
when he pulled up to a nearby hotel.

I was too afraid to say anything in case whatever came out
would be the dead last thing I wanted to share. I couldn't risk
screwing up the conversation before it had even begun.

So I stood there mutely as he handed over his credit card at
the front desk and then signed a few quick autographs for the
employees before he was able to claim his room key. The
longer we waited to break the silence, the more crucial it felt
that the first statement be something really powerful. Something
that would set the right tone for everything that followed it.

And I had absolutely no idea how to salvage what was left
of the night . . . or the relationship between us that was

plummeting at roughly the same speed the elevator was raising us to our hideaway.

Tim unlocked the room with a quick flick of the plastic key card, turned on the light, and didn't slow his purposeful stride until he sank down on the bed. "So, what do you want to discuss, Corey?"

"I love you," I blurted out, feeling a surge of relief when Tim's shoulders slowly began to relax.

"Okay . . ."

"But you can't move to Portland."

Tim crossed his arms. "Excuse me, are you the Portland police?"

I knew he meant it as a joke, but I didn't want to laugh off this conversation. It was too important to take the coward's way out and hide between a smile and a *Sure, sweetie. Everything is just fiiiine* response.

"You can't move out here for me." I sat on the edge of the bed and twisted slightly so that I met his steady gaze. It was supposed to make it easier for me to read his emotions, but I felt swamped by the hazel depths of his eyes. "I love you, Tim, but you can't base these huge life decisions on me. I can't handle that kind of pressure."

"So you'd rather we keep this long distance?" Tim raked a hand through his hair in frustration. "Aren't you sick of comparing schedules and texting and pretending that it's enough?"

"Of course I am! But if you move here and we break up . . . then what? I'm the guy who interrupted every aspect of your life for nothing!"

Tim went deadly quiet. "It sounds like you've already decided you want out."

"*No!* I want to be with you, Tim. I want to find a way to make this work, but that doesn't mean I want to screw up your career and become your Yoko Ono."

"You know Lennon's marriage to Yoko Ono was *not* the way most people picture it."

I threw my arms up in the air. "I don't want to discuss the history of The Beatles! I just . . . I want to keep this thing between us private! Is that really too much to ask?"

"So let me get this straight: You love me. You want to be with me. But you don't want me to move to Oregon, and you never want us to be caught together in public. Why did you even bother coming out if you wanted to keep your life tucked away in the closet?"

I felt like I'd been sucker punched. "There's a difference," I said quietly, "between being comfortable with who I am and seeing our relationship in the tabloids."

"I can't control that!" Tim jumped off the bed and began pacing the room like an imprisoned animal. "I can't wave a magic wand and make the press back off. Why do you think I avoided going public in the first place?!"

"Because you were afraid being gay would damage your career. You thought I would only drag you down. And you were right." I couldn't keep going past the lump that had formed in my throat. I felt shredded, eviscerated—as those few words finally gave voice to the dark, twisted fears I'd never been able to shake.

Tim pulled up short, but all I could see was the broad expanse of his back. He didn't turn around and I found myself grateful for the distance. The only thing worse than seeing a misery in his eyes that matched my own, would be seeing he was devoid of all emotion. For Tim to be completely unaffected.

Either way, it would just lead to pain.

"I'm sorry, Corey," Tim said slowly, his voice hoarser than I'd ever heard it before. "I shouldn't have said . . . I didn't . . ." He scrubbed his face with one of his palms and then tried again. "I hope you find someone who can give you what you need."

My heart crumpled. It collapsed like a soufflé that had been trying so hard to keep its shape and lost the inevitable war with gravity.

He didn't want me.

Not enough.

It was over.

I fought back the rush of tears that threatened to trickle their way down my jaw and onto the suit I had worn for him. There was no way I wanted him to see me crying over him. Not when he was probably already dismissing me as a foolish mistake—as a fanboy who couldn't handle the life of a rock star without the rose-colored glasses firmly in place at all times.

Rising to my feet seemed impossible, but I did it because that's what you do when you run out of other options.

"I, uh . . ." I cleared my throat roughly. "I know you probably don't believe this anymore, but I do love you, Tim. Just . . . take care of yourself, okay?"

He flinched.

And I lost the fight against my tear glands and swiped away the salty streaks with the back of my hand as I walked toward the door.

I hesitated with one hand on the handle, desperately hoping he would call out behind me that he didn't want this to be good-bye. That he thought what we had was worth fighting to preserve. That he loved me too much to quit.

But he didn't.

The deafening silence between us propelled me to step out into the hallway. I couldn't linger in that room with my broken heart seeping into the cream-colored carpeting beneath his feet. I couldn't do it anymore.

My legs gave out beneath me as I heard the door snick shut and watched the keycard slot flash red, just in case I wasn't clear on the whole *you are not wanted here* message.

I leaned against the wallpapered hallway as I struggled to breathe through the pain that ripped into me. Nobody passed me on their way to the elevators, but at that moment I didn't care if every student at Smith High School marched down the hallway so they could all laugh at the gay boy who had been stupid enough to believe that out of everyone in the world, Timothy Goff would pick him. Fight for him.

Love *him*.

Every painful moment flooded through me then. I hugged my knees and began shivering uncontrollably as I replayed every shove in the cafeteria, every pointed glare in the boys' locker room, every homophobic joke I'd been forced to endure with gritted teeth, because if I spoke up I'd be told to get a sense of humor. Every time someone referred to me as Mackenzie's gay best friend, because they assumed that label summed up everything they needed to know about me, and yet those same people would never consider dismissing Jane as her straight best friend.

The shame and fear and guilt and rage flooded me, but none of it could drown out the layer of pain that throbbed underneath.

Tim was finished with me.

I pushed myself off the wall and then focused my full attention on the one physical barrier that separated me from the only boy who made me feel like I could be myself and that was more than enough.

And I began pounding on it with all my strength.

Bam. Bam. Bam.

"Open the door, Tim!" I yelled. "I'm not finished with you!"

A head poked out of a nearby room. "It's past ten o'clock, kid. Shut up!"

"Not until my boyfriend talks to me." I pitched my voice louder. "You hear that, Tim? I'm not going *anywhere* until you talk to me. So open the door!"

"Pipe down!"

"This is ridiculous. I'm not paying for some crazy kid to keep me up all night. Honey, call the desk downstairs!"

I did my best to ignore the voices as I continued pounding away. "If you *don't* open the door, I'm going to be arrested for disturbing the peace. Do you really want that to happen, Tim? For me to spend my prom night in *jail?*"

That did the trick.

Tim yanked it open and glared at me through red-rimmed eyes. "That was a low blow."

"Absolutely." I shoved him back and let the door close behind me. "Ask me if I care."

"Do you care?"

"About making a scene and fighting dirty? Not a bit. About you?" I dug my hands into his hair and slammed him into a full-bodied kiss that contained everything I had. Every bit of passion and hunger and love and fear, it was all in there. And when he gripped me tightly, as if to reassure himself that I was really there, I felt the last of my fear slip away.

"I. Love. You." I punctuated every word with a deep kiss, before I forced myself to pull back a little. "And I know you love me back."

Tim looked adorably confused. "Of course I do."

"Good. Well, I'm going to need you to remind me of that fact every now and then. America doesn't know what you see in me, and sometimes I don't either."

This time it was Tim who dove in for a kiss, and as the slight scruff on his jaw abraded my chin, I didn't care too much if we postponed the conversation for a few hours . . . or days . . .

"I love that you stood up there on stage and spoke your mind," Tim said fiercely when we finally came up for air. "I love your courage, and your snark, and your great, big—"

He kissed his way over to my left ear as I laughed like, well, a high school kid in love.

"Heart," Tim finished as we sank down onto the bed.

"Sometimes I have trouble seeing myself that way."

"I can remind you."

"And sometimes the media attention is going to freak me out. I'm still not entirely sure how we're going to deal with that one."

The pad of Tim's thumb rubbed slow, lazy circles behind my ear. "We'll take it one day at a time."

I rested my hand on his, halting the movement, which was turning my brain to mush. "Promise?"

"Promise." He abandoned the gentle massage and instead slid his hand into mine . . . and he held it. I could feel a foolish grin spreading across my face as he gave it a quick squeeze.

I was holding my boyfriend's hand, just like every one of those couples I had envied at the dance.

Suddenly I wished that we had posed for prom photos together, because I wanted to remember this night forever. *This* was the moment I wanted to think of first when my parents inevitably asked if I'd enjoyed the dance, even though I intended to keep that little fact to myself.

I nearly burst out laughing when it hit me that we didn't need the photobooth—the paparazzi had taken care of that for us. Action movie style.

"Whether or not I move to Portland, there will be times when I won't leave the studio for days at a time. Sleep will become a distant memory, and if I do manage to text, they will probably be pretty generic messages. And you're going to have to keep loving me anyway."

I nodded calmly. "I can do that. But afterward I'm going to want to hole up in a hotel with you for three days."

Tim's laughter died abruptly when he got a good look at my face. "You're serious."

"Absolutely. I'm going to fight for you, Tim. And that means I'm going to help you spend a whole bunch of vacation days. But right now . . . let's just focus on tonight, okay?"

The heart-stopping kiss we shared was answer enough for me.

Marni's High School Survival Playlist

Taylor Swift: "Mean"
Okay, let's be honest: There are some people in high school (cough, Fake and Bake, cough) who are just straight-up mean. It's important to keep in mind that high school doesn't last forever . . . and that your happiness is the best possible revenge. Trust me.

Kate Nash: "Do-Wah-Doo"
When confronted with someone unpleasant, reading a book is always a viable option!

Ben Folds: "There's Always Someone Cooler Than You"
This song is directed at anyone who tries to make you feel tiny in order to make themself feel tall. And yes, there is always someone cooler than you. But the really cool people are the ones who become your best friends. (They also think that you're pretty damn awesome.)

Ingrid Michaelson: "The Way I Am"
I'm incredibly lucky to have found people who take me the way I am, but that wasn't always the case. So don't stress out if even your high school friends don't always get you. Support networks can take time to build.

Sara Bareilles: "Brave"
This song always gives me a boost of courage. It's just so completely made of awesome! I love it.

India.Arie: "Video"
I listened to this song nonstop in high school. It was sometimes a struggle for me to remember that my worth wasn't connected to my looks. Whenever I heard this song I felt a little less self-conscious about my body.

P!nk: "F*ckin' Perfect"
You are perfect to me.

Bridgit Mendler: "Postcard"
Never let anyone make you shy away from your dream by referring to your gender/religion/race/sexual orientation/awkwardness/any other ridiculous reason meant to keep you down. Don't give the jerks of the world that kind of power over you.

Natasha Bedingfield: "Strip Me"
Nobody can steal your voice.

Katy Perry: "Roar"
I take a whole bunch of dance breaks to this song.

Estelle: "Do My Thing"
I wish this song had been playing in my head every single time someone asked about my writing plans when I was first starting out. I was told many, many times that I needed to follow a more conventional career path. I'm so glad I decided to do my thing. I hope you do yours!

Hot Hot Heat: "Middle of Nowhere"
The future still freaks me out. That's okay. I think it scares everybody. Adults are just better at hiding the fact that they're in the middle of nowhere too.

Andy Grammer: "Keep Your Head Up"
You really are going to turn out fine. I promise.

Happy Reading!
—Marni